A Candy Shop Christmas

A Novel by
JOEY JONES

ISBN: 978-1-948978-25-5 (PRINT)

ISBN: 978-1-948978-26-2 (EPUB)

ISBN: 978-1-948978-27-9 (MOBI)

For Michelle:
This novel is better because of you.
Thank you for your love and support. I love you.

Also by Joey Jones

THE ROOTS BENEATH US

"Writing my first book was an experience I will never take for granted! But being able to get lost in the pages of an exceptional read like this will forever be my love language." —Dr. Courtney Evans, Bestselling Author—Uncaged

ALONG THE DUSTY ROAD

"'*Life is about love. About giving love and receiving love.*' This is my favorite line from Joey Jones's new book, Along the Dusty Road. Written with a poetic honesty, Joey brings Luke to life on every page and carries us through Luke's conflicting search for his happy ever after. Sometimes sweet and sometimes intensely emotional, this story hits every mark." —Lacey Baker, USA Today Bestselling Author

WHERE THE RAINBOW FALLS
(The Rivers Series, Book 2)

"A riveting story with an ending sure to make your heart swell, WHERE THE RAINBOW FALLS is a novel that leaves you feeling satisfied and accomplished." —Brittany Curry, Librarian

WHEN THE RIVERS RISE
(The Rivers Series, Book 1)

"A threatening hurricane is on the horizon and love is on the line . . . this captivating story of love and loss will keep you turning the pages and wishing for more. This is Joey Jones delivering what his fans have come to expect!" —Riley Costello, Author of *Waiting at Hayden's,* a shopfiction™ novel

THE DATE NIGHT JAR

"A beautiful love story, capturing the poignancy of both new affection and the power of deep, lasting devotion. Readers of Nicholas Sparks, Debbie Macomber, and Nicholas Evans should add THE DATE NIGHT JAR to their reading list." —Jeff Gunhus, *USA TODAY* Bestselling Author

A FIELD OF FIREFLIES

"This is a tale of tragedy, romance, heartbreak and, ultimately, redemption. With lyrical writing and strong character development, Joey Jones effortlessly pulls readers in." —Kristy Woodson Harvey, *NEW YORK TIMES* Bestselling Author

LOSING LONDON

"I read the entire book in one day... I could not put it down! WOW!! LOSING LONDON was incredible; I laughed, I cried, and I'm still in shock." —Erica Latrice, TV Host, Be Inspired

A BRIDGE APART

"Filled with romance, suspense, heartbreak, and a tense plot line, Joey Jones's first novel is a must-read. It is the kind of book you can lend to your mom and best friend." —Suzanne Lucey, Page 158 Books

Acknowledgments

I have always wanted to write a Christmas novel, and here it is on the 10th anniversary of my debut novel. I am incredibly grateful to have one of the most amazing supporting casts an author could imagine. So many people have stood behind me, beside me, and led me through every step of this journey. First and foremost, I would like to thank God for giving me the ability to write and planting that passion within my soul. Branden, my oldest son, is a fantastic father to a three-year-old girl. Parker is now a third grader who is wise beyond his years. Spending our days together brings so much joy to my life. I love watching him grow, learn, and impact this world in a positive way.

I would also like to thank my wonderful family. My parents Joe and Patsy Jones taught me how to become a responsible adult, and I hope to leave a legacy that makes them proud. My dad now resides in Heaven, and I miss him dearly. My mom, my breakfast partner and one of my best friends, is the humblest person I know. My brothers and sisters DeAnn, Judy, Lee, Penny, and Richard are some of my closest friends. In many ways, their support is my foundation.

My editor Donna Matthews is incredibly talented at polishing my writing. My graphics designer Meredith Walsh did a fantastic job with each of my novel covers and supporting pieces. Polgarus Studio made the intricate process of formatting the interior of this novel a breeze. Once again, Deborah Dove worked her magic in creating the book blurb. Mashal Smith, who travels the world photographing mesmerizing landscapes, captured my biography photo gracefully.

Lastly, I want to thank some people who have been influential throughout my life: some for a season but each for a reason. Thank you to Alan & Kathy Hammer, Andrew Haywood, BJ Horne, Billy Nobles, Bob Peele, Cathy Errick, Courtney Haywood, Diane Tyndall, Erin Haywood, Jan Raynor, Jeanette Towne, Josh Haywood, Josh Towne, Kenny Ford, Kim Jones, Michelle Ferricher, Mitch Fortescue, Nicholas Sparks, Ray White, Rebekah Jones, Richard Banks, Steve Cobb, Steven Harrell, and Steve Haywood. It is a privilege to call each of you my friend.

A Candy Shop Christmas

1

The candy shop and Christmastime went together like Santa and his reindeer, like Jesus and the manger, like Frosty and snow. In Noel Puckett's emerald green eyes, one couldn't exist without the other. When small enough to sit on her daddy's lap, he used to nestle an unmistakable red hat with a floppy white cottontail puff on her head and tell her as long as she kept it on, she wore all the colors of Christmas.

"Because of my eyes?" she would ask, smiling.

"Yes, and they are prettier than any jewel in the world."

Santa hats marked one of the many traditions Noel carried into adulthood. On Thanksgiving Day, which the calendar flipped to this morning, the hats came out of the box holding them since January, and she proudly donned hers throughout the season. Of course the sizes changed over the twenty-eight years of her life, but the look and feel remained pretty much the same. As a child, she wore her Santa hat everywhere: while helping in the family's old-fashioned candy store, sitting at the breakfast table, studying at her school desk, and even when walking, running, or riding her bicycle around the most magical town on Earth—Beaufort, North Carolina.

The red and gold Beaufort Candy Company sign on the two-story brick building matched the name on the map which attracted people from across the country and beyond to this little slice of coastal paradise, especially during the summertime. The historic downtown shop, conveniently nestled between Front Street and Taylor Creek, overlooked the waterfront separating the town from Carrot Island, an uninhabited stretch of land also known as the Rachel Carson Reserve known for the magnificent wild horses that roamed freely.

On both the land and water side, a sidewalk paralleled the main road and waterfront where dozens of docks invited boaters from all over to visit. The deep channel made the area accessible to most vessels of any size, and the waterways that stretched around either side of the nearby visible island created somewhat of a maze through various other islands, marshes, and shoals. Creeks, rivers, inlets, bays, and sounds all intertwined to create countless opportunities for adventures and lead to the nearby Atlantic Ocean.

The candy shop blended in with many other stores on the outside until passersby caught a glimpse of the colorful window displays on either side of the large wooden doors leading to a place that brought smiles to the faces of children and adults alike year-round. The red-bricked walls, high industrial ceiling with exposed wooden beams and black piping, antique wooden floors, and decorative barrels, shelves, and display cases filled with thousands of pieces of every type of candy, pies, and fudge the heart could desire gave this place unique character. At Christmastime the magic reached levels strong enough to power Santa's sleigh.

Adjusting her own hat this year, the light brown hair spilling out curved around Noel's oval face and dangled just below her chin. She wore the red and black flannel pajamas that matched the ones she gave Levi and Laney last night before snuggling on the couch to watch a movie with her two favorite eight-year-olds. A moment later with the opened box at her feet, she studied the candy shop and remembered how much work today brought. By bedtime she and her team of elves needed to turn this place into a Christmas wonderland.

In so many ways, year in and year out, this particular morning felt like Christmas. Last night while the children slept, Noel snuck downstairs and pulled out dozens of boxes filled with decorations as well as those loaded with Christmas candy. Red, green, white, and gold colored wrapping would replace orange, brown, and burgundy to signify the season change. The remaining candy corn, pumpkins, chocolate turkeys, and pilgrim lollipops would be moved to a small clearance section in the back corner and would be a colossal hit tomorrow—the best Black Friday deal around, in fact.

Noel called Levi's and Laney's names, and seconds later she heard the pitter-patter of little feet running down the stairs playing one of the greatest instruments in the universe—original floorboards that creaked making sounds that echoed off the walls of the otherwise quiet store.

A few minutes ago, she asked the children to wait patiently at the top of the stairs while she checked on some things, which meant fluffing their hats and hanging their stockings because she forgot those final touches last night. Thankfully, Noel remembered to fill them with goodies which took a little time. Based on prior experiences, she had a hunch that as soon as she descended the stairs, the kids fell flat on their pajama-covered bellies just above the top step for a peek through the spindles. However, she knew they couldn't quite see the front counter from there.

"What is it, Mommy?" Levi asked, running past heavy wooden barrels of taffy and gummies.

When he and Laney rounded the corner and saw Noel sitting behind the counter with a smile on her face and a little Santa hat in each hand, their faces lit up.

"Our Christmas hats!" Laney declared for all to hear although the locked door kept others at bay until the floodgates opened early tomorrow morning.

"Which one is mine?" Levi asked, his stringy brown hair begging for a comb.

"This one," Noel replied with a grin, sliding it over his head, and grateful it seemed to fit just right while hiding the bedhead sprouts. "And this one belongs to you, Laney."

Grinning from ear to ear, Laney attempted perfect posture while being crowned like a queen. The freckles dotting her adorable face seemed to glow majestically.

"Is it beautiful, Aunt Noel?" she checked.

"Of course," Noel guaranteed confidently. "Both of you look like cute little elves ready for heaps of Christmas fun," she announced exactly like her dad because *Christmas fun* sounded much more exciting than Christmas work. She spoke the same positive affirmations to herself leading up to the big day and even this morning in the mirror when she woke before sunrise.

Instead of building toys in a workshop, they would decorate the whole store and place candy using a planogram she created.

"Do you remember your special treat?" Noel quizzed.

"Christmas stockings," the two shouted in unison while searching for them like an elf on the shelf.

Not many kids received such a gift on Thanksgiving Day, but the children of the owners of this candy shop always had and always would. Noel pointed at the old fireplace, the focal point behind the register area. If memory served her correctly, her great-grandfather laid the bricks by hand.

"I see mine," Laney announced while mouthing her name as she read it.

"Mine is right there," Levi added, pointing his finger.

They each grabbed their respective stockings and dropped to the floor crisscross applesauce style as if accordions made up their lower bodies. A moment later an assortment of wrapped candy scattered across the hardwood like marbles. As tradition, one of each Christmas candy that would be put on the sales floor today made up the loot.

"How many can we eat now?" Laney asked furrowing her brow as she tried to recall the amount allowed 365 days ago.

"Start with two, and throughout the day you will have the opportunity to eat all of them."

"Really?" Levi checked, his eyes bulging as if he never heard those words before.

Noel's mother always said the kids needed the extra energy for such a busy day of helping the adults. Noel popped a few pieces in her mouth last night while sorting and placing boxes and even snuck one in this morning. She sure wished her mom and dad were here, dressed in their silly Christmas attire resembling Mr. and Mrs. Claus. The way the candy store had been passed down to her so abruptly hadn't been the blessing she expected to receive one day. If a positive existed, it disguised itself in the fact that she now spent so much time doing what so many hands once did that it kept her mind occupied.

"Every time the cuckoo clock sounds on the hour, you can eat two more pieces," Noel reminded the kids.

Levi and Laney glanced eagerly at the old gingerbread house time-telling machine above the mantle. Almost every kid who came into the shop pointed it out in fascination.

"It's already seven o'clock," Laney calculated, unwrapping a peanut butter cup and stuffing it into her mouth.

"The first seven o'clock," Levi added while peeling the foil surrounding a milk chocolate ball.

"A.M.," Laney said sounding all educated.

"I am glad your third-grade teacher is showing you how to tell time," Noel noted.

"Daddy taught me first," Levi shared.

As the kids chewed and swallowed their initial pieces of candy,

Noel swallowed a lump that suddenly appeared in her throat. Fletcher's hands were the ones Noel missed most. She missed them helping in the candy shop, with the dishes at home, and, most of all, touching her. Her husband had a way of making her forget all her worries, even on the hardest of days. He listened to her the same way he touched her, slowly and gently, and as the little hairs on the back of her neck stood at attention, she swore she could feel Fletcher's fingers tracing her skin now.

"Why do you have that look on your face?" Laney asked perplexed.

Noel's shoulders shuddered back to reality. "What look?"

"Like you seen a ghost?" Laney explained.

"Ghosts are at Halloween," Levi snickered. "It's Christmas."

"It's Thanksgiving," Laney corrected.

Noel chimed in. "In the candy shop, today is Thanksgiving as well as Christmastime kickoff, so you are both right."

Laney's and Levi's eyes smiled widely as they looked up at Noel.

"The best day of the year," Levi reported, unwrapping his peanut butter cup and dropping it into his mouth.

"I'm opening this one next," Laney reported as she ripped the clear plastic from around a multi-colored mini candy cane.

"Smart girl," Noel pointed out. "That one will last for a while if you suck on it rather than chew."

"So will my chocolate," Levi shared, sticking out his brown tongue.

"You're silly," Noel replied. "Make sure the wrappers go into the trash can."

As she finished the sentence, they snatched up their wrappers like little vacuums and ran to the end of the counter where a wooden barrel lined with an empty plastic bag doubled as a finish line at cleanup time.

A moment later a knock came at the front door, and a pair of eyes cupped by hands on either side peered through the glass.

"Mrs. Madelyn," Laney and Levi shrilled, and another race

ensued to a broad-shouldered lady with wavy white hair and large-rimmed black glasses.

A crisp November morning breeze blew through the doorframe while Levi and Laney temporarily held Mrs. Madelyn there, each wrapped around either of her legs.

She squeezed the balls of their Santa hats as if they might toot like bicycle horns.

"How are my two favorite munchkins?" Mrs. Madelyn inquired through a belly laugh that entered the store before she did.

The children responded quickly by each grabbing a hand. "Come see what we got," Laney encouraged.

"Yeah, it's candy," Levi blurted out.

Elbows rested on the counter, Noel's palms held her chin while she watched the greeting with a tired smile.

"I brought coffee," Mrs. Madelyn announced when she finally spotted Noel.

"Oh, so sorry," Noel blurted out. "Where are my manners? I was so engrossed in the reunion that I didn't even realize you had hot coffee in your hands," she confessed as she jumped from the stool and waltzed toward the front of the store. "Wait, you don't have coffee in your hands, you have little hands in your hands."

"Fret not," Mrs. Madelyn responded. "I anticipated this greeting and placed the beverages on the sidewalk outside the door."

"Wisdom," Noel gleaned, "I will grab them."

A few stray leaves swirled on the sidewalk as Noel shivered in response to the difference in the outside temperature, making the warmth radiating from the inside of the coffee cups comforting. Once she turned the lock and made it to the counter, she found her three elves huddled around the candy like a fire as Levi and Laney explained each piece to Mrs. Madelyn.

"Now that everyone is here," Noel announced after the kids plucked Mrs. Madelyn's Santa hat from the box and mangled her hairdo, "are you all ready for the Christmas fun to begin?"

"It already has," Laney proclaimed.

"But now it's even more fun because Mrs. Madelyn is here," Levi added.

"That's right, and now we can decorate the Christmas tree and the whole shop then put out the new candy," Mrs. Madelyn reminded them.

"The Christmas tree," Levi and Laney shouted when Mrs. Madelyn's and Noel's eyes followed her impactful words to the back of the store where a twenty-foot live Eastern Red Cedar Christmas tree awaited its dressing."

Noel smiled from ear to ear. The children had been so excited about their Santa hats and stockings that they ran right by the beautiful present the local Christmas tree farm delivered late last night.

"It's so big," Laney remarked.

"They always bring us the biggest one," Mrs. Madelyn reported.

Last night Noel repeatedly thanked the farm's owner when he showed up with two helpers to unload, set, and even fluff the tree. It made one less thing to worry about.

"It's taller than all of us if we stood on each other's heads," Levi proclaimed.

The kids ran to the base of the tree and stretched their necks as if stargazing.

Noel and Mrs. Madelyn took their first sips of coffee as they watched the children from afar in awe.

"What are you asking for this Christmas?" Mrs. Madelyn whispered to Noel.

"I already have everything I need," Noel stated.

"How about a handsome man?"

Noel's eyes closed, and her lips fell open. She had a handsome man—*once*. "There is no replacement for Fletcher Puckett."

"Of course not but every person deserves a companion and a

helpmate. You run yourself ragged around here taking care of this shop and those two beautiful children; one of whom is more yours than your brother's, whom I pray a miracle over every day."

"With all due respect, Mrs. Madelyn, I don't want any other man."

"My dear, there is an overlap between wants and needs," she disclosed. "There are lots of days when I don't want Jack Brown, but I need him regardless of whether my pride allows me to admit the truth. Not in the way these culturally confused modern women say they don't need a man but to fulfill the deepest desires of the human soul."

Noel snickered. "Jack is a treasure," she acknowledged by attempting to turn the conversation towards Mrs. Madelyn's marriage rather than discussing the hole in her own heart.

"He's a pot of gold where the rainbow falls," Mrs. Madelyn granted.

"Don't you mean *at the end of the rainbow*?" Noel questioned yet thankful for the lead-in to a new topic.

"I like to imagine that rainbows never end. They just rise and fall on the earth, and beneath us they make a circle underground that we can't see with our eyes but can feel in our hearts."

The visual played out in Noel's mind. "Sounds peaceful."

"Something tells me that God might have a surprise gift in store for you this Christmas season," Mrs. Madelyn predicted before taking another sip of her coffee.

Noel nearly spit out the words that came to mind: *You better not try to play matchmaker during this busy holiday season.* Thankfully the kids came running back over with ornaments in their hands putting an end to a silly conversation.

2

avin Dawson fastened each button on a perfectly ironed burnt orange shirt and then straightened the collar while looking in the mirror beside which his dark brown suit coat hung. His flight into Atlanta last night kept him up later than expected because of a weather delay. However, the limousine his dad's assistant scheduled still managed to reach the gate at his parents' estate by midnight.

Neither of his parents waited up, but the butler granted access and ensured his belongings made it to his bedroom. Even though he couldn't remember perspiring all day, Cavin knew his mother would have a fit if he didn't shower before climbing into fresh linens. One of the family's staff members took responsibility for washing all the laundry, so he never quite understood why it ruffled her feathers. After toweling off, he opted to go straight to bed rather than finish the paperwork from the deal he closed before stepping onto the airplane in Oklahoma; putting off the final details until tomorrow would make it easier to wake up in time for the traditional Dawson Thanksgiving breakfast.

The next morning he freshened up, and while he skipped down the spiral staircase in the spacious open foyer with his jet-black hair parted neatly and slicked back, he absentmindedly connected his cuff links. Passing through another room, he greeted one of the workers on his way to the formal dining room, where he found his mother and father awaiting his arrival.

Sitting properly in a new yellow dress at one end of a table for twelve where each place setting displayed a plate, silverware, and fine linens, Cavin's mother glanced at her wristwatch. "We were beginning to wonder if you overslept."

"Your mother was afraid you stayed out late with a woman," Cavin's father offered halfheartedly from the head of the table.

Cavin approached his mother gracefully and kissed her cheek. "You look beautiful," he complimented before replying to the comments. "My connecting flight was delayed," he revealed.

"Thank you. Now please sit with us," Cavin's mother requested. "We can discuss the details of your trip as George and the others serve the meal they have generously prepared."

As Cavin's father stood to shake his son's hand, his brown tie covered the buttons down the shirt neatly tucked into his dress pants. A moment later, Cavin sat in his usual spot midway along the table on the right side while the other chairs remained empty as usual during this meal. He immediately noticed the lavishly designed tablescape featuring a centerpiece layered with pumpkins of various sizes; autumn colors and associated fruits spilled across a black and orange checkered table runner.

Fall-themed decorations and trinkets accented the room as well as every other area Cavin made his way through this morning and last night. The house decor, inside and out, changed with each season. At last count he recalled his family having thirty-one Christmas trees—one for each room and a handful on the porches.

"I was delighted to hear that you reached our goals in Oklahoma," Cavin's father announced as the staff quietly carried out dishes and set them gingerly in the appropriate places.

"That is fabulous news," his mother commended, smiling at Cavin before turning her attention to her husband. "Luther, when will you purchase a private jet so our son can be on time for holiday meals?"

"Mother, I left my bedroom a few minutes before eight, and I am confident the walk did not take that long," he postulated and then sipped the iced water next to his place setting.

"If you are on time, you are late," she reminded him.

Growing up, Cavin heard that phrase hundreds if not thousands of times, and he expected that George, who began to uncover each dish so the others could insert the appropriate serving utensils, could verify that.

"Would you be late to a business meeting?"

"No, Mother."

"Then please treat your father and me with the same respect."

"Ruth, he is here, it is Thanksgiving, and he closed the deal we have been working on for a month."

She forced a smile as George and the staff filled their plates with ham, eggs, bacon, and other breakfast delicacies. "Wonderful, now can we afford the airplane?"

"Maybe a helicopter," Cavin's father responded.

"We previously discussed that idea," Cavin's mother reminded everyone.

"Did we?" her husband checked.

"Mother feels it is not a safe mode of transportation," Cavin reminded him. "I happen to agree."

"When Cavin closes the deal in Beaufort, maybe we can shop for an airplane," his father proposed.

"Beaufort?" Cavin inquired with a furrowed brow.

"Beaufort is a little town on the coast of North Carolina, and it is ready for big changes."

"I thought Beaufort was in South Carolina," Cavin's mother interjected.

"That is Beaufort," Cavin's father clarified, pronouncing the South Carolina city as Bew-fort. "Beaufort," he explained, pronounced Bow-fort, "is our next masterpiece."

"When will I travel to Beaufort?" Cavin asked carefully considering the appropriate way to say the town's name. Once he arrived, he would not want to slip up in front of the locals. Mistakes like that often offended people and built unnecessary walls.

"This deal needs to be finalized before Christmas," Cavin's father stated with expectant eyes locked on Cavin.

The skin between Cavin's eyebrows crinkled as he did the math. "You promised me a week of vacation when I returned from Oklahoma," he reminded his father. "Remember, I have a flight booked for Cancun that leaves on Sunday." He looked forward to spending a few days with his parents, catching up with old friends in the area, and then heading to a tropical paradise to work on his tan and meet that woman his mother mentioned to his father earlier.

"Sandra already took care of that," Cavin's father explained.

Ruth watched the dialogue as she scooted food around her plate with her fork.

"What do you mean by took care of that?" Cavin inquired.

"The Cancun flight is postponed until after the holidays," he reported. "Now you have a flight scheduled into North Carolina."

While Cavin loved having someone take care of his travel arrangements, he didn't appreciate not having a say or at least a briefing prior to plans being altered. "So you want me to fly to North Carolina on Sunday?"

"Cavin, you need every day available to work your magic in Beaufort," his dad reasoned. "You know how things are during the holidays, especially in small towns, with people taking time off."

Cavin stuffed a forkful of ham into his mouth, hoping that chewing would keep him from speaking his mind. *Think positively*, he advised himself. At least he could relax for the next couple of days, play golf with his buddies, look up an old flame or two, talk business with his father in person, and play tennis with his mother.

"Son, did you turn into a Neanderthal while in Oklahoma?" his mother asked, staring disapprovingly at his chipmunk-like cheeks.

"Believe it or not," Cavin's father added to his previous statement, "Black Friday is not a very busy day at the airport, so Sandra was able to book a flight for tomorrow morning."

Cavin forcefully pushed his fork against the table causing a thud to echo throughout the formal dining room. "Are you serious?" he questioned. "This is Thanksgiving, Dad, not April Fool's Day. This sounds like a prank, but I have a feeling it is not."

Cavin welcomed the demands of his job. He strived under pressure. He took joy in meeting deadlines. He even enjoyed the adventure of living in a different city every month while working miracles as a property acquisition and development specialist. He felt like he owned the city when things went his way, and they almost always did. The goal to transform a town gave him purpose.

"Can we discuss business later?" Cavin's mom suggested sternly. "Perhaps we can have a peaceful meal together while giving thanks for all that this family has received?"

"Ruth, if Cavin reaches our goal in Beaufort, we can all give thanks for a private airplane," Cavin's father announced, hoping to diffuse the tension. "Cavin, I will even ensure you get the personal assistant you requested."

The frown on Ruth's face evaporated as a pleasurable smile quickly took residence.

Cavin pulled in a deep breath and let it out slowly. "Please do not promise me things you cannot give me," he replied. "Like a vacation," he added with a dagger.

"Son, have you ever known me not to come through on my word regarding business?"

Cavin's mind raced. "No."

"You will have an assistant. We will have a private plane for company and family use. You can be the first to use it for your trip to Cancun in the New Year."

Cavin knew negotiating like turkeys knew Thanksgiving although this opportunity presented itself at an inopportune time. *Always be prepared to close the deal because you might not get a second chance*, the man on the other side of this negotiation taught him years ago, and the advice worked flawlessly. "I want two weeks in Cancun, and from now on, my assistant, whom I interview and hire, will make my travel arrangements, and every decision about my schedule must go through me," he insisted.

"Land the deal, and your requests will be granted," his father promised as he stood to shake Cavin's hand.

3

The first step of transforming the candy store into a Christmas wonderland required pulling all the Thanksgiving decorations. The kids and Noel started at the front of the shop and worked toward the back where Mrs. Madelyn sorted the items into the appropriate pre-labeled bins to make things easier for next year. The candy went to the back corner clearance section to the left of the giant Christmas tree and would be organized later. Levi and Laney ran up and down the aisles collecting all the turkeys and pumpkins they could find.

"If it is brown or orange," Mrs. Madelyn instructed, "bring it to me."

She only had to ask the two little elves to return a couple of items that needed to stay put. One of the funniest moments came when Levi asked if they needed to roll all the brown candy barrels to the back of the store.

"Those remain in place year-round," Noel reminded them.

Noel focused on removing fall-related signage and erasing chalkboards with quotes and drawings of leaves. She climbed up and down the ladder, what felt like a hundred times, giving her legs a holiday workout and hopefully clearing room for turkey, dressing, candied yams, sweet potato fluff, cornbread stuffing, mac-and-cheese, pumpkin pie, and all the other traditional dishes.

The annual community Thanksgiving feast would take place within walking distance of the candy shop. Residents and their extended families and friends came together there every year for fellowship, fun, and food provided by the local restaurants. One of the best things about Beaufort was that almost everyone knew each other, and everything anyone needed could be found in the heart of the town: a general store, clothing boutiques, ice cream, furniture, groceries, and dining.

Beaufort Candy Company always provided pies and fudge made in-house along with a few trays of leftover Thanksgiving candy. A full-service kitchen beyond the back wall of the shop, which no one in the store would ever know existed if the sweet aromas didn't give away the secret, allowed Noel and Mrs. Madelyn to create most of the bakery items as well as a lot of the candy on display. It often surprised tourists when they explained that nearly everything was made from scratch on the premises.

Living upstairs helped Noel keep up with supply and demand. In the evenings after the shop closed, she could scurry in and out of the kitchen preparing and baking for the next day while the kids worked on homework, watched a movie, or played outside. Once they went to bed, she often spent an hour or two downstairs taking care of the final touches and refilling the displays.

Selling their old house after the tragic boating accident that took the lives of her husband, mother, father, and sister-in-law had been the only viable option. Before that, her parents lived upstairs. Noel never wanted to sell the house she bought with her husband, but with only one income, she couldn't afford the mortgage. She and Fletcher talked about life insurance for years but never got around to making it happen.

Learning the hard way, she now encouraged everyone, especially those with children, to pick a plan immediately. She even mentioned it to random strangers when a conversation ignited in the shop. Her parents' term policies ran out years ago limiting their inheritance to the candy shop and the apartment above which Noel thanked God for daily; otherwise, she didn't know where she and the kids would live. In some ways their living quarters came as an upgrade since not many families her age owned a waterfront residence. For that, she remained grateful.

Noel knew about a decline in candy sales recently but didn't realize the hole her parents dug to keep the place open. Come to find out, they hadn't been paying themselves like they used to; only she and Mrs. Madelyn's salaries showed up in the books that her father guarded so tightly. On the one hand she found it sweet that they gave up an income to keep Beaufort Candy Company in business, but at the same time she wished she knew, so she could have had the option to plan for her future accordingly or possibly come up with ideas to increase business. However, the new things she tried so far hadn't helped the bottom line.

"Unless a miracle happens tomorrow, the store will be in the red after Black Friday," Noel told Mrs. Madelyn when they found a moment alone in the kitchen where the pies for today's event waited to be delivered via the little red wagons the kids liked to play with.

"I'm so sorry, darling," Mrs. Madelyn replied sincerely. "You have worked so hard this year to move the store into the black."

When setting the goal earlier in the year, Noel researched the true meaning of Black Friday and found it seemed debatable and ultimately mingled over time. One explanation came from the idea that retailers hoped to move out of the red negative numbers and into the black positive ones by or on this day each year. Apparently this thought process began circulating in the 1980s; however, historically, the title referred to throngs of factory workers claiming sickness to prolong their holiday break. Later, traffic officers in Philadelphia used the term to describe long shifts and terrible traffic due to holiday shopping coinciding with an annual football game. Regardless of the origin, the term stuck, and now retailers like Noel hoped for significant sales volume on Black Friday.

"We," Noel corrected. "We have worked so hard. You have put in more hours than ever before," she reminded her friend who had been like an aunt to her growing up. Somehow in the wake of the tragedy, Mrs. Madelyn seamlessly took on the role of the adult mother turned best friend whom Noel missed dearly.

"I wish I could do more."

"You do more than your share," Noel reminded her. She initially thought she could hire employees to take on the hours her parents put into the shop although she doubted anyone would be able to match the output their experience afforded. However, since they hadn't been drawing a salary, the funds to hire additional help didn't exist.

"Honestly, I am not sure how long I can keep it up," Mrs. Madelyn revealed. The demands of Halloween and Thanksgiving at the candy shop took a toll on her body. "Being on my feet all day wears me out more than it used to; I could once skip around this store like you do. Your mother, God rest her soul, and I both could."

The two of them had acted like sisters and were the best of friends. They went to grade school together, graduated high school the same year, and worked in the candy store pretty much their whole lives. Mrs. Madelyn married a farmer whose family owned a successful farm, so she never needed much income. Early on she helped at the shop for fun, but in more recent years she helped out of need, and Noel could tell her joy faded at times.

"You know you don't have to pay me, Noel."

"There is no way I am taking advantage of completely free labor," Noel rebutted.

"What do you mean by completely free labor?"

"I know you have been clocking in well after arrival and clocking out way before you leave."

"Honey, I'm old, it takes time to put away my purse, drink a little coffee, indulge in a bakery item, and take care of all the other personal things I don't intend to do on the clock."

Noel laughed. "We both know you work way more hours than you get paid for."

Mrs. Madelyn waved a hand. "Minor details," she responded, brushing aside the truth. "If I cut back, how will you afford to hire someone to compensate for the extra hours?"

Noel fought back the tears springing up inside her. "I will have to find a way. Maybe I can put in more time myself."

"Sweetheart, you run on fumes," she noted. "Those children deserve your free time more than this shop needs it."

"What other option do I have?"

"You can always sell the store."

Noel closed her eyes, tucked her lips inward, and bit down. Of course the idea of selling the candy shop filtered through her mind a time or two, especially when sifting through the numbers in the wee hours of the morning.

Mrs. Madelyn continued, "This location has a lot of value. That would give you enough to buy a cute little house somewhere and take care of your needs while you get your feet on the ground with a new career."

"I can't talk about this, not today," Noel admitted with tears streaming down her cheeks. She already lost so much; she couldn't fathom voluntarily letting go of the legacy her family built. "This is supposed to be a happy day."

Mrs. Madelyn's ensuing bear hug swallowed Noel. When the kids came running into the kitchen, Noel wiped her tears on one of the woman's broad shoulders and sucked up the ones yet to fall.

"Hey kiddos," Mrs. Madelyn called out while giving Noel time to pull herself together.

"What's wrong?" Laney asked.

"Is Mommy crying?" Levi inquired.

"Mommy is happy," Mrs. Madelyn replied. "Do you know why?"

"Why?" the children asked in unison.

"Because all of us are together and because it is time for us to load up all these pies for the big lunch."

"Yay," Laney declared.

"I am going to eat too much turkey and pies," Levi predicted, rubbing his belly and inciting a round of laughter.

Noel painted a smile on her face and spun around with all the enthusiasm she could muster. "Who's going to get the little red wagons?" she queried.

"I am," Laney shouted.

"We are," Levi answered enthusiastically.

"Both of you grab one and come help Mrs. Madelyn and me fill them with enough pies, fudge, and candy for the whole town."

The kids hastily retrieved the wagons, parked them haphazardly near the stainless steel island occupying the middle of the kitchen, and helped position the goodies one at a time with a sense of pride.

When the carts became full, Noel said, "Let's run upstairs to change outfits for the community Thanksgiving feast."

"I want to wear my Christmas pajamas," Levi pleaded with folded hands and a cheesy grin.

"Me too," Laney begged.

This request didn't surprise Noel. "I think we might look a little out of place showing up for Thanksgiving lunch wearing Christmas outfits, especially pajamas," she pointed out. "I will make a deal with you. You have to change out of your pajamas, but you can wear your Christmas hats."

Laney and Levi looked at one another as if trading their deepest thoughts. "Okay," both giggled and ran up the stairs.

"I set out outfits for each of you on your beds," Noel called up the staircase as she walked in that direction before turning to Mrs. Madelyn. "Would you like to come up and relax while we change?"

"No, thanks. With these old hips, I don't want to climb those stairs more than necessary," she laughed. "I will wheel the carts up front and straighten a few things around the register while you all freshen up."

"Thank you," Noel replied with a genuine smile. She didn't know what she would have done without this woman.

Noel skipped up the steps and hustled into her bedroom. She wanted to be early so the desserts and candy could be set on the serving tables before the guests arrived. Even though dessert traditionally came after the meal, experience taught her that plenty of hands would want first dibs on the baked goods, and little hands would find the candy quickly.

While changing into wide-leg chocolate brown linen pants, which Noel bought for the color name, and because they looked cute, of course, she studied her body in the bathroom mirror. Unsure whether her diet or lack of appetite helped her keep a slim waist, she found herself thankful that she could eat more than her share today and not fear the consequences.

Fletcher always told her how beautiful she looked no matter what she wore or if she gained or lost ten pounds. She sure missed his words of affirmation. Noel didn't feel unpretty now; however, she lacked the confidence she once possessed. She missed walking into places like today's festivities with her arm anchored around her husband's.

Noel wrapped a belt through the loops circling her waist and then pulled on a tan long-sleeved turtleneck. Adjusting her hair, she clasped a gold necklace with a turkey pendant around her slim neck and added the matching earrings. Lastly, she spent a few minutes fixing her hair before stepping into a pair of shoes for the occasion.

Prior to walking downstairs, she called for Levi and Laney, but neither answered. She then glanced out the back windows and spotted a colt standing beside his mother on Carrot Island. The view that had been a lifesaver after the accident kept her occupied for a few moments. When Noel made it down the steps, she found the children near the front door being silly with Mrs. Madelyn, and when she took in the sight of their outfits, a large grin stretched across Noel's face.

"Don't you two look adorable?"

Noel picked out a brown dress with a white undershirt for Laney and brown pants and an apple-red collared shirt for Levi. The Santa hats topped off the outfits brilliantly.

"Mrs. Madelyn said she will wear her Santa hat to the feast if you do," Laney announced.

Noel's smile shone through her green eyes. "Of course I will," she agreed, "but one of you will have to run upstairs and get it for me; I left it on my bed."

Without a single word, the race began. Each kid took a different route through the candy shop, and Laney made it up the stairs first. Running indoors wasn't allowed anytime the store was open for business, but Noel's father always let her and her brother play freely when the closed sign hung; she permitted the same for these little ones.

Somehow Levi made it down with the hat dangling from his grip.

"Levi took the hat from me," Laney complained with a frown.

"Did not, we both grabbed it."

"I had it first, and then you yanked it from my hand."

Analyzing the situation, Noel studied their faces. "I know who made it up the stairs first," she announced glaring at Levi. "Did Laney have it to begin with?"

"Maybe," he answered, "but she dropped it and I got it then."

"You two are a team," Noel reminded them. "You need to help each other rather than work against the other."

"I did. I picked up the hat for her."

"Wouldn't a team player hand it back?" Noel asked.

Levi shrugged his shoulders.

"How about you hand it to Laney now," Noel recommended, "and, Laney, you can put it on my head like I did yours."

"I get to crown you like a queen?" Laney asked as the corners of her lips swiftly turned upward.

"Yes," Noel replied.

Levi handed it over with a slight hesitance, and Laney beamed as she slid it onto Noel's hair causing it to curl out more than before.

"You three get together for a picture," Mrs. Madelyn suggested while pulling her phone from the enormous purse draped across her forearm.

Standing behind the little red wagons staged for a photo shoot, each kiddo wrapped an arm around Noel while Mrs. Madelyn snapped several pictures. Then Noel talked her into getting into a shot, and Noel held out the phone and took a selfie of the whole gang.

After Noel twisted the lock, the four of them walked down the sidewalk with the kids in charge of the wagons. Noel and Mrs. Madelyn played the role of the caboose in case anything fell out since Levi and Laney knew the best route to the feast as well as anyone. They played on these streets nearly every day after school and during the summers; the two roamed Beaufort like pirates once did. Nowadays it was a safe town, low in crime, and high on the phrase *it takes a village*. The one rule the children must abide by was staying together at all times. They also kept high-powered walkie-talkies to report back to Noel and to allow her to check in on them.

When they entered the grassy lawn between two buildings where the community Thanksgiving feast took place each year, a large circus-style tent covered a slew of chairs and tables for dining, and a few buffet bars occupied the far corner. Although the sun shone brightly, a regular breeze blew through the trees that dotted the park-like area.

Noel instantly spotted a cluster of volunteers with familiar faces who quickly made their way with Thanksgiving greetings, hugs, and outstretched arms. She loved and appreciated all of these folks—or at least most of them—but she wondered when the extra emotional support for the poor, pitiful widow and children would end.

4

The mayor led the charge. Alongside him several city council members broke free from helping the restaurant owners. The employees set out dishes being carted in from various directions. Police officers and firefighters, who were bringing in the last chairs, greeted Levi and Laney with fist bumps and smiles. The two knew most of the first responders by name and vice versa.

"Let us help you," the mayor offered after the lengthy pleasantries subsided.

"The kids are excited about wheeling the carts to the dessert table and unloading all the goodies, but you all are welcome to join us for the pie guessing game," Noel stated, turning her attention to the mayor's wife.

The woman's face bubbled at the thought of the tradition. "Yes, let's do," she agreed.

The farmers' market manager pointed Noel to the dessert table, and nearly everyone gathered around to ooh and aah.

Cornucopias decorated the tables, and Noel was glad to see dark tablecloths in case one of the kids or anyone else spilled food. Once they set out all the pies, the crowd of inquiring minds waited for the mayor's wife to begin.

"Oh heavens, you all brought lots of unique pies this year," she observed. The mayor stood beside his bride with bulging eyes. The two were regular customers, and Noel was almost certain the enthusiastic woman tasted every dessert ever made at the shop. The most informally formal person Noel ever met went on to point at each pie as she carefully thought and then called out the name: "Apple, pumpkin, pecan, sweet potato, butternut squash, lemon, chocolate silk, cranberry, coconut, and French silk."

Those were all the ones she guessed correctly, Noel confirmed, and after several guesses at the remaining pies, she gave up.

"What's that one?" the mayor asked, pointing.

"Maple syrup pie," Noel answered.

The mayor rubbed his oversized belly. "You all stay away from this pie," he warned the onlookers with a heavy grin. "It has my name written all over it."

Laney gave the man the eye because he picked her favorite.

"Is that an oatmeal pie?" the farmers' market manager asked.

"Sure is," Mrs. Madelyn divulged.

"I haven't seen one of those in years."

Noel remembered her grandmother teaching her how to make that particular pie as a young child.

"And that one?" a city council member asked.

"Pumpkin cheesecake pie," Noel revealed.

"How about that beauty?" a police officer standing next to Levi checked.

"Caramel apple pie with streusel topping," Noel shared.

His eyes grew as large as the muscles stretching his sleeves.

"That pie has my name on it," Levi announced, and a round of genuine laughter ensued.

Witnessing all the interest excited Noel. Although she had yet to set out the name plates for each pie because of the annual guessing game, she made sure to add that touch because she knew members of the community would take note. She prayed for lots of orders between now and Christmas. She did the same with the fudge which would be a hit as well.

"They are all decorated so beautifully," a familiar voice spoke.

Noel turned. "Jack, you made it," she announced then hugged him carefully after a firefighter friend pushed his wheelchair close to the dessert bar.

Mrs. Madelyn stepped toward her husband, and when she bent down to greet him, he kissed her on the cheek.

"Aw, you two are the sweetest," Noel noted.

"Plenty of years of practice," Jack stated with a grin.

"He's been in love with that woman since middle school," the mayor's wife reminded everyone.

They all grew up together. Beaufort was one of those towns a person didn't want to leave once they figured out what they wanted in life. Some wandered off for college, careers, relationships, and all kinds of other reasons, but many circled back to what Noel called *the roots beneath us*. She thought of this phrase one day while meandering through the large live oaks on the courthouse grounds where the Olde Beaufort Farmers' Market assembled every Saturday from April through November.

The locals missed having the market during the winter months, but they looked forward to the Olde Fashioned Holiday Market, a one-of-a-kind Christmas event that took place every December. Vendors squeezed into every nook and cranny with the best gifts around: homemade candles, soaps, dog treats, Alpaca socks, novels, jewelry, ocean-inspired art, and so many other unique items. They also sold the freshest fruits and vegetables available from local farmers like Jack, as well as freshly caught seafood.

Anything related to fishing, boats, and water made Noel's mind drift to Fletcher. He fished for a living. The man knew the waterways like the back of his hand.

She remembered her dad often saying when introducing Fletcher to others, "He's not a fisher; he's a catcher."

Her man sure knew how to bait a hook to reel in the big ones, the little ones, and everything in between. He taught Levi how to fish, and Laney tagged along, too. The two of them still fished, and Noel wondered if being by the sea helped Levi feel close to his dad. Personally, she hadn't stepped onto a pier or a boat since the accident. She hadn't swum in the creek, the river, or the ocean. She had no desire.

"Noel," a voice called out. "Noel, did you hear me?"

Noel shook away her thoughts. "I'm sorry, what?" she asked, realizing nearly everyone dispersed while memories of Fletcher paralyzed her. Now she stood alone at the dessert table with Walter Benson, a local businessman with deep pockets and influence, who also happened to be her accountant. "I think I zoned out," Noel added, fluttering back to reality.

"Have you thought about my proposal?" Walter asked enthusiastically in his perfectly fitting suit and tie which he adjusted while awaiting an answer.

"Yes," Noel answered simply without further remark, still trying to find her bearings.

"The offer is quite lucrative," he suggested, moving in close to provide his full attention.

Uncomfortable with the lack of distance between them even though his short, well-fed stature did little to intimidate her, Noel stepped back. She wanted to sock him and knock the expensive frames right off his nose. "I have no interest in selling the candy shop."

Walter's face soured a hint then quickly transitioned to his pondering look as he pressed his thumb and forefinger against his chin. "Noel, my dear, I want to make sure you see the whole picture?" he conveyed as he adjusted his hands to create a large frame in midair.

"What whole picture?" she asked, ignoring his gesture with folded arms while looking for Laney and Levi or any reason to walk away.

"Maybe a new perspective will help you make a more informed decision."

"Excuse me?" she shot back focusing on his cold eyes.

"I have no interest in your candy store," Walter clarified, giving the comment a moment to settle. "Just the building," he reminded her, knowing he explained this in the past but maybe not as clearly as needed. "You can keep the business open; I can even help you move your little shop somewhere down the street where the cost of real estate is more affordable."

Noel frowned. While most people in town supported her after the accident, Walter did a poor job of hiding his intentions of taking advantage of her in times of weakness. The two of them graduated from high school around the same time, and Walter moved off for college then worked his way up at an accounting firm in Virginia. His father passed away not long before hers, and Walter subsequently moved back home to take over his family's accounting business.

Noel knew Walter had conversations with her dad about the building in the short time between each of their parents' deaths. Although Noel's father never shared the details, he made it clear he didn't like doing business with the guy stating several times that he was nothing like the standup gentleman his father had always been. A couple of weeks after Noel's father passed, Walter came into the candy shop with a bouquet of flowers in one hand and a sales proposal in the other; he went on to explain that the deal would remove a lot of the stress from Noel's life. Ever since, he continued hounding her with offers and options.

"Remind me why you want my family's store so bad?"

"Noel, there is no hiding the fact that the building you own is a diamond in the rough. I want it as an investment; that's what I do, remember? I own twenty percent of the buildings in the downtown area."

Noel scoffed, recalling when he initially tried to convince her that the building was in disrepair and of little value. The irony was that he owned the building attached to hers, and the two were nearly identical in every way. "I am not in the market to sell, Walter."

"Numbers are what I do, Noel," he reminded her. "As your accountant, I know yours quite well. Costs of goods are up, and sales are down. It's only a matter of time before you go out of business and are forced to sell the property or, heaven forbid, lose it to foreclosure," he stated matter-of-factly. "I am trying to help you."

"All you care about is numbers, and that's another reason I have no interest in selling my family's building to you," she relayed harshly all the while realizing some truths in his statement.

"I care about Beaufort and doing what is best for the whole community, including you," Walter replied. "I can see your mind is made up for now, but I am always available; however, the offer may not be the same the next time we meet," he concluded, holding out a business card to accompany his signature salesman grin.

"Thanks, but no thanks," Noel responded. "I have dozens of your cards." Actually, the kids ran most of them to the trash can as soon as the bell jingled on Walter's way out each time.

"Happy Thanksgiving, Noel," Walter offered. "I look forward to enjoying some of your delicious pies and fudge."

Noel forced a smile. "Happy Thanksgiving," she uttered and then caught a glimpse of the kids roaming around with a group of police officers communicating on their walkie-talkies. A while back, Officer Rainey, a guy she grew up with who married her good friend Chelsea, found a channel for them to reach the officers. Ever since, Levi and Laney believed they were junior officers.

"The kids are helping us track down a missing turkey," Officer Rainey relayed seriously to Noel when she neared his position at the far corner of the tent.

"Oh really," she laughed.

"This is important police business," he rebutted.

"I bet," she replied with raised eyebrows.

"Noel, it is Thanksgiving Day; we can't have missing turkeys wandering around the streets of Beaufort. People need to eat."

Noel chuckled. "Are you sure the kids are not bothering you all?" she asked seriously.

"Ma'am, you are the one impeding this investigation," he remarked with a smirk. Noel shook her head and watched him press a button on the radio attached to the shoulder area of his uniform. While studying her from head to toe, he spoke into the receiver. "Detectives Levi and Laney, be on the lookout for a woman about five feet and six inches, wearing a pair of brown pants, a tan turtleneck, and a Santa Claus hat," he relayed. "She may be involved in the heist."

Noel swatted him on the opposite shoulder with the back of her hand. "Stop it," she spewed. "The instigator here is the man in uniform with broad shoulders about six foot four, maybe 250 pounds, and a slick bald head from which all his hair fell onto the rest of his body."

"Copy that," Levi interrupted through the radio, and then Laney followed suit.

Rainey pressed the button again. "Word on the street is that this woman assaulted an officer," Rainey added, trying not to let out the snicker tickling his insides.

"Are you attempting to turn the kids against me?"

"Just doing my job, ma'am."

"Quit calling me ma'am; we are the same age."

"Yes, ma'am."

She held up her fist. "No pie, fudge, or candy for you today," Noel teased.

"Is that also what you just told Walter Benson?" he inquired. "The way you were looking at him I thought I might have to break up a fight," he chuckled, knowing the history.

"Nope, I only banned you," Noel retorted.

Rainey reached for the button once more and turned his mouth toward his shoulder. "This lady is also withholding desserts from police officers."

"Is it Mommy?" Levi's voice asked while snickering.

"She's a possible suspect," Officer Rainey confirmed.

"Want us to arrest her?" Laney's voice questioned authoritatively.

"Yes, but approach with caution; she may be armed and dangerous."

Noel snuck away into the thickening crowd and began talking to folks; some she saw regularly and others she hadn't seen since last year's event. She remembered that particular Thanksgiving feast all too well. She and her elves had brought in the pies, and then she hid from everyone as best as possible. Noel quickly found that sitting alone at a secluded corner table caused her to stand out like the nearby Cape Lookout Lighthouse with a light swiveling on top of her head every fifteen seconds. People followed that beacon right up to her table, and as she quietly pushed the food around on her plate, they insisted on offering their well-meaning condolences. Meanwhile, the kids played as usual; however, they checked in more frequently due to newly acquired insecurities from their recent losses. When the kids were occupied, Noel often excused herself and ducked around the corners of nearby buildings to release the built-up tears. A couple of times, she wandered into a vacant restroom and dropped her head into her hands. She eventually went back to the candy shop early and left the kids with Mrs. Madelyn, who understood without question.

Shaking away that memory, Noel spotted Chelsea—tall with long blonde hair, beautiful blue eyes, and a lean figure—walking from a nearby parking spot. Once her friend made it to the shelter, the two became lost in conversation.

Suddenly a handcuff circled Noel's dangling wrist, and before she could turn around, it clicked.

"You are under arrest," Levi announced proudly.

Laney grabbed Noel's other wrist assisting Levi in the capture and pulled her aunt's hands together behind her back. "You have the right to remain—" she trailed off searching her memory for the word.

"Silent," Rainey's wife whispered.

Noel shot her friend a look of betrayal.

"Silent," Laney copied.

"If you talk, we will tell on you," Levi stated while securing the second cuff on his mother's other wrist.

Noel and Chelsea laughed out loud.

"You can hire a lawman," Laney added.

Levi turned his attention to Mrs. Chelsea. "Do you know anything about the missing turkey?" he interrogated.

Chelsea held up her hands. "No, don't arrest me, I don't even know this woman," she uttered, smirking. "In fact she tried to tempt me with the dessert table before the meal started."

"You traitor," Noel declared, shaking her head although unable to keep a straight face.

Rainey walked onto the scene, but before he could speak, a boisterous and familiar voice caused Noel's head to turn.

"Hey, Sis, I'm usually the one in handcuffs," Keaton Bradley protested.

5

"I guess trouble with the law runs in the family," Keaton added with a snicker, cutting his eyes at Rainey before wrapping his arms around Noel.

With her hands secured behind her back, Noel couldn't reciprocate the hug properly, but she pushed herself into her brother's embrace and caught a whiff of the alcohol on his breath. Thankfully, he looked halfway put together wearing a pair of jeans and a wrinkled, heavy button-up shirt with pockets on either side. She wasn't sure if he left the top two buttons unbuttoned on purpose, but the chest hair spilling out begged for an undershirt. As for the thick black hair on top of his head, she couldn't tell if he combed it or not since he and a lot of others often sported a messy look these days.

"Daddy," Laney called out enthusiastically, clinging to her father's leg like a koala bear.

"Hey, little bug," he said, lifting her as far as his hands would stretch toward the white tent's cathedral ceiling. "I missed you."

"I missed you too, Daddy," she replied with unadulterated joy lining her voice.

"Uncle Keat," Levi chimed.

"My main man," Keaton spoke vehemently, giving his nephew a turn in the air.

"Throw me up high," Levi requested, recalling the thrill of previous experiences.

"Maybe not right now," Noel quickly warned, not knowing how much her brother drank this morning.

"Mommy's orders trump our fun," Keaton concluded with a sideways grin surrounded by the stubble on his tired face.

"Hey, Keaton," Chelsea greeted after waiting for her turn. She stepped toward him and gave him a side hug. Like Noel, she noticed his breath and wished he wouldn't drink in the mornings.

Hugging her back, Keaton shared a short stare with Rainey who stood on the other side of his wife with an uneasy look covering his face.

"Keaton," Rainey greeted simply.

"Rainey," he responded with a nod.

At that moment a voice vibrated the speakers set up around the tent which interrupted the reunion.

"Ladies and gentlemen, Happy Thanksgiving," the mayor offered enthusiastically and then gave a short speech while the crowd settled. Most found seats, some stood in groups, and others inched toward the food. The aroma of the Thanksgiving meal tempted everyone's senses as volunteers lifted the covers from the dishes and dashed around taking care of last-minute preparations. "I won't ramble on because I know you all are hungry. I am going to hand the microphone over to our dear friend who will say grace for this wonderful meal created by our local restaurants and dessert donated by Beaufort Candy Company. Make sure you find these fine folks and give them thanks for their generosity."

Last year, Noel cringed when she heard those words and subsequently found people's eyes darting in her direction. She remembered wanting to crawl underneath the table and hide like the kids had while playing. This time around, it didn't sound all that bad although she wouldn't have invited the attention, but, hopefully, it would drum up some much needed business.

A local pastor blessed the food, and then several lines quickly formed at the buffet tables.

"Can Mommy's handcuffs be removed now so that I can eat lunch?" Noel asked Levi using her soft motherly voice.

Levi looked at Rainey for approval.

"I think some of the officers found the missing turkey," Rainey announced then shrugged. "It looks like your mom is innocent after all, so we better release her so she doesn't become hangry."

Laney and Levi giggled. Keaton glanced at the kids and then at Rainey.

"We don't want that," Chelsea agreed, lifting her eyebrows for emphasis as a breeze caused her blonde hair to swish like streamers on a little girl's bicycle.

"You have to watch out for these officers," Keaton warned with a sarcastic snicker. "You think they're your friends and then all of a sudden they turn on you," he reminisced, cutting his eyes at Rainey.

Rainey's shoulders broadened, and he turned his body toward Keaton.

Chelsea grabbed her husband's hand. "Not here," she whispered, wrapping her body into his as if about to dance. "Especially in front of the kids," she added.

At that moment one of Noel's hands became free of the cuffs, and she instantly used it to clutch her brother's wrist. "Stop it," she hissed in his ear and rolled her eyes at him. "The kids are having fun."

Noel hated the animosity between Rainey and Keaton these days. It kept her up at night sometimes as her mind spun, and on many occasions the animosity made her cry even in front of them a few times. In a small town avoiding people proved difficult, especially those within the same circle of friends.

Keaton and Rainey grew up best buds nearly inseparable like

Levi and Laney. They ran around the streets of Beaufort having fun, swimming in the creeks and rivers, playing sports, and enjoying life to the fullest. As adults, they carried on many of those same activities and added new ones like listening to live music on the waterfront. Noel and Chelsea always joined in on the fun although at certain stages the boys had been too cool for the girls and vice versa.

Now Keaton and Rainey couldn't be in the same room without arguing, and sometimes the disagreements led to physical altercations. Pushing and shoving started wrestling matches which on a few occasions turned into blows, and both of the stubborn men walked away bleeding and bruised more than once. Noel knew that anytime they all got together Keaton would say something he shouldn't, and Rainey never backed down. She couldn't count the number of times she and Chelsea stood in the middle of the two grown men although both were about the same size and strong enough to throw either of the ladies out of the way with one arm. Thankfully neither did that, but Noel feared her brother might accidentally hurt an innocent bystander on one of these nights when alcohol called the shots.

Keaton was lucky Rainey never pressed charges. In a way their scuffles reminded her of fights the two boys got into as kids when something didn't go their way and they didn't know how to control their emotions. Nowadays, Rainey controlled his temper well. Dealing with criminals on a regular basis required knowing when to use words and when to assert physical force. On the other hand, Keaton, who had been cool, calm, and collected up until the tragedy, let alcohol and anger do the talking for him. Whether Noel liked to admit it or not, her brother had been arrested several times and served short-term jail sentences.

These days Noel made sure not to invite Keaton anytime Rainey would be around. Of course Rainey and Chelsea didn't invite him to their get-togethers either, and the same went for the rest of their friends. The downsides of this trend held many negative consequences. An alcoholic often doesn't do well alone or with a group of friends who wait at the bar with open arms and similar problems.

Most importantly, Noel didn't want the kids around Keaton when he drank which happened way too frequently these days. When Noel's and Keaton's parents and spouses died in the boating accident—on the trip where her father planned to share some big news—Noel knew two options existed. She could let her emotions control her, or she could fight with every ounce of energy possible to control her emotions. She elected the latter as often as possible while Keaton chose to give in fully to the grief. When Noel hit her knees and crawled to friends and God, Keaton ran to isolation and alcohol.

Early on, Noel let Laney stay at her house because Keaton admitted he could barely take care of himself let alone his little girl. At the time his realization of his struggles seemed admirable, and Noel thought everything, including the turn to the bottle, would be temporary. However, what started out as a day or two here and there became a weekend, and then a week, and before she realized it, Laney basically moved in with her and Levi.

Little by little Laney's clothes, toys, and other belongings filled up the dresser and space in the guest room which slowly became hers. Eventually Noel took Laney to pick out a bedspread, curtains, and other things for her room so it would feel like home. Laney chose a beautiful stars and moons theme, and they even created a solar system on her ceiling. However, at bedtime Laney always wanted to crawl into bed with Levi, and Noel understood firsthand why they didn't want to sleep alone because she didn't either.

Rainey and Chelsea wandered to the other side of the tent, and Noel, Keaton, and the kids headed for the long buffet line. After standing there for about ten minutes slowly inching forward, Noel came up with an idea.

"If it's okay with Keaton, why don't you kids go play, and we will make you a plate?" Noel suggested.

"That's fine with me, Sis."

Laney and Levi instantly joined a group of children playing tag in the open lawn while the bright sunshine cast shadows under the tent as they ran around. Either the temperature increased over the past hour, or the number of attendants warmed the area even though a breeze kept people chasing napkins and other lightweight objects brought to the event. The tension of the brief encounter between Keaton and Rainey may have also been a factor in boiling Noel's blood.

"Why do you feel the need to give Rainey a hard time about being a police officer?" Noel asked her brother quietly.

"Why do you think?" he questioned with a furrowed brow.

"Because he arrested you?"

"Bingo."

"You never seemed to have a problem with him being a police officer before that incident," Noel reminded Keaton.

"Yeah exactly."

"What was he supposed to do when he responded to a call and found you kicking a car while onlookers videoed the whole thing?"

"Haven't we had this conversation?" Keaton checked, holding his finger to his chin. "About ten times."

"Probably."

They shuffled a few feet ahead when the line moved.

"Can we just eat Thanksgiving lunch and talk about something different?" Keaton proposed.

"Sure, if you promise you won't start anything with Rainey while we're here."

"I'm not that stupid, Noel. I realize we are in public, and pretty much the whole town is here," Keaton said while looking around.

At least ten people walked by and said hello while Keaton and Noel shuffled forward. Some knew about Keaton's struggles, but others didn't; although in a small town, it didn't take long to get relabeled.

"We were in public when you pushed Rainey on Halloween night while the kids trick-or-treated," Noel reminded her brother.

"That's because he told me I needed to go home when I was simply trying to spend a fun evening with my daughter."

"Do you remember why he said you should go home?" Noel asked, impressed that her brother kept the conversation to a low volume this long. She already decided that if she thought anyone nearby could hear she would change the subject.

"Rainey accused me of being drunk."

"You were drunk," Noel reminded him. "Are you drunk now?"

"No," he insisted.

"But you have been drinking."

"What makes you think I've been drinking?" he questioned with raised brows.

Noel peered into her brother's green eyes, a little darker than hers. "Did you brush your teeth with alcohol this morning?" she asked harshly.

Keaton took a step back. "Is it that obvious?" he asked.

"It always is," she sighed.

"I only had a couple beers," he replied, brushing it off.

"Yeah, and it's only noon."

"It's Thanksgiving; I'm celebrating," he reasoned with a snicker.

Noel searched for the silver lining. Thankfully Keaton's speech wasn't slurred, and more importantly he showed up for the community meal to spend some time with his daughter, nephew, and her on the holiday.

"I am glad you are here," Noel acknowledged as she tried to let go of the other thoughts.

When they reached the first table, each grabbed two plates,

utensils, and napkins. From there they slid the trays down the line, piling on turkey, ham, sweet potato fluff, stuffing, cornbread, rolls, green bean casserole, cranberry sauce, mashed potatoes, corn on the cob, deviled eggs, and lots of baked macaroni and cheese for the kids.

Noel glanced at the dessert table surrounded by smiling faces and laughter, and it made her heart happy to see that so many people enjoyed the treats she, Mrs. Madelyn, and the kids prepared.

"It looks like your sweets are a hit as always," Keaton noted.

"I'm so glad," Noel replied. "Do you see anything you want before it all disappears?" she asked.

"I see a lot of things I want," Keaton replied, "but I only have two hands," he pointed out while carefully balancing the overflowing plates.

"Noel," a lady, who Noel recognized but didn't know by name, called out from across the table, "I can't wait to try this apple pie; it looks delicious!"

Others at the table bombarded Noel with generous comments and questions about the pies and fudge. She patiently responded to everyone, and then she and Keaton found a few empty seats at the end of a table on the side of the canopy where the kids played.

"Laney, Levi," Keaton hollered, the tone of his voice causing several groups in the area to halt their conversations because of the interruption.

Noel noticed a few awkward glances, some prolonged stares, and gossipy whispers, but after a few moments everyone seemed to turn their attention back to their meals and conversations.

"We need beverages," Noel realized out loud.

The kids hurried over still wearing their Santa hats to Noel's surprise. She feared they would be lost by now.

"You guys come with me so we can get drinks for all of us," Keaton encouraged them as he motioned toward the beverage station.

Noel loved seeing her brother interact with the kids and knew he wasn't drunk because he hadn't been short with them every time they spoke. As they walked away, each of them grabbed one of his hands, and Noel fixated on the sight that was cute enough for a picture frame.

After bringing back drinks, Levi and Laney ate most everything Noel expected and left the rest for her and Keaton. The conversations went smoothly with lots of laughter, and for a while Noel felt like they were a normal family again. They chatted with the people who sat nearby and even shared some things they were thankful for this year. Levi and Laney said playing police and tag, and Noel and Keaton mentioned family and friends.

Even though Keaton was a different person from the man Noel knew up until last year, he was her only adult family member left other than distant relatives, and she prayed that her brother found his way back one day soon.

6

"We would love for you to come back to the shop with us and help decorate for Christmas," Noel mentioned eagerly to Keaton after wrapping the leftovers with foil.

She purposely waited until the kids ran off to the dessert table out of earshot of the question to avoid the chance that her brother's answer would disappoint them.

"I wish I could, but I promised my buddies I would watch football with them," Keaton answered apologetically.

Noel hoped he would spend the rest of the holiday with family, but she knew beggars shouldn't be choosers. Although she invited him to the feast today, she initially doubted he would show up. However, he proved her wrong, and for that, gratefulness filled her healing heart.

With messy fingers, Levi devoured a piece of the pie he called dibs on earlier, and Laney forked a few bites of the slice she chose. Noel and Mrs. Madelyn deliberately cut the pieces much smaller, knowing that kids and even some adults wouldn't have room for a regular helping. Most usually sported bigger eyes than appetites after a full Thanksgiving meal, and from what Noel saw in the buffet line, the local restaurants prepared all of the traditional dishes and even added a few contemporary favorites.

When Keaton announced his departure, Laney responded with a question that nearly broke Noel's heart. "Daddy, will you help us decorate the Christmas tree?" she asked sweetly with her fingers bonded as if kneeling at her bedside for a prayer. However, if a prayer would bring her father back into her life more regularly, it would have happened a while ago.

Keaton lifted his daughter up again. "You know I would love to, but I have to meet some people."

"What people?" she asked inquisitively.

"Friends," he answered simply as if the rebuttal stunned him.

"Are they more important than us?" she wondered aloud with childlike sincerity.

Noel pressed her lips together hoping Laney's question would warm her father's heart.

"Absolutely not," Keaton replied. "No one is more important than you, Levi, and Aunt Noel."

Is football more important? Noel wanted to ask. *How about beer?* However, she kept her lips together as if bonded by glue.

"So you'll come?" Laney assumed hopefully.

"I can't cancel my plans at the last minute, little bug."

You could Noel thought. *You should.*

"Maybe your dad will come by the candy shop soon and see all the hard work you and Levi have done," Noel suggested, hoping to soften the blow.

"Yeah Daddy, do that."

"I will," he promised.

Maybe he would, maybe he wouldn't, but for now the answer seemed sufficient for Laney.

When Keaton disappeared after a round of hugs, Noel and the kids tracked down Rainey, Chelsea, Mrs. Madelyn, and Jack. Rainey wheeled Jack back to his vehicle, and then the rest of them headed to Beaufort Candy Company to decorate for Christmas.

Laney and Levi pulled the empty wagons along the sidewalk, and Noel reminded them that all the leftovers would be donated to the homeless shelter.

"The tree is so huge," Levi told Rainey, his eyes mirroring the word choice as he and Laney led the group along the boardwalk overlooking Taylor Creek, the most scenic route.

Tiny waves rippled across the water causing the surface to shimmer like diamonds. Most of the boats remained docked while everyone celebrated Thanksgiving although a few meandered through the no-wake zone. Several families on their vessels' decks appeared to be enjoying the sunshine and the view as a pod of dolphins graced everyone with their presence moving at a pace similar to the wagon-themed walk.

After Noel twisted the key in the lock and everyone spilled through the entrance, Rainey's eyes stretched the distance of the store, the space more than twice as long as the width. "Wow, the Christmas tree really is massive."

"Told you so," Levi declared.

"It smells so good," Chelsea pointed out sniffing the open air as if a candle rested beneath her nose.

"I have always loved the smell that the fresh candy and live Christmas tree create," Mrs. Madelyn commented as she became lost in the thought of all the years of experiencing the distinct aroma. It reminded her of the dear friends who introduced her to this shop—two people who embodied the Christmas spirit year round.

"Rainey, you get to climb the ladder to wrap the lights around the top and hang the ornaments on the branches that are too high for the rest of us to reach," Noel announced.

"I knew you all had an ulterior motive for inviting me," Rainey responded with a smirk.

In the past only family and Mrs. Madelyn decorated the store, but this year Noel decided at the last minute to solicit the help of friends. She waited until the end of the Thanksgiving feast to ask since she hoped Keaton would be the one climbing the ladder as usual. This would mark the first time without him present for the occasion. Last year he still participated in most family traditions. None of the adults gave fully into decorating the candy shop last season, and Noel knew it showed visually and in the books. This year she held high hopes.

Chelsea smacked her husband on the shoulder. "You are the second woman to hit me today," Rainey acknowledged.

"Oh yeah, who was the first?" she inquired. "I want to know so that I can thank her for helping keep you in line."

Rainey glared at Noel as she locked up the store behind the crew, grinning as the conversation between her friends took residence in her ears.

"Thank you, Noel," Chelsea noted.

"My pleasure."

The cuckoo clock sounded letting everyone know that two o'clock arrived. More importantly, the kids, helping prove Pavlov's bell theory, sprinted to the spot where they left their stockings. Levi slid across the wooden floor like a baseball player trying to score the winning run.

"Did we miss eating any of our special candy while we were at Thanksgiving?" Laney investigated suspecting they had.

"I think the two of you ate more than your share of candy at the community feast," Noel declared as she recalled seeing them run to and from the dessert table often along with scores of other children. "But yes, you missed two, and you can eat them whenever you want."

"Or you can give them to me," Rainey encouraged.

"No way," Levi replied.

"You can have my two extras," Laney offered. "I'm stuffed like a turkey."

Everyone laughed at the comment and the exasperated facial expression that accompanied her cute little face.

"You can have one of mine," Levi decided.

After the three kids—one much bigger than the others—finished unwrapping and eating candy, Noel held a quick huddle with the group to discuss the planogram she created to turn the candy shop into a Christmas wonderland.

Once the helpers understood their roles, Rainey fetched a couple of fifteen-foot extension ladders from the back room to add to the two ten-foot ladders on the floor from earlier. Mrs. Madelyn and the kids started wrapping multi-colored lights around the base of the Christmas tree while Noel and Chelsea strung white icicle lights from the lowest ceiling beams, interchanging the ladders to reach the desired points.

When the kids and Mrs. Madelyn made it as high up the tree as their arms would allow from floor level, Rainey circled the tree with lights until reaching the very top. While he worked on that, the kids hung ornaments and candy canes on all the low branches, and then Rainey did the same up the tree. Noel fussed at him when she caught him letting the children climb the ladder to add items, but he promised he would support them with his hands the whole time.

"Rainey's a big, strong police officer, Mommy," Levi stated while flexing his biceps.

Noel grinned and shook her head. Keaton did the same thing in previous years, and she imagined Levi and Laney brought up the idea this time around.

As traditional Christmas carols filled the store, the volume a bit higher than during business hours, Noel snuck peeks at the tree while she and Chelsea worked their way toward the back of the shop taking turns climbing and holding the ladders for each other.

"This is a workout," Chelsea mentioned several times.

"I told you it was hard work."

"I thought you were exaggerating," she countered, playfully rolling her eyes.

Rainey paused his part of the Christmas tree project several times to help his wife and Noel reach spots beyond their limits. Mrs. Madelyn constantly reminded everyone to test each strand of lights before installing them, a comment Noel's mother used to be in charge of making. Every time the clock sounded, the kids ran for their candy, and Rainey stopped, too, to unwrap treats with them. Noel gave him permission to pick whatever he wanted in the store as payment for helping.

"You might regret making that deal," he surmised.

At nearly the exact time Levi topped the tree with the giant star, Noel and Chelsea hung the last strand of icicle lights. Rather than letting Levi and Laney argue about who got to put the star on, Noel asked if one wanted to perform that task and the other shut off all the lights in the store except for the Christmas ones.

"That's when the magic really comes to life," Mrs. Madelyn reported.

Laney quickly opted for the latter, and the timing seemed impeccable because as they worked and the clock hands circled, the sun sank below the horizon, and eventually darkness took over the view on the other side of the windows.

Everyone stood together and counted down from twenty-five. When Laney flipped the switch off at zero, a collective gasp floated through the air above where the ice cycle lights glistened like snow falling through the breath of winter. Each set of eyes in the room followed the strands from the front of the candy shop to the back where the brightly lit and decorated Christmas tree took center stage. The room glowed majestically thanks to the thousands of tiny bulbs flickering like a field of fireflies dancing in the night sky. Although the store required more light for enhanced displays and customer safety, the current illumination throughout the maze of aisles flowing around the barrels, baskets, and stands made walking through while basking in the beauty of the Christmas scene they created feasible.

A few years ago Noel's father installed electrical lighting that allowed every hardwired light in the store to be dimmed and raised by the movement of a switch. Noel adjusted the small lever to where they would keep it set during business hours, but at nighttime all the lights except for the Christmas ones would be shut off, so people wandering the sidewalks would be drawn to the scene. Many stopped and cuffed their hands over the windows for peeks inside, especially the children. Noel's family learned to keep extra window cleaner in stock for just that reason.

After finishing this first major step, Noel announced that it was almost time for the kids to fill the bins with Christmas candy under the direction of Mrs. Madelyn while she, Chelsea, and Rainey hung lighted wreaths on the walls and decorated the fireplace with green garland and Christmas trinkets to go along with the stockings. First, however, Noel retrieved from the refrigerator pre-made Christmas fruit bowls filled with red and green fruits, including strawberries, kiwi, raspberries, and pomegranate, as well as grapes and apple slices in both colors. She mixed in local honey which the shop sold year round.

Years of experience proved that this light dinner worked much better than leftovers after such a heavy Thanksgiving lunch. It didn't take long for her to remember that the kids and adults needed extra napkins as fingers became sticky and little faces decorated with fruit juice lit up the room as brightly as the assortment of lights.

"This is so yummy," Laney announced after sucking on a strawberry.

"The hot chocolate is the best," Levi added.

"Chocolate and fruit work well together, so why not hot chocolate and fruit?" Chelsea queried pretty sure this marked the first time she tried the unexpected combination.

Rainey licked his fingers. "We need to make this an annual tradition," he insisted.

"It is," Levi and Laney answered simultaneously.

"Jinx," they both shouted hurriedly, and everyone laughed out loud.

"What?" Rainey replied. "Why haven't you invited me before?" he asked the kids.

"You've probably been busy arresting bad guys," Levi assumed.

Another round of laughter filled the air as the Christmas lights continued to glow like stars in the night's sky.

"Is my daddy a bad guy?" Laney asked Rainey.

Rainey pondered the question as he chewed on an apple slice. Meanwhile Noel and Mrs. Madelyn glanced at each other wondering if they should provide the answer. As they waited Noel held a grape near her mouth while Mrs. Madelyn lowered her ceramic snowman cup.

"Sometimes people make bad decisions, but that doesn't necessarily make them bad people," Rainey articulated. "Your dad has made way more good decisions in his life than he has bad ones."

Noel felt tears bubbling behind her eyes and instantly knew she made the right decision to keep her mouth shut.

"Mama said I was the best decision she and Daddy ever made," Laney shared.

A fresh batch of tears formed in every adult's eyes.

"You sure were," Noel agreed without hesitation.

"Your daddy will always remember that," Mrs. Madelyn added.

"I hope so, especially at Christmastime," Laney proclaimed.

"Mommy, was I the best decision you and Daddy made?" Levi checked.

Noel nestled herself between Levi and Laney, pulling each of them close. "Yes, you are the best decision ever. Both of you are," she confirmed.

Levi and Laney grinned, and then Levi broke the silence as everyone smeared tears across their faces. "I thought we were going to put out candy," he reminded them as the idea suddenly hopped into his mind.

Red, green, and gold packaged candy quickly took over the barrels, bins, and baskets as Levi and Laney poured piece after piece from boxes like milk into a cereal bowl. All the while smiles and laughter erupted from their faces. The wreaths went up quickly thanks to the pre-hung nails, but lining the fireplace with garland took a little longer. Noel wanted everything to look just right for the big day.

The final two projects allowed the kids to roam around carrying gift boxes wrapped with bows. They placed an assortment under the tree and then added some on the shelves and in any other empty spaces found in the store. Mrs. Madelyn followed behind adjusting things where needed, but overall, the kids' placements pleased her.

Noel and Chelsea worked on the window displays while Rainey ran back and forth fetching supplies. By the time the ladies stepped out of the windows, each area showcased the most inviting gingerbread house village anyone ever set eyes on, and the giant candy canes and lollipops in large glass jars really stood out. Noel couldn't wait to see people's faces light up and hear their responses.

Lastly, Noel asked Levi and Laney to update the numbers on the countdown to Christmas signs—one they kept on the sidewalk and the other just inside the front door. The outdoor chalkboard always drew attention, and indoors, a candy cane-themed pole held a red octagon similar to a stop sign at which nearly every child stopped upon entering. When Levi and Laney fixed the numbers, the signs read *Only 27 Days Until Christmas!* However, Noel knew those days would fly by as quickly as Santa's reindeer. After today the kids would take turns flipping the numbers on each sign which they often ran to first thing in the mornings.

"I think that's a wrap," Noel announced as the cuckoo clock

sounded ten times. "You two kiddos need to get some sleep because tomorrow is another big day," she added as they ran for one last round of candy.

"Black Friday," Chelsea announced excitedly. "Every shopper's dream."

"Let's hope those shoppers dream of candy tonight," Noel replied with a smirk.

"These two sure will," Mrs. Madelyn noted, rubbing the tops of Levi's and Laney's Santa hats.

"I think I had way too much sugar today," Rainey claimed, holding his stomach.

"You have too much candy every day," Chelsea responded. "It sure must be nice to have a high metabolism. Some of us have to eat healthy and work out."

"What's a mabolism?" Laney questioned.

"Metabolism," Noel corrected. "It is our body's ability to burn off what it takes in."

"Our bodies are on fire?" Levi questioned with bulging eyes.

"No, silly, it's just a saying," Mrs. Madelyn answered. "But my eyes feel like they are on fire because they've been open way too long. I'm going home to Mr. Jack."

Noel let everyone who didn't live upstairs out the front door then put Levi and Laney to bed. Although they seemed wired until the moment their little heads hit the pillows, that soft touch did the trick. Within moments as she prayed for them like she did every night, their eyelids collapsed.

Noel wished she could join the kids in sleepyland, but instead she spent nearly two hours downstairs tidying up. When the clock struck midnight, she knew it was time for bed. Whatever hadn't been accomplished today would have to wait until tomorrow or whenever the first free moment of the busiest shopping day of the year occurred which would probably be at closing time.

7

Cavin cleared the sleep from his eyes as the family's limousine slowly came to a halt at the departures entrance of the Hartsfield-Jackson Atlanta International Airport. The beams from the headlights of the other cars reminded him that most people were still in bed this early in the morning.

"Sit tight while I collect your bags for you, Mr. Dawson," the driver offered.

"I will grab them this time," Cavin insisted, holding up a hand. "I only have two to check, and you probably have better things to do on Black Friday than work."

"This is what I signed up for," the gentleman dressed in a fancy tuxedo replied with a half-hearted smile.

"I have better things to do," Cavin reported begrudgingly while strapping a backpack over his shoulders and then reaching for his laptop. Before opening the door, he handed the driver a $100 bill. "Go buy your wife something nice."

Once the soles of Cavin's dress shoes hit the asphalt, he pulled two hefty suitcases from the vehicle, steadied their wheels, and popped up the handle. The contents would need to keep him clothed for nearly a month. A few seconds later he entered through the automatic sliding doors and made his way to the check-in counter, knowing he could find it with his eyes closed. Like clockwork he handed the attendant his driver's license and plopped his bags onto the designated weighing area.

"Heading to New Bern, huh, Mr. Dawson?" the blonde-haired woman confirmed with a trained smile.

"Beaufort, actually," Cavin mentioned mostly to keep the pronunciation of the town at the forefront of his mind, yet he feigned interest in her, especially the way she filled out her uniform but didn't quite flaunt the features beneath the clothing. Even if he didn't find the woman on the other side of the tall counter attractive, he would have studied her closely as he did everyone with whom he came into contact. His father raised him to notice the details, such as a person's name, the style of watch on their wrist, the brand of shoes on their feet, and whether or not they made eye contact. "I guess New Bern has the closest airport," Cavin added, making small talk which often helped start meaningful conversations in his line of work.

"Are you flying there to see family for the holidays?" the lady around his age asked while handing him his ticket.

Cavin knew many of the airline's workers' names at this airport, but he never encountered this woman before. "Nope, I am going there for work on Black Friday of all days," he replied with a snicker.

She smiled genuinely as her head cocked to the right ever so slightly. "At least I'm not the only one working the holiday," she teased.

"If you weren't working, I would invite you to explore coastal North Carolina with me, Grace," he suggested with a grin after reading her nametag and checking her ring finger.

The woman blushed and shrugged her shoulders. "Maybe another time."

Cavin grinned. "Don't work too hard today, Grace."

People loved hearing their names, and he knew that. He used

all types of tactics to remember names, including saying them multiple times in conversations, especially upon meeting someone new, relating their name to another person he knew or a celebrity, or writing it down along with a few important characteristics about the person.

At the security checkpoint, Cavin followed protocol by setting all his belongings in the bins on the conveyor belt, including his belt, cufflinks, watch, and cell phone. He removed his shoes last and watched the bins move along the line while stepping into the revolving scanner to lift his hands above his head as the picture showed.

"Good morning, Tom," he greeted.

The security officer on the other side of the machine that Cavin had walked through hundreds of times nodded. "Mr. Dawson, I hope you and your family enjoyed a wonderful Thanksgiving."

Stepping in his direction, Cavin performed the typical circular rub of the stomach. "It was fabulous; I just ate too much." It impressed him when others remembered his name, especially someone like Tom, a retired military officer, who saw thousands of people daily. He took this job for something to do rather than the pay after his wife passed a couple of years ago. His son lived abroad, so he didn't see him often. It amazed Cavin how much could be learned about people by spending only a couple of minutes in their presence every now and then.

Tom tapped his own plump stomach. "I eat too much every day, my friend," he responded with a chuckle.

"Airport food will do that to us," Cavin concluded with a laugh.

A few minutes later Cavin reached the gate specified on the mobile ticket and boarded the airplane with the first group.

"Welcome aboard, Mr. Dawson," the flight attendant greeted as Cavin entered the airplane. She stood next to the pilot who shook another man's hand before recognizing Cavin.

"Thank you, Darlene, it's good to see you again," Cavin

acknowledged. "How are those two children of yours?"

"Crazy as ever," she replied with her typical spicy demeanor laughing louder than socially acceptable, but everyone always seemed to quickly embrace her jolliness.

"Cavin, happy Thanksgiving," the pilot offered.

"Truman, Thanksgiving was yesterday," Darlene broadcasted. She didn't need the intercom for her voice to reach the back of the plane. "Today is Black Friday; tomorrow is Small Business Saturday; and Monday is Cyber Monday."

Truman shook his head and laughed, and Cavin chuckled in unison. "Happy Thanksgiving, Black Friday, and all the rest to both of you," Cavin remarked. Because of the flight rotations, keeping up with the pilots' and flight attendants' names proved more challenging than for some of the other airline workers.

"She keeps me on my toes," Truman teased. "What is Sunday?"

"A day of rest," she retorted.

"On another note, Dad says he's buying a private jet for the family business in the New Year," Cavin disclosed. "We might have to hire you two to keep us on our toes and in the air."

"We know how to do that," Truman replied. "That's exciting news. Keep us posted."

"Truman, you better treat me right," Darlene encouraged. "This is the second job offer I've received this week."

With a smile on his face, Cavin took a seat in the first-class section and stretched out in the leather chair while rummaging through his bag for a pair of earphones. By the time he picked a movie, the wheels lifted off the runway, and his ears popped. Out of habit he tossed a peppermint into his mouth. Normally, Cavin would listen to a business-related podcast during the flight, but to celebrate the holiday weekend which his dad cut short, he opted for mindless entertainment. Darlene brought him a beverage and a snack and checked on him several times while, thanks to the window seat view, Cavin watched the sunrise above a layer of puffy cotton clouds that could easily be mistaken for snow-capped mountains. One of the perks of getting up this early in the morning to catch a flight was the unique perspective of the golden rays of the sun filtering through the clouds.

The plane touched down in Charlotte well before the film ended, but Cavin figured he would pick back up where he left off after the short layover.

Unfortunately, the second flight landed in New Bern before Cavin finished the movie, but he was glad to be on the ground. Maybe he would watch the rest later but probably not. He had more important things to accomplish. The newly renovated yet quaint airport allowed him to gather his checked bags quickly and locate the reserved rental vehicle within a matter of minutes.

The GPS in the full-size black SUV promptly informed him that a mere forty-mile drive to Beaufort lay ahead. That would put him there around the time most businesses opened on a regular weekday morning. Leave it to his dad to ensure he literally had every available hour in town. However, with Black Friday not being a typical day, he imagined most banks, real estate firms, and other business offices would likely be closed while the retail shops probably opened earlier than normal.

The rumble in Cavin's stomach made him think about grabbing breakfast in New Bern or while driving through one of the other small towns on his route—Havelock or Morehead City— but he decided he would rather kick off his business trip dining with the locals. Highway 70, which he learned would soon become Interstate 42, thanks to a couple of construction zones where the road shifted from two lanes to one for short periods, took him all the way to Turner Street which led into the heart of Beaufort, North Carolina.

A short and curvy high-rise bridge just before the horseshoe turn into the quaint town offered a view that made his heart smile as he heard the cha-ching sound slot machines make in his mind.

A picturesque glimpse into Beaufort featuring an inviting body of water dotted with docks filled with sailboats and other vessels welcomed everyone showcasing an area that resembled a small port city. It reminded Cavin of the cover of a movie he saw when scrolling through options on the airplane. A cute little sign made the location as clear as the blue sky on the other side of the open sunroof.

Cavin rolled down the windows and drove slowly wanting to take in every little detail of his first impression of this town. The air smelled like the beach as a short bridge just above sea level crossed the waterway previously visible from the taller bridge now observable on his right. The body of water pretty much ended flush with this bridge along with what resembled a kayak trail leading through an uninhabitable marshy area on the left. He imagined specific breeds of wildlife probably loved that terrain.

A few blocks lined with cute houses slowly gave way to the waterfront business district after Cavin passed a small old convenience store named Big Daddy Wesley's, at which he chuckled, and the courthouse. As the tires circled so did the thoughts in his entrepreneurial mind—all the homes located along this entry route could be acquired and converted to retail space allowing for a next-level wow factor for tourists. He envisioned a boardwalk along the first waterfront that resembled the one the GPS map showed when Turner Street came to an abrupt end at Taylor Creek.

Pedestrians filled the sidewalks on either side of the road and the walkway on the other side of the road in front of him which formed a T. While sitting at the stop sign that forced motorists to take a right or left, Cavin read the words Front Street on the green street sign located on the corner while waiting for a family and a few stragglers to filter across the white-lined crosswalk. This seemed like the hub of the Beaufort waterfront area.

When the coast cleared, he maneuvered the steering wheel

clockwise following the road that paralleled the creek on the left though a row of standalone buildings obstructed the full view of the water. He noticed a couple of restaurants, some small shops, and what looked like a boat-building facility with a large opening on either side that allowed passersby to peer straight through to the creek. Cavin, taking in the buzzing sounds of saws and sanders, made a mental note to visit that facility. He could already smell the pleasant aroma of freshly cut wood.

The North Carolina Maritime Museum sat on the right side of the street before giving way to a few blocks of nice homes, while the opposite side of the road suddenly offered an open view of the creek and what looked like private docks stretching into the waterway, and there he spotted several boats cruising along the calm water. The words *potential, potential, potential* darted across Cavin's mind like a banner ad in Times Square.

The town already embodied a Hallmark movie, but this place could grow significantly without losing its charm. Although not an island, Beaufort felt like one which spoke volumes about the potential for this gold mine. Vacationers wanted to unplug from reality, and nothing accomplished that feat quicker than living on island time in a quaint town. So many people were fed up with big cities—the busy streets, the ridiculous crime rates, and all the rest—yet they still wanted to visit a spot featuring everything they needed and more. Cavin's land acquisition and business development goals were to achieve this feat without losing the small town's ambiance.

A few blocks from where he initially turned, Cavin reached a cul-de-sac that required traffic to turn around and head back in the direction from which it came. Before spinning the wheel, he stopped to take in the view since the rearview mirror showed no cars directly behind him. A few stray benches in grassy areas overlapped by live oak trees overlooked marsh grass and the waterway that circled this end of Beaufort. Across the channel he captured the sight of a slew of fishing boats with large nets strung high while the crews rested somewhere else.

Cavin doubted they got much more time off than he did but maybe the fishermen were home with their families for the long holiday weekend. He imagined Beaufort's makeup included many native residents as well as wealthy outsiders who retired here. That rang true for most small waterfront towns these days. Often an ongoing battle existed between the two groups, the former wanting to maintain the status quo of a slow-paced environment while the latter pursued change in the form of adding modern amenities.

Cavin hoped to find a middle ground between the different perspectives. That goal provided him an opportunity to appeal to each group although the ice on which he had to tread was usually as thin as paper. Nonetheless, he welcomed the challenge.

Pivers Island, housing the Duke University Marine Lab, came into view on the left across the channel, close enough that Cavin could pull an iron from his golf bag and send a ball over there without a problem. He wished he had brought his clubs with him but knew he could rent some at a local country club if he wanted to play. There was a good probability he would meet other business professionals who enjoyed the game, and he would treat them to a round of golf while discussing the endless possibilities his family's firm could offer the area.

Heading back in the other direction, Cavin noted that the town would benefit from a boardwalk on this end of the road to meet up with the one he spotted on the map earlier. When he made it back to that point where Turner Street met Front Street, he kept driving straight with the creek now on his right yet hidden by a row of two-story shops. On the left the buildings resembled those in a normal small downtown area. After passing a candy store with a mouth-watering display of festive holiday treats in the windows, he pulled into a parking lot overlooking the waterway.

"Waterfronts are not for parking lots," he murmured to himself, although he appreciated the spectacular view.

Across the street Cavin couldn't miss the long red sign with bold white lettering on the front of Clawson's 1905 Restaurant & Pub. After closing the SUV's windows and sunroof, he ventured in that direction hoping to find a delicious breakfast and some chatty locals who might divulge information about prospective real estate development opportunities.

8

oel barely slept a wink last night, and this morning she ran around like a madwoman straightening items she overlooked yesterday. She found a few leftover Thanksgiving decorations that needed to be put away and picked up a handful of random pieces of candy the kids must have dropped on the floor at some point. She thought about letting Levi and Laney sleep in while she opened the store at eight o'clock but then decided against the idea. Last year when she did that, they eventually wandered downstairs in their pajamas with their hair all a mess, asking for breakfast and wanting to snuggle like the three of them often did in the mornings.

At this point Noel still sacrificed breakfast, but the kids had cereal and changed into regular clothes while she worked. All three of them proudly wore their Santa hats. Noel adjusted the light dimmer one more time trying to get the lighting just right for this time of morning. She knew she would shift it throughout the day depending on the sun's location, cloud coverage, and whatever other variables happened to occur.

A knock came at the door, and Noel jumped. When she collected herself, she headed toward the front of the store, but the person outside had her back to the door as if surveying the street.

Noel glanced at the cuckoo clock and twisted the lock to open although it wasn't quite time for the Black Friday kickoff.

"Good morning," Noel greeted enthusiastically, running on adrenaline rather than sleep.

Mrs. Madelyn turned around in her oversized coat. "Where are all the people?" she asked.

"What people?"

Noel scanned the sidewalks and saw a fair number of pedestrians wandering in winter clothes: coats, boots, toboggans, and all the warm items that begged for snow Beaufort rarely received. She wondered if some shops opened early, or if everyone came out for breakfast or a cup of coffee to warm their bones before shopping.

"The Black Friday shoppers," Mrs. Madelyn exclaimed. "I thought I would have to wiggle my way through a line of hungry folks waiting for the complimentary cinnamon rolls."

Noel's green eyes suddenly bulged. "Oh no," she called out and then covered her mouth with both hands. "Oh no."

Noel grabbed Mrs. Madelyn's glove-covered hand and pulled her into the warm store.

"What's wrong, Noel?"

"I forgot," she realized out loud, her energy instantly sagging.

"Forgot what?"

"The cinnamon rolls, the social media posts—everything," she exclaimed in one rushed phrase.

"Calm down, sweetie, we will take care of all of it, and no one will ever know the difference."

"I thought I remembered all the details this year," Noel claimed, standing near the register and staring at the time which was shouting to her that the eight o'clock tune would sound in less than ten minutes. "I wrote check-off lists so I wouldn't drop any balls. How did I forget to invite the first fifty customers for the complimentary cinnamon rolls that I also forgot to bake?"

As the words spilled out of Noel's mouth, the bell on the door jingled.

"I even forgot to lock the door," she uttered louder than intended.

A gentleman around her age wearing a dark full-length overcoat let the door close behind him but stopped his gait just inside as he apparently tried to decipher the meaning of her comment.

"Good morning, handsome," Mrs. Madelyn greeted with a smile. "Welcome to Beaufort Candy Company."

"Morning, ma'am. It sounds like I may have shown up at an inconvenient time. If you will be kind enough to point me in the right direction, I can come back later for some of your delicious-smelling candy," the customer responded. "I just arrived in town and was wondering where I might find the best breakfast Beaufort, North Carolina has to offer. I tried the restaurant across the street, but apparently they aren't open."

"We aren't open yet either," Noel spouted.

"Yes, we are," Mrs. Madelyn countered wondering if Noel even heard a word the guy spoke.

The man with slicked-back black hair stood there appearing confused. He glanced back and forth between them seemingly waiting for a conclusive response.

"How does a complimentary cinnamon roll for breakfast sound?" Mrs. Madelyn invited.

"It sounds delicious," the man accepted.

"But," Noel started then she stopped glancing at the customer and back to Mrs. Madelyn. "We don't have cinnamon rolls."

"Sweetie, we have cinnamon rolls. I placed them in the refrigerator last night before I left for the evening. We just need to turn on the oven and bake them."

The man furrowed his brow. "I can come back another time," he mentioned again wondering what he stepped into the middle of.

"That might—" Noel began.

Mrs. Madelyn immediately cut her off. "Absolutely not, you are our first Black Friday customer, and you and the next forty-nine guests receive a complimentary cinnamon roll."

Mrs. Madelyn set her purse on the counter, reached in for her wallet, and turned back to the man. "What is your name, sir?"

As soon as the question reached his ears, cackles erupted from the stairway as Levi and Laney ran down exuberantly making a grand entrance. "Mrs. Madelyn," they hollered in unison. "It's Black Friday," Laney shouted.

All eyes focused on the children as they hurried in for hugs.

"Good morning, Levi and Laney, my Santa hat darlings."

A moment later the customer interjected, "Apparently, you are Mrs. Madelyn, a very special person to these two beautiful children." He paused temporarily to smile as the attention turned to him. "I am Cavin Dawson," he shared, answering her previous question.

"Kevin," Levi called out as Mrs. Madelyn reached for his outstretched hand. "You are wearing your Black Friday coat."

Cavin glanced down at the black overcoat he picked out this morning.

"It's not a Black Friday coat," Noel corrected. "That's not a thing."

Cavin let go of Mrs. Madelyn's hand, looked up at Noel, and then turned his gaze to Levi. "Actually, I am," Cavin agreed. "This is my Black Friday coat, but I didn't think anyone would realize it. You are a very observant little boy, Levi."

Levi chuckled. "I knew it," he mumbled confidently with a cute smirk covering his proud face.

Mrs. Madelyn handed Cavin a twenty-dollar bill.

"What is this for?" he inquired with a wrinkle between his eyebrows. "Does the first customer receive twenty dollars to spend on candy?" he asserted, glancing around at the edible merchandise taking in a scene that reminded him of childhood.

He could almost taste the chocolate, and another smell also stood out, but he couldn't quite put his finger on it.

"Coffee," Mrs. Madelyn announced. "We need coffee," she insisted. "Me, you, and Noel all need coffee."

"I like coffee," Cavin replied jubilantly, shrugging his shoulders and then looking down at Laney. "Now I know everyone's name. You are Laney," he deduced reaching down to squeeze the ball on the end of her hat before looking up at Noel. "That means you are Noel."

Noel's gaze shifted to his warm brown eyes. "Yes," she confirmed. "And I need to bake fifty cinnamon rolls in record time."

"By the time you return with coffee, yours will be ready," Mrs. Madelyn promised with a smile.

Without another word Noel scurried down the center aisle toward the Christmas tree before vanishing through the door leading to the kitchen.

"She's not always this high strung, Mr. Dawson," Mrs. Madelyn reported.

"Maybe the coffee will help," he surmised with a grin.

"Mom loves coffee," Levi shared.

"She drinks it every morning," Laney disclosed, drawing out the words. "But maybe she forgot today," she added with a shrug.

"Where might I find this coffee?" Cavin pondered aloud.

"That's right; you mentioned you are new in town," Mrs. Madelyn murmured. "Cru is just around the corner," she acknowledged, pointing him in the right direction.

His brows rose toward his hairline. "Cru?"

"Cru is a coffee shop and wine bar," Mrs. Madelyn explained. "Best coffee around."

"How do you take your coffee, Mrs. Madelyn?" Cavin inquired. "And what does Noel prefer?"

Mrs. Madelyn answered Cavin's questions while Levi and Laney ran to the countdown to Christmas signs, where they flipped the numbers to twenty-six. After making the day official, the two skipped around the store reacquainting themselves with all the new Christmas candy. This morning during breakfast they talked about how they looked forward to showing their friends from school where to find all the good stuff when they came in with their families today.

"That's a lot of information; would you like me to write it down?" Mrs. Madelyn asked Cavin.

"No ma'am, I think I can remember the order."

"I don't need any money back," she noted. "I am buying your coffee, too, and you can keep the change."

"That's mighty kind of you," Cavin replied.

"Oh, one more thing," Mrs. Madelyn interjected. "Tell everyone you see that the first fifty customers receive a free cinnamon roll fresh out of the oven. If you have the social media, tell those people, too."

"Yes, ma'am," Cavin agreed with a grin on his face, somehow able to hold in the chuckle in response to her arrangement of the words the social media.

When the cuckoo clock sounded, Cavin turned and walked out the door, and Mrs. Madelyn hustled to the cash register area to remove her coat and put away her things. Since no one else entered the store by the time she felt put together enough to start work, she scurried back to the kitchen to check on Noel.

"How are things going in here?" Mrs. Madelyn inquired while taking in the scene.

"You're acting differently this morning," Noel announced rather than pointing out she already pulled the first batch of cinnamon rolls out of the fridge to slide into the preheating oven as soon as the temperature reached the desired level. She figured all of that appeared obvious anyway.

"You think I'm the one acting differently?" Mrs. Madelyn

quipped while she humored her friend.

"You called that man handsome," Noel retorted as she set two cups of icing on the stainless steel counter.

"He is handsome; didn't you notice?"

"Of course I noticed, but why did you offer him a cinnamon roll that he has to stand out there and wait fifteen minutes for?"

"He's not waiting," Mrs. Madelyn shared.

A puzzled expression appeared on Noel's face. "He left?"

"He's gone to get coffee for us, remember?"

Noel's hands quit moving for the first time since Mrs. Madelyn stepped into the kitchen. "You gave a stranger twenty dollars *and* asked him to get coffee for us," she asserted emphasizing the word and. "Don't you think that qualifies as strange?"

"Cavin seems like a nice enough fellow, and I figured it would give him something to do while waiting for the best breakfast in Beaufort," she replied with a grin. "Plus, did you see the coat he wore?"

"The Black Friday coat?" Noel laughed while feeling herself relax a little for the first time since Mrs. Madelyn arrived. "What about it?"

"The man doesn't need twenty dollars," she pointed out. "But he does need coffee and breakfast. And he is not wearing a wedding ring," she added with a wink.

9

Upon reaching the other side of the crosswalk, Cavin turned and looked back at Beaufort Candy Company with an unusual expression. *What just happened in there?* This thought rattled around in his mind; he never imagined his stay in Beaufort starting out with running errands for the first locals he met. However, he figured he now had four new friends, or at least three, since he was unsure about Noel. The woman seemed irritated by his presence from the moment he walked into the store, and things didn't seem any better by the time she disappeared into the back. She had cute kids, though, and Cavin wondered if Mrs. Madelyn was their grandmother. She made him laugh a lot. Even now he still chuckled inside about the way she phrased *the social media.*

"Beaufort Candy Company has complimentary cinnamon rolls for the first fifty guests this morning," Cavin randomly shared with a family standing on the corner where he temporarily paused his journey. He pointed to the building he just left.

The little boy tugged on his mom's jacket. "I want one," he whispered with excitement.

"Thanks," the dad replied. "We'll check it out."

"Tell Mrs. Madelyn that Cavin sent you."

Cavin walked past a building that looked like a bank as he read the names of some of the shops on the other side of the street. For some reason Sweet Lilly Ru stood out to him. Maybe because he once dated a woman named Lilly.

"Free cinnamon rolls at Beaufort Candy Company," Cavin announced to a couple of teenagers walking past him.

They blushed and said nothing, but once they passed by, he heard them laughing which made him smile.

Cavin found Cru, the coffee shop, a little way down the sidewalk, exactly where Mrs. Madelyn explained. He opened the door as a woman walked out and stepped back to give her room to exit while holding the handle.

"Thank you, sir," she offered with a friendly smile.

"My pleasure," he replied. "Beaufort Candy Company has a complimentary cinnamon roll that would go great with your coffee," he commented.

Her smile grew. "Sounds delicious."

When Cavin entered, the place was hopping with patrons. It took a moment to find an open spot to stand as he studied the menu on the brick wall behind the counter. He quickly realized the establishment offered much more than coffee. Photos of flatbreads, bagels, and pizza stood out, and he even noticed a glass-cased freezer next to the counter featuring ice cream. They sold other goodies as well, so he figured he shouldn't announce the free cinnamon rolls to anyone else in here.

Potentially making enemies on the first day in town wouldn't bode well for his plan, and he knew from experience that most shop owners and even some employees were heavily invested in their downtown community. He needed everyone on his good side including Noel. Maybe he would take her something extra, he considered while eyeing the other customers' selections. Then Cavin remembered he hadn't done anything wrong; he simply walked into Noel's store, or at least he assumed the shop belonged to her. Something about her demeanor made it seem as though she was in charge although she and the older lady acted like best friends who could say anything around each other without being offended. Maybe Mrs. Madelyn or someone else owned the store, he considered.

By the time Cavin made it to the front of the line, he decided on an iced latte for himself to go along with Mrs. Madelyn's and Noel's orders, and he decided to add a couple of extra items that he hoped would go over well upon his return.

During the breezy walk back to Beaufort Candy Company, Cavin told three more strangers about the giveaway. One man looked a lot like Santa Claus and seemed equally as jolly. Another person told him she ate already, but she might grab one for her husband. The third contestant said they loved cinnamon rolls.

Cavin's mom and dad told him that from an early age he talked to everyone he encountered whether in public, at company parties, or at family gatherings. They said he always wanted to be the life of the party. So, as an adult, communicating with people came easily. He didn't mind taking no for an answer. Although as he learned how to talk to people, he became pretty good at convincing others to see things his way.

When Cavin stepped into Beaufort Candy Company the second time around, the vibe felt completely different. The store seemed alive. Smiling shoppers meandered up and down the aisles reaching for candy in the bins and barrels before placing it in their baskets; Christmas music played softly in the background; and the smell of fresh-baked cinnamon rolls wafted through the air. Mrs. Madelyn moved in a seasoned pattern behind the counter weighing candy, placing it in cute little bags, and ringing up customers in the short line one by one as if nothing else in the world mattered. Noel waltzed from one person to another while balancing the tray of cinnamon rolls while the kids handed the excited recipients a small paper plate and a napkin.

"Welcome back, Mr. Dawson," Mrs. Madelyn called out between customers.

He smiled, set two drink trays on the end of the counter near a bowl of gold-covered chocolate coins, and held up her coffee. "This one is for you, Mrs. Madelyn."

"Thanks, and we also appreciate you sending people over for the cinnamon rolls. I think about ten people said you sent them. The Hanson family walked in within minutes of you leaving, and some girls came with their boyfriends. I think they could have eaten two or three each," Mrs. Madelyn laughed.

"Kevin," Levi called out when he spotted him. "Come get your cinnamon roll."

Cavin's eyes twinkled. The way Levi called him Kevin sounded so cute. Maybe the little guy couldn't quite pronounce Cavin, or maybe he initially heard the name Kevin in his mind. It didn't matter either way, and this didn't mark the first time someone renamed him. Adults often made the same mistake although he usually chose to correct anyone over twelve gently.

"It's free," Laney reminded him.

Cavin rubbed his hands together as if about to start a fire with his excitement then looked at Noel as he reached into the beverage carrier. "Levi and Laney, if it's okay with your mom, I will trade each of you a hot chocolate for one of those delicious-smelling treats."

Their eyes bulged nearly causing their brows to rise into their Santa hats. "I love hot chocolate," Levi shouted.

"Hot chocolate is the best," Laney added.

Noel glanced at the kids and then at Cavin. "Yes, it's fine," she agreed as she stretched the tray in his direction. Laney traded him a plate for the hot chocolate while Levi handed Cavin a napkin and grabbed his beverage quickly as if someone else might claim it if he didn't. "I believe you deserve one of these," Noel offered with a calm voice.

"They smell delicious, Noel," Cavin replied. "In fact the whole store smells amazing," he added while looking around at the decorations and tree that seemed to accent all the festive candy colors perfectly.

"Christmas," Noel said as her eyelids closed ever so briefly while taking in the aroma. "It smells like Christmas."

"I love the scent of Christmas," Cavin declared. "Oh and here is your coffee, Noel," he added, reaching for her cup.

"Thank you," she acknowledged, steadying the empty tray in one hand while receiving the coffee with the other. "You really didn't have to do that."

Levi and Laney made their way to a cutout area underneath the front counter, accessible from the back. They named it their fort, and the hideout offered a place for them to relax and unwind when needing a break. The oversized cubby, complete with soft blankets, a pillow, and a few stuffed animals, allowed Noel and Mrs. Madelyn to keep an eye on the kids. It also gave Levi and Laney a place to eat during business hours rather than having to go upstairs for snacks or even meals.

"It was my privilege," Cavin responded. "The new guy in town has to accept and endure initiation," he added with a laugh.

"Welcome to Beaufort," Noel finally offered. "I should have said that earlier, but I was a bit frazzled."

"Life happens, and in the retail world Black Friday is always unpredictable," he acknowledged. "Is this a family business?" he asked using his pointer finger on the hand holding his coffee cup to reference the candy shop.

He took a quick bite of the cinnamon roll, and as soon as he began chewing, the warmth, softness, and sweetness simultaneously laser-beamed a message from his taste buds to his brain, and Cavin imagined his subsequent facial expression highlighted his genuine approval. He thought Noel would answer the question while he chewed delicately, but she didn't say anything right away, and eventually, he swallowed the remnants of the first bite.

Noel's head dropped when she heard the words *family business*. Although unsure why, she instantly thought of the accident that took half of her family. She missed Fletcher, her parents, and her sister-in-law Lexi tremendously during the holidays. They used to have so much fun living life together and running this family candy business. Even though her husband made a living captaining a fishing boat, he still pitched in here especially on days like yesterday and today when an extra set of hands made a huge impact.

If Fletcher were here, I wouldn't have forgotten the cinnamon rolls or the social media posts. That thought flashed through Noel's mind, and she nearly said it aloud which for some reason made her blush. Suddenly, she wanted to slip away from this man with perfect teeth standing in front of her waiting for an answer.

"Yes, this is a family business," she eventually uttered.

Cavin noticed the sudden change in Noel's demeanor and knew better than to ask the follow-up question that came to mind. "That's wonderful, and this is the best cinnamon roll I have ever tasted," he divulged. "It was definitely worth the wait. In fact I think making customers wait for this piece of perfection might be the best tactic to lure them in to buy candy."

"Thank you," Noel said simply. "I am sorry Mrs. Madelyn twisted your arm to get us coffee."

"You must have trained her well," Cavin remarked before taking another bite of the sticky treat.

Noel snickered. "That woman trained me."

Cavin glanced toward the counter as he finished chewing. "I like her."

"She's one of a kind," Noel reported as she momentarily locked eyes with Mrs. Madelyn who had been sneaking peeks in her direction this entire conversation.

"Noel, I imagine you have a lot to do with it being Black Friday including baking more of these delicious cinnamon rolls for your customers, so I will let you get back to it while I pick out some candy."

Noel smirked. "Thanks again for the coffee and even more for getting hot chocolate for the kids."

"Anytime."

Remembering she had given Cavin the last cinnamon roll on the tray, Noel turned and headed for the kitchen realizing the next batch should be ready soon.

Cavin wandered through the aisles with mixed emotions. Although he loved the taste of candy like most other human beings, he rarely ate sugary delights, and he couldn't recall the last time he partook of something sweet for breakfast. He usually stuck with healthy options like eggs and fruit smoothies. However, it didn't take long for nostalgia to set in as he reunited with candies from his childhood, some that he hadn't come across in years. He noticed that the store offered their own homemade candy rather than the name brands.

A handful of minutes later at the register, Cavin waited in line behind a couple of customers before Mrs. Madelyn greeted him again.

"The coffee is delicious," she said, touching her cup. "I hope you enjoyed your cinnamon roll."

"So far it's the best breakfast in Beaufort, Mrs. Madelyn."

She laughed out loud. "I told you."

With customers standing in line behind Cavin, Mrs. Madelyn placed the items he chose on the scale. "Did you bring your wife or girlfriend with you to Beaufort?" she inquired with a grin.

"I left both of them at home," Cavin teased without missing a beat, and then he noticed a puzzled expression take over Mrs. Madelyn's face. "Just kidding, of course," he quickly clarified. "It's just me," he confirmed.

"Well if you need to know about all the best places in town, you know where to find us," she suggested while punching in numbers on the old-timey cash register.

"I will keep that in mind, Mrs. Madelyn," Cavin agreed. "Thank you for the cinnamon roll and coffee."

"Thank you for retrieving the coffee and helping us resolve this morning's catastrophe."

"Anytime."

"Kids, say goodbye to Mr. Dawson," Mrs. Madelyn said, peeking underneath the counter.

"I thought I saw them run back there earlier."

Laney and Levi stood, each of their little heads just above the tall counter. They wore noticeable hot chocolate mustaches which caused Cavin to grin.

"They have a little fort back here," Mrs. Madelyn shared with a smile.

"Bye, Kevin," Levi said while Laney waved dramatically.

"Thanks for the hot chocolate," Laney offered.

"It was yummilicious," Levi added.

"Levi and Laney, maybe next time I will have one with you."

Mrs. Madelyn handed each of the kids a napkin before the next customer set a basket of goodies on the counter.

When the bell jingled as Cavin pushed open the door to exit the store, Noel stepped out of the kitchen with a fresh tray of cinnamon rolls just in time to catch a fleeting glimpse of the dark-haired newcomer before he disappeared onto the sidewalk.

10

Cavin spent the next few hours walking around the downtown waterfront area of Beaufort which was even more beautiful on foot at a slow pace. He slid his long, thin fingers along the rail separating the boardwalk from Taylor Creek and noticed a neatly placed Christmas wreath hung on each concrete pillar he passed. The rows of docked boats stretching toward Carrot Island offered a unique and inviting nautical vibe that seemingly attracted people from all walks of life.

With the wind blowing Cavin's coattail rather fiercely, he stopped to lean against the railing overlooking the creek hoping for a few moments of reprieve from the chilly weather. He nestled his cold hands into his pockets and studied the wide array of vessels from canoes to sailboats to yachts as the water slapped against the barrier beneath his feet. One boat in particular captured his attention, and most likely caught the eyes of every passerby.

At the end of one of the docks rested a fancy superyacht twice as long as the next largest yacht in the water's parking lot. The three enormous decks brought it to a height that surpassed the others by a wide margin, and its sleek design with long, darkly tinted windows was mesmerizing.

Cavin wondered who owned the yacht and what they did for a

living. He imagined their net worth must be at least a billion dollars which meant this individual probably owned a large corporation, was a famous celebrity, or made a fortune some other way. The impressive boat could even belong to one of the top social media influencers with all the money they raked in these days. Regardless, Cavin made a note to meet the owner and work his magic to find a way onto the yacht for a tour if nothing else. Having a contact who played in a league like that would be a major asset.

Walking a little further, Cavin discovered John Newton Park, a small area accessorized with benches beneath spidery live oaks that overlooked the rippling creek. A cute little red and white barn-style Santa house sat in the middle with a tall chair out front. He figured families would line up here soon to have pictures of their children taken with the big guy. Assorted colored lights lined the A-frame roofline; a wreath hung above the doors; and flat wooden trees painted green flanked either side of the entrance.

After some time studying the layout of the scenic waterfront, Cavin went into nearly every shop on Front Street and met as many people as possible. In some places he talked to the business owners, and in others, he made acquaintances with employees. Many of the stores were already decorated for Christmas or at least in the process of adding special touches like trees, lights, ornaments, and snowmen.

Early on in his career, Cavin learned not to step up to the counter and start asking questions or for the owner, but to peruse each store with a purpose. In nearly every shop, he purchased at least one item. He carried bags around with him so that the staff would realize his intention to shop, and when the merchandise became too bulky, he dropped it off at the rental vehicle. While perusing the stores, he asked for help, opinions, directions, and all kinds of other things. He learned as many names as possible and listened for the names of the key players in town that those he met mentioned.

Every small town had a powerful group who pretty much ran things, and those were the people he wanted to influence. It could consist of the sheriff, a retired professional athlete, the mayor, a respected farmer, business owners, or just about anyone. Cavin kept a small notebook in his shirt pocket, and each time after visiting a new store, he took notes. It didn't take much prodding to figure out which businesses were popular and which ones struggled in this tourist town. He didn't need to ask who owned each location because that information was readily accessible online, and he studied the details before going into every establishment. Most often he would have done this homework on the airplane, and now he kicked himself for watching the movie instead because it slowed down progress during the available hours to work in the field today.

Cavin focused on the ages of the owners and paid attention to which ones sounded tired or worn out from a long year. Most talked about how business boomed in the summer, but that wintertime brought along a different story. Nearly everyone noted the sales uptick the holidays offered, but many mentioned that once foot traffic dropped off in January, the little town slowed down drastically. The locals would shop some but not enough to remain open full-time. Most shops would then run on limited days and hours until the tourist season kicked in come spring.

Cavin listened intently to these familiar stories. Most of the small coastal towns he visited dealt with the feast and famine that the weather promised. Some business owners could handle it, and others couldn't. He made careful notes about his first impressions knowing his predictions often proved true. On the ground, he also began mapping out which properties he wanted to acquire most. The parking lot next to the candy shop interested him more than anything he saw so far, and the Beaufort Candy Company building and the connected structures were high on the list as well. The more land and buildings he could acquire on adjacent properties, the more opportunities they would bring.

A large, carefully designed hotel would be a wonderful addition to the waterfront area. Cavin imagined an aesthetically pleasing parking deck at the street level, shops and restaurants accessible from the outside and inside on the second floor, and rooms from the third up. About six stories would probably allow the new structure to fit in well with the town's current charm, and the location would demand a premium room rate.

Cavin ate lunch at Clawson's 1905 Restaurant & Pub with Luther Perkins, the owner of a prospective property. The guy talked his ear off in his store earlier, and when Cavin asked about a good place to eat, the man invited him to have lunch. In his mid-sixties or so, Luther clearly indulged in many meals. He wore large glasses and the top of his head was completely bald, reminding Cavin that he never understood why people like Luther didn't just shave off all their hair rather than leaving the remnants on the side, but he didn't dare ask.

"The first place anyone new to Beaufort should eat is Clawson's," Luther insisted with a thick southern drawl.

Cavin instantly recognized the name of the restaurant as the one he'd hoped served breakfast. The popular establishment with classic hardwood floors, brick walls, nostalgic décor, and high-backed wooden booths proved to be as charming as the town itself. Teaming with customers, Cavin figured he and his new friend settled into the last open booth just after the busboy wiped it down for them. Cavin felt certain this place would make his top ten favorite spots in Beaufort.

"What is the story behind this building?" Cavin inquired, still taking in the warm, homey, and Christmassy surroundings.

"Clawson's began as a grocery store in the late 1800s."

"Really?" Cavin interjected, trying to imagine what this space might have looked like over 200 years ago filled with aisles of food. He knew for sure the products on the shelves wouldn't have included all the dyes and preservatives found in the middle aisles of the grocery stores these days. When shopping for meals and snacks, Cavin tried his best to stick to the outer edges of the store in order to keep himself healthy which reminded him that he needed to find a gym to utilize during this trip. This was the type of thing he needed his own assistant to handle.

Luther noticed Cavin's wandering eyes. "This location isn't the original Clawson's," he pointed out. "The grocery store was across the street on the waterfront. It was destroyed by a hurricane, unfortunately, and later rebuilt in this spot. There's a brick building out behind this place which can't be seen from Front Street, and it is said to be the oldest standing structure in Beaufort. It was Clawson's bakery."

"Does every business in this town have a bakery?" Cavin asked with a hint of laughter under his breath. "I visited the candy store and the coffee shop this morning, and both offer baked goods."

Chewing a piece of popcorn shrimp, Luther laughed through his nose. "The old bakery is now Backstreet Pub," he eventually revealed.

"So pubs and bakeries are the town theme, huh?" Cavin replied with a gentle smile.

"We love to eat and drink around here," Luther admitted rubbing his oversized belly while forking another bite off his plate.

"Who doesn't?" Cavin offered in agreement. "I imagine hurricanes have relocated a lot of businesses in Beaufort over the years."

"Yes, sir."

"Does it ever concern you that a hurricane could take out the business you have built?" Cavin inquired knowing the risk of hurricanes often weighed heavily in the minds of coastal business owners, especially small businesses.

"Not really," Luther replied. "What bothers me is the rising cost of insurance."

Cavin chuckled at the serious joke. "Cheers to that," he acknowledged, holding up his half-full glass of iced cold water.

Luther picked up his nearly empty soda and tapped glasses with a heavy hand; however, with all the white noise circling the enchanting environment, no one else seemed to notice.

While Cavin savored the taste of Mahi Mahi served over rice and perfectly seasoned veggies, he asked Luther well-thought-out questions. In return Luther spilled the beans on local politics, pointed out all the people he knew in the restaurant, and introduced Cavin to several locals.

"Cavin Dawson works for a firm in Atlanta in business development," Luther told each one of them.

Cavin carefully crafted those words years ago and repeated them to Luther and everyone else he met today. He steered clear of phrases like real estate and land acquisition management, knowing that they often raised red flags, especially the latter. Most people didn't like change at least not until he could show them the dollar signs that came with improving their town.

"Cavin is here on vacation, but he likes to mix business with pleasure," was another phrase Luther took in earlier and spat out a few times to his friends which often brought on smiles and seemed to set others at ease. Cavin almost scrapped the line for this trip because every time he said or heard it, his mind went to Cancun where he should be right now lying on a beach next to beautiful women in bikinis.

Cavin geared his conversations toward helping businesses reach their potential while maximizing profits. In order to do that, he needed to know as many details as possible, and when business owners realized he was willing to offer them complimentary advice while they became friends, they often opened the corporate books, business plans, marketing strategies, and all the rest. In fact Cavin made plans to play golf tomorrow with a well-respected banker who had been at the restaurant's bar having a few drinks on his day off until Luther waved him over.

"It's a great day to have banker's hours," Cavin offered with a grin when Luther introduced them.

"It's almost as nice as being on vacation," the clever fellow replied.

"You have one-upped me there, Jeff," Cavin laughed while the waitress cleared the plates.

Jeff sat down with them after standing beside their table for several minutes in conversation. While that might have seemed rude in a fancy Atlanta restaurant, in a small town that's what people did, and it usually worked in Cavin's favor. The more friends he could make, the better. He found out that Jeff was a scratch golfer which he appreciated. Now he wouldn't have to let the guy win purposely.

"Luther, would you like to play eighteen holes with us?" Cavin asked.

Luther snickered. "You fellows call me when you play a round of putt-putt."

Everyone laughed.

"Jeff, you should invite a couple of friends to join us," Cavin suggested.

"I will see who I can scrounge up."

"Tell them the outing is on me," Cavin offered. He carried a healthy budget for wining and dining, and he would pay for the meal he and Luther just ate even though Luther invited him. "That might entice them."

"We will likely have a line of people waiting to play," Jeff teased.

"The more the merrier."

Cavin needed a local to have some drinks with this evening so he could check out the nightlife on his first Friday in Beaufort. He considered asking Luther or Jeff, but neither seemed like the type. Both wore wedding rings and probably had a family at home. Cavin thought back through the people he met today—the names he wrote in his notebook and the business cards with phone numbers. He would prefer to meet an attractive woman who could show him around town, and if it turned into something more, that would be an added bonus, especially since he would be in Beaufort for a while.

Cavin recalled meeting a few cute ladies today. Some he imagined could show him a pretty good time, but for some reason one in particular stood out. In fact his interaction with Noel Puckett crossed his mind several times as he familiarized himself with this place. She had kids, though, making the chances she could go out on a whim on a Friday night seem unlikely. He would also feel a little awkward going back into her store for a second, or technically a third, time today.

Cavin blinked his eyes realizing he lost track of the conversation the two gentlemen sitting across from him were having in reality. When they reached a stopping point, he asked a question his mind had been pondering.

"So who owns the fancy yacht?"

11

The morning hours at the candy shop flew by along with the gusts of wind that swirled outdoors. Lunchtime came and went, and the only thing Noel found time to eat was leftover fruit from last night. The fifty cinnamon rolls disappeared within an hour, and she could proudly say she never indulged. Instead she burned calories racing around the shop doing everything from showing customers to the candy of their liking to sweeping up an entire box of malt balls that somehow got spilled to working the cash register when Mrs. Madelyn needed a break.

Mrs. Madelyn preferred to work the front counter because it allowed her to sit on the stool for the most part which kept the pressure off her knees that came with working the floor. She knew Noel's young body could handle the bending, random ladder climbing, and walking countless laps around the maze of candy barrels and bins. She nearly had to force Noel to sit on the stool up front while she devoured the sandwich she brought for lunch. Her husband packed it for her knowing a busy day lay ahead. He always did sweet things like that.

Levi and Laney nibbled from the fruit bowl here and there as they showed the younger customers around the store, tackled random projects Noel and Mrs. Madelyn needed help with, and ran up and down the stairs a hundred times like usual. They also made sure each kid who entered the shop received a hand-delivered miniature candy cane from the basket near the tree or the one by the front door depending on where they were when they noticed them.

"Have you seen my Santa hat?" Noel figured she heard this question ten times today as the kids ran around the store, mostly helping but also playing. When they got hot or tired of wearing the decorative hats, they ended up in the most random places. Thankfully, Noel hadn't had to ask them to slow down many times, and in each missing item situation, one of them or Mrs. Madelyn found the hat.

The kids weren't the only ones asking questions. "Do you think we are busier than last year's Black Friday?" Noel asked Mrs. Madelyn on more than one occasion. She knew a steady stream of customers meandered through the store, but she made a pact with herself not to be distracted by looking at the sales numbers throughout the day. Instead, she would wait for the big reveal after closing.

"It's hard to say, but I know I have rung up a lot of customers," Mrs. Madelyn answered optimistically.

The afternoon hours seemed to move like the fast-forward feature on a television as Noel cut and weighed countless slices of fudge while tackling other random tasks that popped up. She loved giving children samples of the fudge that looked or sounded best to them, and then watching their eyes light up like the Christmas trees their families decorated this time of year. Many of the kids wanted to keep the tiny spoons, but the downside to their excitement about the miniature utensils was having to collect them from the most peculiar places in the store. However, there was always an opportunity for a positive spin, and the one for this dilemma was that Levi and Laney enjoyed having Where's Waldo hunts to see who could find the most. On the other hand, neither of them wanted to clean the mirage of fingerprints off the glass display case, so Noel often found herself with the window cleaner and paper towels in her hands.

The Christmas tree needed watering daily, and that didn't click in Noel's brain until late in the day. The kids filled a water pitcher in the kitchen sink, and she followed behind, wiping up a trail of droplets they left in their wake.

Throughout the day it brought Noel joy to see so many familiar faces, even ones she saw just yesterday at the Thanksgiving feast, as well as to meet new customers. Some she hadn't seen frequently enough to recognize, and others said this marked their first visit to the candy shop. She made an effort to tell every customer how much she appreciated their business whether they purchased a handful of candy or walked out with bags full in each hand. Everyone seemed so full of energy, and Noel imagined hearing Christmas music for the first time of the season and seeing the store decorated for the holiday may have had something to do with that. She received numerous compliments on the tree, the icicle lights, and the window displays.

The mayor's wife stopped by for her favorite pie and promised to order more for upcoming festivities. The jolly woman threw more parties than anyone Noel ever met which delighted her because she regularly ordered pies, fudge, candy, or an assortment of all of these goodies. Just today Noel wrote down a handful of orders for the lady including one for the book club and another for her bridge group.

When the cuckoo clock sounded at five, Mrs. Madelyn finished ringing up the customers in line, and Noel held open the door for each of them. Mrs. Madelyn walked the final customer to the exit where they all stood talking for several minutes with their hair blowing across their shoulders.

While the adults remained occupied, Laney and Levi scurried like little mice down the stairs and snuck into their hideout underneath the cash register. Laney threw a blanket over their heads and held her pointer finger to her lips.

"Stay quiet so we can surprise them," she whispered excitedly.

Noel pushed the door against the wind, turned the lock, and hurried to the cash register to pull up the sales data on the monitor. Mrs. Madelyn knew her motive, and she too was eager to see the Black Friday totals. She stood over Noel's shoulder as they scanned the list showing the number of transactions, average ticket amount, and all kinds of other helpful data. However, the figure that interested Noel the most was at the bottom, and when she mouthed it as Mrs. Madelyn read it, her head and heart sank into her hands.

Mrs. Madelyn sighed and rubbed Noel's back gently. "Oh, honey, it's just one day," she reminded her friend.

"It's supposed to be the biggest day of the year," Noel murmured beneath her palms.

"It probably was," Mrs. Madelyn replied looking on the bright side.

"Yeah, but not big enough. I can't hire anyone to help if sales aren't up enough even for me to pay myself a decent wage."

"I'll be here as much as I can," Mrs. Madelyn offered hoping to cheer her up a bit.

"The problem is bigger than staffing, and I can't let you work yourself to death like I'm doing." Noel paused for a moment to let her thoughts settle. "If a miracle doesn't happen between now and Christmas, I think I will be forced to close the store at the beginning of the New Year," Noel disclosed. She couldn't help but wonder if that was the big news her dad mentioned sharing on their family trip that she missed, and he didn't make it home from.

"Oh, darling."

"Levi and Laney will be devastated," Noel voiced. "I'll be devastated," she cried. "I am devastated."

Beneath the counter, worry crept onto Levi's and Laney's little faces. Neither needed to hold a finger to their mouth to remind the other to remain quiet. Each realized the words shared were not intended for their ears.

"Black Friday isn't just one day of sales, it's a predictor for the rest of the Christmas season," Noel reminded Mrs. Madelyn.

Mrs. Madelyn knew that all too well from many years of experience. "Let's just take it one day at a time, sweet girl, and see what God has in store."

Eventually Noel and Mrs. Madelyn busied themselves tidying up the shop, and Laney and Levi snuck back upstairs like little elves just in time for Noel to call them down.

"Who wants to sweep?"

"I'll get the broom," Laney shouted quickly.

Laney's enthusiasm after such a long day surprised Noel and actually brought a smirk to her face even after the bad news she discovered at the register.

"Levi, will you help replenish the candy bins?"

"Of course, Mom."

Noel appreciated her son's positive response as well. "Thank you both."

Standing near the Christmas tree, a smile traveled across Mrs. Madelyn's face as she straightened several branches and ornaments tainted by little hands. She wondered if Laney and Levi could sense Noel's sadness knowing children had a way of humbling their hearts when adults needed them the most.

By the time cleanup and restocking finished, everyone was zonked, and Noel ended up putting the kids to bed around eight thirty because she knew that Shop Small Saturday would bring in a crowd of locals. The year-over-year customer count had been down some today, but the average ticket decline worried Noel the most. People seemed to be holding on to their money a little tighter this year or spending it somewhere else. These thoughts became front and center in Noel's mind again as she walked out of the kids' bedroom.

"What are we going to do to help Mom keep the candy shop open?" Levi whispered from his pillow after his mother disappeared.

An inch of light filtered through a small sliver between the door and the frame into the otherwise dark room.

Lying still on the adjacent pillow while facing her cousin, Laney reminded Levi of what the two of them quietly talked about earlier after overhearing the news and scurrying upstairs into this very room. "We have to work harder," she murmured.

"Maybe if we help enough, the store will stay open."

"We need to make some money, too," Laney suggested.

"What if we have a bake sale like the one at school?" Levi considered remembering their school hosting a bake sale to raise funds for new playground equipment.

Laney scrunched her nose. "I think we should do something different than treats since the candy shop already has so many."

"How about lemonade?" Levi proposed. "Everybody loves lemonade."

Laney could make out the whites of her cousin's eyes as they talked between pillows. "Yeah, we can make a lemonade stand in front of the candy shop!"

"Actually, I think I have an even better idea," Levi decided with extra enthusiasm as he recalled what Kevin brought them earlier. "Since it's Christmastime, we should have a hot chocolate stand instead of lemonade."

"Yeah, that's the best idea. Lemonade tastes better in the summertime, but hot chocolate is best when it's cold. The cocoa Cavin brought us this morning warmed up my bones."

"It was so good," Levi agreed. "We can sell lots of hot chocolate and give Mom all the money to keep the candy shop open."

"We can charge one dollar for every cup. If we sell 100 cups, we would make $100," Laney predicted excitedly.

"We need to make a poster that shows the price," Levi suggested, recalling one he helped create during art class.

"We can use the markers we use for our school projects."

"This is going to be so much fun," Levi exclaimed. "Do you want to make the poster now?"

Laney sighed. "Let's do it in the morning. I'm tired."

Levi yawned. "Me too."

12

After lunch Cavin nearly wandered back to the Beaufort Candy Company, but wanting to avoid appearing desperate, he instead visited additional businesses and introduced himself to more townspeople. He met an attractive woman in a clothing boutique and another at a jewelry store; however, he never felt the desire to request a tour of the Beaufort nightlife from either of them.

Around five o'clock Cavin nearly caved. He even walked into Cru and stood in line to buy Noel the coffee she liked. He thought she might appreciate a little boost at the end of what must have been a long and tiring day. The notebook he pulled from his pocket reminded him of her preference, and he would get something for Mrs. Madelyn and the kids, too. However, he ducked out at the last minute, deciding that mixing business with pleasure on this occasion might not be the best idea.

Cavin really wanted to acquire Noel's property, and he wasn't sure whether getting to know her personally would help or hurt his chances. He needed more time to think that through, so he opened the email from his dad's assistant and clicked on the link with the rental house address she booked. The route led him further down Front Street where the shops, restaurants, and businesses gave way to gorgeous southern homes featuring tall columns and widow's walks overlooking Taylor Creek on the opposite side of the road.

On the creek side, a sidewalk extending all the way from the business district paralleled the street, and boat docks stretched into the water like wooden fingers. Most of the houses stood two or three stories, many of them white with wraparound porches on each level. When Cavin turned into the driveway, the elegant plantation style home in front of him with a perfectly manicured lawn reminded him of a conversation he once had with his dad as a child.

"Why do you stay in such big houses when you go on a business trip by yourself?" Cavin inquired as his father showed pictures highlighting another of his successful ventures.

"Son, when we promote our wealth, we attract wealthy people, and that's good for business," he informed his future successor. "We show our wealth through homes, vehicles, clothing, accessories, and all the material items we possess. On business trips this is of utmost importance."

Sitting in the oversized SUV that fit in nicely in the driveway, Cavin glanced at the key code in the email. Upon making it to the enormous front door with his laptop strapped over his shoulder, the numbers worked like a charm. As he unloaded the vehicle, he noticed that some nearby homeowners already put up decorations. Having a Christmas tree on the porch seemed to be popular, and he decided he liked the look.

After a few trips it felt nice to kick off his shoes and collapse on the couch. A quick tap on the watch wrapped around his wrist told him he walked 20,000 steps today. No wonder he felt a bit spent. He knew he couldn't keep his head on the fluffy pillows long, however, or he would fall asleep and miss opportunities to network this evening.

Rather than eating dinner out, Cavin ordered delivery and spent the next few hours going over his notes from today and researching the properties further online. He found out that Noel's family had owned the candy shop building for ages. He figured it was most likely paid off, which probably didn't bode well for his case. It wasn't like she was near retirement age, and he could dangle the idea of a nest egg in front of her. Other than being stressed about the cinnamon rolls, the woman seemed to have her ducks in a row. However, with all the hustle and bustle at the candy store this morning, he hadn't been able to gather any information on what their sales situation looked like or if she enjoyed the environment.

With darkness fully settled in and the moon casting an illustrious glow on the creek visible through the long row of extravagant windows, Cavin ran a quick search on his phone for a list of local weekend hot spots. He soon discovered that one of the waterfront restaurants offered live music. From there he contemplated whether to drive or walk, and ultimately slipped into comfortable shoes, a pair of khakis, and a nice sweater.

As soon as he stepped outside, the wind slapped his face like an angry girlfriend, and he instantly second-guessed the decision to travel on foot. At least this way, he could enjoy a few drinks and not have to worry about whether he had too much to operate a motor vehicle.

"Getting into any type of trouble with the police will instantly ruin your reputation in a small town where you are trying to make friends and win influence," his dad hammered into his head before nearly every trip.

Thankfully Cavin steered clear of run-ins with the law thus far, and with that thought in mind, he shoved his hands into his pockets and walked briskly down the sidewalk noticing details he missed on the drive to the house. He spotted a kayak launch, a little free library box, gazebos, and other neat things along the waterfront. On the opposite side of the road, he appreciated the fancy houses and their Christmas decorations, especially the traditional green garland draped along the balcony railings and white picket fences.

The trek took longer than expected, probably because Cavin's bones shivered from the inside out, but as he closed in on the glow of lights, he began to hear music drifting in his direction. When he reached the source, surprisingly he found a slew of people on the outdoor patio at Dock House Restaurant where a band played beach music in the corner. He assumed the music would be indoors considering the weather, but there appeared to be portable heaters set up all around the outdoor tables at the white planked two-story establishment. Most people appeared to be dressed warmly with drinks in their hands and smiles on their faces.

Cavin weaved his way through the crowd to the bar where every seat was taken. It didn't take long to recognize a place designated for walk-up orders, and he patiently waited his turn while he people-watched and chit-chatted with the others in line and in the vicinity. He learned that was the best way to make friends when alone in a bar. Talking to everyone made an individual look less awkward and more approachable. Having short conversations about the weather, the song playing at the moment, or the best drinks came easily.

"What can I get for you?" a tall middle-aged fellow with a thick beard asked when Cavin stepped up to bat.

Cavin ordered a drink recommended by a guy sitting on the closest stool. They chatted about the game on the television while he waited for it to be mixed, and Cavin wondered if he would run into anyone he met today. So far he saw no familiar faces, but he enjoyed meeting new people. A wide array of ages and social statuses made up the crowd who seemed to love singing Jimmy Buffett lyrics off-key.

Cavin found the best way to meet a woman was to make friends with the guys in the place who would eventually introduce him to other people they knew. However, the first woman he met startled him in a very unexpected way. When he turned with his drink in hand, she ran smack dab into his chest and not only caused his beverage to spill, but the impact loosened his grip, and the glass shattered on the concrete floor.

Although the music continued to play, the conversation halted as if a casket was being rolled down the aisle at a funeral. All eyes were suddenly on Cavin and the woman who immediately began to pat him compulsively with a cocktail napkin as if the drink soiled his clothes, but it hadn't. Maybe a few drops landed on his sweater, and a splash probably reached his shoes and pants legs, but thankfully, the all-too-familiar bar scene that could ruin a fun night way too early had been avoided. Who carried a pair of dry clothes in the car for situations like that, Cavin considered, although he chose not to have a vehicle here anyway.

"I am so sorry," the lady, who appeared a little older than he, offered apologetically staring into his eyes as if trying to determine if he was mad. "I was trying to get away from that guy, and all of a sudden, there you were."

Cavin glanced around for the person she mentioned but didn't see anyone who fit the bill. The bartender motioned to Cavin letting him know the glass would be taken care of and then made eye contact with a server who seemed to be on the case. It didn't take long for the roar of conversations to fill the air again once the other patrons understood the commotion.

Cavin smiled at the woman. "It's not my glass," he laughed.

"Oh, was it your girlfriend's?" she replied with a raised eyebrow.

Cavin chuckled. "I don't have a girlfriend," he shared. "But what I meant is that the glass belonged to the restaurant."

She shrugged her narrow shoulders, covered by a burgundy dress and a black jacket. "That's funny," she replied. "You're funny."

"I'm not a comedian, but I've been known to make people laugh."

Her first laugh rolled into the second one. "See, you did it again."

Cavin held out his hand. "My name is Cavin Dawson," he said. His dad taught him to introduce himself by always using his first and last name.

"I'm Georgia," she replied, "like the state."

The server began to sweep the broken glass into a dust pan as everyone stood clear of the area that Cavin and Georgia slowly moved away from.

Cavin smiled. "It's nice to meet you, Georgia."

"You ever been there?"

"I live there," he relayed, his eyes widening.

"Are you kidding me, Mr. Comedian?"

"I'm as serious as a stroke."

Her eyebrows shifted upward. "Don't you mean a heart attack?"

"Nope, that's what everyone says. I'm different."

"You sure are," she acknowledged. "What part of my name are you from?"

Cavin belted out a laugh. "That's pretty funny."

She winked at him. "You're not the only one with jokes, Cavin Dawson from Georgia."

It impressed him that she caught and recalled his last name. "I live in Atlanta, but I travel a lot."

"What brought you to Beaufort?" she inquired. "And don't say an airplane or car," she added with a snicker.

Cavin liked her wit and found her blonde hair and blue eyes attractive although he determined she was probably ten years his elder. However, the makeup she applied hid the wrinkles well, and she took great care of herself. He imagined she could introduce him to a local gym.

"I am here on vacation, but I like to mix business with pleasure," he reeled off with a wink.

Georgia blushed at the flirty nature of his banter. "Let me buy you another drink," she offered.

"How about I buy you two drinks and you give one of them to me," Cavin insisted.

"Is that your pick-up line for all the ladies?" she smirked.

"Only the ones who are strong enough to knock a drink out of my hands and make the glass shatter on the floor," he acknowledged while glancing down.

Georgia smiled and flexed her bicep although well hidden by layers of clothing.

When Cavin and Georgia stepped up to the bar, the bartender filled their order but only charged Cavin for one drink.

"It's on the house," he offered with a snicker, "since Georgia spilled yours."

Tilting her head, Georgia squinted her eyes at him. "You're too kind, Louie."

"Thanks," Cavin replied to Louie, nodding at him before returning his gaze to Georgia. "You must be a regular here if you are on a first-name basis with the bartender," he added as they drifted from the bar.

"Cavin, this is a small town. Everybody knows everybody," she explained. "Plus when you are a town councilwoman, you can't get away with anything."

"I see. So you run the show here in Beaufort," Cavin postulated with a smile.

"I help keep things running smoothly."

"You must be an intelligent woman," Cavin ascertained.

"I can hold my own."

"I have noticed."

"Before I ran into you—literally," she laughed, "I was sitting with some friends. You should join us."

Cavin knew better than to pass up such an opportunity. "I would be honored."

Cavin followed Georgia through the maze of people before shaking hands with a table full of locals including the mayor and his wife, another town councilperson, a doctor, and an insurance agent.

"It is a pleasure to meet each of you."

Within thirty minutes of filling a chair at the table, Cavin received an invitation to the mayor's party tomorrow night, an acceptance to join the Saturday morning golf outing, and a handful of business cards. It appeared that meeting Georgia, whom he learned was an attorney, might have been his golden ticket.

"Would you like to dance, City Boy?" Georgia confidently asked Cavin as people shuffled to the dance floor at the onset of a popular song.

"Of course," Cavin accepted.

Cavin quickly figured out that Georgia knew her way around a dance floor, and he sure was glad his mother forced him to start taking dance classes at age twelve. "It is a sure-fire way to meet and get close to pretty girls," his father told him when Cavin initially scoffed at the idea. At the time Cavin didn't realize the skill would continue to reap benefits well into adulthood.

"You and I might need to sign up for one of those reality dancing shows," Georgia mentioned acknowledging Cavin's abilities.

They danced, drank, and mingled with the group as well as other patrons who eagerly flocked to their table and then danced some more. Cavin never expected songs like "Run Run Rudolph" to cause so much commotion, but everyone hurried to the dance floor every time the band started a Christmas tune.

When Georgia asked how Cavin kept in such great shape, he told her about his rigorous workout routine. During that conversation she recommended the local gym where she said she worked out daily.

Although unsure how many drinks he consumed, Cavin knew when to call it quits. Another rule his father taught him was that getting drunk in the presence of intelligent business people was a terrible idea, especially in public. "You will show your hand to them if you have more than your share of alcohol, and if you aren't careful, you will show your rear end as well," his dad preached. "Instead buy them drinks and let them show you their cards and whatever else they can't control."

Most of the people at this table, or at any table where he sat, didn't need anyone to buy them drinks; however, the gesture often received value well beyond the monetary kind. As the evening wound down, Cavin picked up the tab for the whole group and walked away from the venue with more than a handful of new friends, one of whom mirrored his every step as the creek slapped against the boardwalk's concrete wall.

"Thanks for buying drinks for me and my friends," Georgia acknowledged. "Bumping into you really paid off," she added with a wink and a simultaneous shoulder tap.

"Was that your plan all along?"

"Do I come across as that type of woman?" she teased.

Before Cavin had the opportunity to respond, a man stepped out from a dark area underneath a large, mysterious live oak tree. "Georgia, who's your new boyfriend?" he slurred.

Cavin and Georgia both stopped in their tracks and turned their attention to the guy. Realizing the fellow knew Georgia by name, Cavin held his tongue.

"He is my friend, and his name is none of your business," Georgia stated calmly and intelligently.

"You don't know his name," the man laughed then turned his attention toward Cavin while stepping close enough for Cavin to smell the alcohol on his breath or maybe he spilled some on his worn jacket. "Dude, she doesn't even know your name."

Cavin squinted his eyes. "What is your name?" he inquired while trying to diffuse the situation.

The guy's eyes bulged. "My name?" he asked slowly and loudly, stumbling back a step. "Georgia knows my name."

Despite the fact that pole lights lit the area well and many people from the bar remained within shouting distance, Cavin still felt uncomfortable. He glanced at Georgia but kept the guy in his peripheral vision.

"Everyone knows your name," Georgia said to the man.

"I know his name," the fellow responded, nearly sticking his finger into Cavin's chest.

"This is the guy who was harassing me earlier . . . right before we met," Georgia explained to Cavin.

The news made Cavin feel even less at ease.

"If you hadn't walked away from me, maybe you would be going home with me instead of this dingbatter," the man contested.

Cavin's brow furrowed. What was a dingbatter? Did the drunk guy just create a new word?

"I doubt that," Georgia hissed.

"You've gone home with me before," he retorted.

"That's the end of this conversation," Georgia exclaimed. "Let's go," she insisted to Cavin. "And don't worry, he's harmless."

"She's right, I'm harmless, but Miss Big Shot here isn't. She's trying to ruin this town," he claimed then paused. "Be careful who you go home with, especially in a small town, mister. Everybody knows everybody's business around here."

"You need to mind your own business," Georgia barked as she reached for Cavin's hand and led them away.

"Don't let her tell you what to do, man. Be a man."

Cavin figured things would likely work out best if he let Georgia's words be the last. Although that guy seemed hammered and obviously jealous not to be the one walking beside this beautiful woman, he actually gave sound advice whether he meant to or not.

"Who is that guy?" Cavin asked once out of earshot.

"His name is Keaton, and although he can be a nuisance, he's not really a bad person. He just has a sad story."

"That's unfortunate," Cavin acknowledged.

"I am sorry he harassed us," Georgia apologized.

Cavin glanced over his shoulder. "Do you think we have to worry about him following us?"

"Probably not," Georgia replied, looking back.

After a few moments of silence, the wind blowing off the creek reminded Cavin of the temperature. "Speaking of stories, what is yours?" he asked, digging his hands into his pockets. "Where are you from and how did you end up in Beaufort?"

"I grew up in Boston, graduated from Boston College, took a position as an attorney for a large corporation, and traveled abroad handling casework for a while, then ended up here a few years ago. Now I am on my own."

"What drew you to Beaufort?"

"My family vacationed here every summer when I was a kid. I absolutely adored the place and still do. I have so many fond memories of swimming in the creek, going out on the boat, getting sunburned on the nearby beaches, and exploring all the coastal areas. I still have friends here now who I met back then. The mayor and his wife are from here."

"I kind of figured that with their accents," Cavin assumed.

"Then I guess you realized I am not from here."

"I speculated you were from up North, but it seems the time spent traveling abroad probably influenced your accent."

"My travels influenced my whole life, which is why I now want to bring more opportunities to Beaufort."

Those words were music to Cavin's ears. "Like what?" he investigated.

"More diverse restaurants, luxury hotels, shopping, gated

communities, golf courses, and the like. This area draws a plethora of wealthy tourists, and I think we can capitalize a lot more on what they bring to the table."

"What's holding Beaufort back?" Cavin asked.

"Tradition, old money, farmers, nostalgia . . ."

"That sounds normal for a small coastal town."

"Yeah. So what is your story, Mr. Dawson?"

"I was born and raised in Atlanta, graduated with a master's degree from Georgia Tech, and I currently work in business development."

Although Cavin was pretty sure he and Georgia were on the same team in this town, he didn't want to reveal too much too early.

"Do you travel frequently?" Georgia inquired, her heels clicking on the sidewalk.

"Yes, quite a bit."

"For business or pleasure?" she asked. "Or both?"

The question made Cavin think more about the Cancun trip he was missing right now than his work travels. If he met someone like Georgia there on the first day, the rest of the stay would be all fun and games. Appearances and outcomes wouldn't be much of a concern.

"Business, but I try to make time for both," Cavin answered cautiously.

"What is your all-time favorite destination?"

Surprisingly, Cavin never really considered this question which struck him as odd as he struggled to find an honest answer. "I am not sure I have one. I like exploring pretty much any new area, but I guess I particularly enjoy small towns like Beaufort."

"Why is that?" Georgia inquired.

"I guess I appreciate the people and, like you, the potential."

"That's a great response, but it doesn't really answer my question," she teased.

"It's hard to pick just one. I really try not to fall in love with any specific place. I appreciate each for what they are; I enjoy the experiences and move on to the next."

Cavin realized that pretty much summed up his romantic life as well. He didn't have time to fall in love. He almost mentioned that he was supposed to be in Cancun, but that would certainly spark questions about his purpose for being here.

"Maybe you can think about it and tell me more next time we see each other."

Next time. Cavin was glad to hear Georgia wanted to get together again, and his excitement split between business and pleasure. He enjoyed her company this evening. She was the type of woman he would have wanted to meet in Cancun—professional, flirty, attractive, carefree.

"This is my current residence," Cavin relayed when he spotted his rental vehicle in the driveway from the creek side of the street. The walk seemed less cold with someone to talk to.

"You have good taste," Georgia complimented.

Cavin grinned. "I appreciate the finer things in life in which category you seem to fall."

Georgia blushed as they came to a stop in front of the house. "You appear to have some valuable qualities yourself."

Only a narrow street stood between them and a warm, inviting house, yet the words of warning the drunk guy delivered earlier flashed through Cavin's mind.

13

oel slept like a rock and woke up on Small Business
Saturday with more energy than expected. She imagined
it would take forever to fall asleep because when she first
crawled into bed, her mind raced about the fate of the candy shop.
She remembered wishing for Fletcher to be lying next to her with
his usual good advice. He probably would have spoken his
encouraging words softly while giving her a back massage although
not expecting anything in return. However, once his fingers
started caressing her body, one thing usually led to another. The
intimacy they shared seemed otherworldly, and she would give
anything to be wrapped up with him in these sheets feeling the
warmth of his skin against hers right now. He always had a way of
setting her at ease. Maybe last night, he found a way to comfort
her because her tired body somehow overpowered her busy mind.
Hopefully that would make life easier today.

"Thanks, Fletch," Noel whispered into the universe that
seemed to swallow her more often than not these days.

Shockingly Noel found the kids not only awake in their bedroom
but also out of bed and on the floor working away at something.

"What are you up to?" she asked as she pushed their door all
the way open.

Laney's and Levi's necks jolted at the sound of her voice, and they wore a guilty expression on their faces.

"Um, we are making signs," Laney announced.

"What kind of signs?"

"Hot chocolate stand signs," Levi exclaimed.

The two kids looked at each other communicating through eye contact about the mission. First thing this morning, they decided that they couldn't keep the hot chocolate stand a secret, but that didn't mean anyone had to know the purpose.

The skin between Noel's eyes wrinkled as if squeezed with a clothespin. "When and where is this hot chocolate stand taking place?" she inquired, holding her chin with her thumb and pointer finger.

The kids held each other's gaze again, and for a moment neither said anything.

"Today," Levi finally confessed. "In front of the candy shop."

"Oh really?" Noel asked amused.

"Yeah, we want to make some money," Laney added.

Levi's eyes bulged a little.

"Do you have an adequate supply of the ingredients?" Noel inquired knowing the kids helped her make homemade hot chocolate mix recently but wondering if they considered the amount needed to sell in bulk. In the candy shop kitchen as well as her own, she always tried to teach Levi and Laney to consider all the possibilities and challenges while still letting them help.

The kids looked at one another each hoping the other knew the answer. "Probably," Levi eventually surmised. "We helped you make some the other day."

"Our homemade hot chocolate is the best ever," Laney stated. "Our customers will love it."

Noel smiled proudly. "Yes, they will. However, I think you will need to make more of the homemade mix. Do you remember the ingredients?"

"Sugar," Levi blurted out quickly.

"Which kind of sugar?"

"Powdered," Laney, her little chef, knew off the top of her head. "Cocoa powder, too."

"And powder milk," Levi blurted out.

"Powdered, but yes," Noel corrected. "What do we add a splash and a dash of?"

"Vanilla and mini chocolate chips," Laney added enthusiastically, vividly recalling making it with her aunt.

"What goes in last, Levi?" Noel checked.

"Marshmallows."

"Yes, little dehydrated marshmallows," Noel noted. "Then what do we mix it with to serve?"

"Milk," Laney answered.

"Mom, will you help us make enough for our customers?" Levi asked energetically.

"Please," Laney added, clasping her hands together.

Noel sighed. "Today is going to be a really busy day at the store," she reminded them, or at least she prayed it would.

"We will do all the work," Laney promised.

How could Noel say no to her little helpers wanting to become entrepreneurs? "I will assist with heating up the hot chocolate and transporting it from the kitchen to the stand, but you two have to do the rest."

"Thanks, Mom."

"You're the best, Aunt Noel."

Noel grinned wondering what she was getting herself into. She couldn't keep her own store afloat, so what made her think she could help the kids start a small sidewalk business?

"You are also going to need a table and jackets because it's cool outside."

Thankfully today's forecast was much nicer than yesterday's. However, almost all November mornings arrived with a chill in the air.

The kids finished making their signs, scarfed down cereal, brushed their teeth, and hustled downstairs to the candy shop kitchen to collect the ingredients from the cabinets and set them on the prep table.

"You are also going to need disposable insulated cups with lids since you are serving this to the public," Noel explained when she joined them in the kitchen. "And we will store the hot chocolate in an urn so that you two won't have to pour such a hot beverage."

"I know where the cups are," Laney claimed.

"I will get an urn," Levi announced.

Before Noel flipped the candy shop's sign to open, the kids set up a table on the sidewalk, complete with a Christmassy tablecloth, an urn full of hot chocolate, paper cups, and two poster board signs affixed to the front of the stand.

"I'm not sure how many people will stop for hot chocolate this early in the morning, but we will see," Noel mentioned.

Mrs. Madelyn appeared on the sidewalk with a large smile. "A hot chocolate stand," she said enthusiastically. "I want a cup."

"You are our first customer," Laney announced.

"It will be one dollar," Levi stated, holding out his little hand.

Mrs. Madelyn rummaged through her purse and pulled out a crisp dollar bill from her wallet. "Where is your tip jar?" she asked.

Laney and Levi shared a puzzled look.

"What's a tip jar?" Laney asked.

"A jar you tip over like a cow?" Levi speculated with a grin.

Noel, Mrs. Madelyn, and Laney all giggled.

"How do you know about cow tipping?" Noel inquired.

"Uncle Keaton," Levi explained.

"Ah, I see," Noel replied.

"A tip jar is nothing like cow tipping, silly. It's a jar that sits on the table so your customers can give you extra money for your good service," Mrs. Madelyn explained.

"We didn't think of that," Noel confessed.

"We definitely need one of those cow tipping jars," Laney proclaimed.

Again, everyone laughed although Laney didn't quite know why what she said was so funny, but she went along with it.

"I will bring you one," Noel promised.

The kids offered their thanks, and then Levi held a cup beneath the spout while Laney flipped the lever.

"There you go," Levi said as he handed over the cup.

Mrs. Madelyn took a sip. "This is delicious," she approved. "You might sell out."

"Hopefully we sell out of candy today, too," Noel wished.

"It is going to be a good day," Mrs. Madelyn predicted.

"Let us know if you need anything," Noel reminded them before heading through the door with her helper.

"Just a tip jar," Laney repeated.

"Oh yeah," Noel responded.

"Be sure to flip the Christmas countdown signs," Mrs. Madelyn advised when she spotted the outdoor chalkboard and candy cane-themed pole holding the red octagon signboard still reflecting yesterday's number. She recalled both parents and children alike reading it aloud with excitement.

Laney immediately raced in her direction. "I almost forgot," she claimed, switching the chalkboard's number to twenty-five.

Levi hustled inside to change the second sign.

A few minutes later Mrs. Madelyn delivered the tip jar and placed three one-dollar bills inside.

"Wow, that's more money than the hot chocolate," Levi exclaimed after she walked away.

Laney high-fived her cousin. "We are going to save the candy store."

14

Cavin woke up excited to play golf with his new friends today. He delighted in how quickly he put together an outing that would combine business and pleasure.

He pulled on golf pants, a polo shirt, and a nice sweater. Looking in the mirror, he straightened his collar then plucked from a nearby bag the golf shoes he would later slip on at the country club. For now, though, he put on a pair of casual business shoes.

Up early he allowed time to grab a cup of coffee at Cru and find a sporting goods store where he could buy a set of clubs. He considered renting some at the country club but ultimately decided having his own set would look more professional.

Feeling good, he walked outside ready to head out for the day, but his mood shifted instantly when he noticed a flat tire on the front of the SUV.

"You gotta be kidding me," he exclaimed into the crisp morning air throwing his hands up. Then his eyes drifted to the back tire on the driver's side. "What the heck," he shouted, realizing it was also flat.

A quick walk around the vehicle revealed two more deflated tires. Baffled, Cavin stood staring at the SUV in utter disbelief. It didn't take a genius to figure out this wasn't a coincidence. One tire maybe but not four. Who would have done this? Neighborhood kids, maybe?

Cavin's mind raced. Nothing like this ever happened on past trips. How would he even go about getting this fixed since this wasn't his vehicle? Would he or the rental car company be held responsible?

Tugging his phone from his pocket, he dialed his dad's assistant. Eventually her voicemail chimed in, and although her position required her to remain on call, Cavin realized she was likely sound asleep on this early Saturday morning. Hopefully she would discover the voicemail soon and get back to him.

Cavin considered reaching out to his dad for guidance but determined he didn't want to involve him unless absolutely necessary. He would likely interrogate him and somehow find a way to blame Cavin by implying that he made an enemy which he hadn't. On second thought, what if the guy from last night who harassed him and Georgia near the bar was responsible? As these thoughts circled in his mind, Cavin quickly decided he would put $100 on him being the culprit. He probably followed them to the house last night. That made Cavin wonder if he flattened the tires last night or this morning. Probably last night, he decided, assuming that the guy was probably hungover this morning.

Cavin's second call went to the rental car company his family used. Glancing at his watch as the recording announced their normal business hours, he realized they weren't receiving calls yet, either. He contemplated searching online for a towing company, but how could a truck tow a vehicle with four flat tires?

Maybe an auto mechanic shop could send someone with an air pump, Cavin surmised. Before checking the listings, he decided to examine the tires more closely to determine if they were slashed or if only the air had been let out.

Cavin bent down next to each tire, trying not to let the knees of the sole pair of golf pants touch the ground. Upon further inspection, he found no evidence of slashes, and feeling for nails made no sense.

A quick glance at the local shops brought bad news. Not a single auto mechanic was open on the weekend.

"That's why this town needs to grow," Cavin growled. Atlanta would have numerous options open twenty-four hours a day.

A few minutes later, Cavin decided to walk to Cru. That would give him time to think through this situation, and then hopefully he would receive a call back from his dad's assistant. As he walked briskly down the sidewalk, Cavin passed the restaurant where he met Georgia, followed shortly by Clawson's where he ate a meal with Luther Perkins and also met Jeff, the banker with whom he was set to play golf today.

As Cavin approached the candy shop, he thought of Noel and spotted a table out front that hadn't been there yesterday. As he closed in on it, he saw two small figures huddled behind the table, and then he heard the sound of crying.

A few seconds later, he recognized it was Laney and Levi sitting on the low-lying window frame embracing one another, but he couldn't tell which was sobbing. When Cavin made it close enough to the table to see their faces, he realized both were in tears.

"Are you guys okay?" Cavin asked.

Startled, they both looked up at him incredulously.

"Dumb question, I know," Cavin admitted. "What's wrong?"

"That mean lady said we can't sell hot chocolate," Laney cried.

Cavin took in the purpose of the table for the first time. "What? Why?"

"We don't have a license," Levi shared.

"A license?"

"Of course we don't have a driver's license," Laney added, still bawling, "we're kids."

Cavin contained a smile. "Where is the lady now?" he asked. "Did you tell your mom?"

"She's inside talking to Mom."

"She called someone who is going to shut us down."

"The health inspector?" Cavin inquired.

Levi and Laney shrugged their little shoulders.

"I will see if I can help," Cavin offered. "I am a pro at conflict resolution."

"A pro at what?" Laney asked, puzzled.

"At helping," Cavin clarified. "First I will take a hot chocolate, please."

"The mean lady told us not to sell any more," Levi shared.

Cavin reached into his wallet and dropped a twenty-dollar bill into the tip jar. "You are not selling the hot chocolate to me," he explained. "You are giving it to me," he added with a wink.

A slow smile crept onto the kids' faces, and then Laney held a cup while Levi flipped the spout. In that moment a short man with a bald head hurriedly approached the table.

"I'm sorry, sir, these kids can't sell you hot chocolate," the man proclaimed authoritatively. "They don't have a street vendor's license."

Cavin purposely stood in front of the cute posters, blocking the price. "These kids are giving away hot chocolate to Small Business Saturday shoppers," Cavin announced. "The jar is for donations, and the money goes to help a good cause," he explained.

The man's brow furrowed, and for a moment he remained motionless with a puzzled expression on his face. "She didn't mention that," he muttered to himself.

When the guy scurried towards the candy shop's window that showcased a stunning array of irresistible sweets, Cavin quickly ripped the taped signs off the table skirt and shoved them beneath the table.

Levi smirked while Laney monitored the man cupping his hands on the glass that Noel cleaned earlier this morning.

"Surely in a small town like Beaufort, a couple of local kids can help the community by giving away hot chocolate during the Christmas season."

The man turned from the window. "I don't see the harm in that, but . . ." he trailed off as if not sure what else to add.

"I am Cavin Dawson," Cavin announced politely introducing himself to the stranger.

"I'm Samuel Lowe, town councilperson."

About the time that Cavin took in the title, Noel came rushing out the front door.

"Kids, I'm afraid . . .," she started before trailing off when she spotted Cavin and Sam.

Then someone else hurried out the door behind her, but Cavin focused his attention on Noel.

"I think we have come to a resolution," Cavin announced.

"A resolution," the woman trailing behind questioned defensively, and when Cavin turned to her, she added, "Cavin, why are you here?" with a surprised expression.

Noel's eyebrows lifted toward the Santa hat atop her head. "You two know each other?" Noel inquired. "I thought you just arrived in town yesterday," she said to Cavin.

Georgia didn't wait for any further responses. "What is this resolution talk?" she questioned interrupting.

Cavin suddenly felt the need to walk on eggshells. He needed all of these people in his corner.

"Georgia, the kids are simply trying to raise money for the community," Sam announced.

"No one mentioned that," Georgia argued.

Noel looked at Sam and then at Cavin.

"They're giving away the hot chocolate. Only accepting donations," Sam offered.

"Wait, they have signs on the front of the table with prices," Georgia recalled. Noel glanced down to where she helped the kids affix the signs as Cavin stepped back and Georgia walked to the front of the table for a better view. "Where did the signs go?"

"Are you sure there were signs?" Cavin asked nonchalantly. "Have you tried this hot chocolate?" he asked as he changed the subject while lifting the cup in her direction. "It is delicious. I might invest in these kids. They are the kind of forward-thinking people this town needs."

Surprising everyone, Georgia took a sip. "It is good," she admitted begrudgingly although her expression remained disgruntled.

"I'll have a cup," Sam said with a large smile.

Georgia chimed in again. "If the hot chocolate is indeed free and this truly is to raise money for the community, which organization is it helping?" she inquired while staring at the kids.

Levi and Laney suddenly appeared even more frozen than throughout the whole confusing ordeal.

A random MISSING DOG poster on a nearby light pole caught Noel's attention. "It's for animals," she reeled off.

"What kind of animals?" Georgia probed. "What's the organization?"

Cavin followed the movement of Noel's eyes, and he imagined Georgia would keep pressing. "Lost animals," he concocted. "The kids are starting a fund to help find missing animals." It was actually a brilliant idea, he thought.

Levi and Laney looked like a couple of spectators at a ping pong match with their little lost eyes bouncing from one person to the next.

"What is the organization's name?"

"We are still working on the details," Noel replied.

"Kids, don't forget to pour me a cup," Sam reminded them, removing a bulky wallet from his dress pants pocket and casually tossing a crisp ten-dollar bill into the tip jar.

Levi and Laney smiled and worked in tandem quickly making another beverage.

If Georgia's eyes had been on a hill, they would have rolled all the way to the bottom. "How do you know so much about this potential nonprofit, Mr. Dawson?" she interrogated studying him closely.

The fact that she used his last name didn't slip past Cavin. "These folks are the first people I met in Beaufort yesterday, and we had a discussion over beverages and cinnamon rolls," Cavin disclosed, purposely leaving the details to the imagination.

"Is that right?" Georgia declared, giving Noel a sideways glance all the while keeping her focus on Cavin. "It doesn't take you long to get around a new town, huh?"

Cavin felt the intensity of her accusation. "I like meeting new people," he countered.

Georgia shifted her gaze to Noel. "The kids can keep the hot chocolate stand up today, but before setting up shop again on the sidewalk, which is a potential insurance liability, you all will need to complete the necessary application paperwork at the municipality office."

"Sure we can do that," Noel offered to appease the woman.

"If you need help, I imagine your business consultant, Mr. Atlanta here, can assist," Georgia proposed, patting Cavin's firm chest. She then painted a smile on her face and altered her tone to match the chirpy birds in a nearby tree, locking eyes with Cavin. "Let's get together again soon," she suggested before winking at Noel as she turned and walked away, her hips moving like a runway model on a mission.

Noel furrowed her brow, scoffed, and with folded arms monitored Cavin's expression closely. She thought his eyes would most likely follow Georgia's departure as Sam's had, but to her surprise Cavin didn't so much as glance in the woman's direction. An instant later his gaze met hers, and the two studied one another for a moment.

"This is the best hot chocolate I've ever tasted," Sam declared, turning his attention back to the table.

Laney and Levi grinned.

"They can sell it by the gallon," Cavin stated and then quickly rephrased, "I meant the kids take donations for a gallon." As soon as Cavin finished the statement, he thought it sounded kind of odd to sell hot chocolate by the gallon; he had never heard of that . . . but why not?

"I'll take a gallon."

"In order to have the hot chocolate available by the gallon, we will need gallon jugs first," Noel proclaimed with an expectant glare in Cavin's direction. "I think Cavin signed up for that task."

"Put me down for one," Sam requested. "Call me when it's ready, and I'll pick it up. Good luck today, kids," he added with a smile before heading down the sidewalk.

"You are quite the businessman, huh, Mr. Dawson," Noel declared.

"Just trying to be helpful," Cavin replied as he tried to decipher the meaning behind her comment.

"In addition to fetching the gallon jugs, you can also help these kids make the hot chocolate," she directed.

"I would, but I am kind of in a pickle this morning and do not have time right now, unfortunately," he explained.

"In that case can I have a word with you in private before you run off?"

"Of course."

"Levi, Laney, keep up the great work. I will come back to check on you in a bit," Noel promised. "Remember, when the urn gets to the one-quarter mark, we need to make more so you don't run out."

"Yes, ma'am," they responded in unison.

Cavin followed Noel into the candy store where Mrs. Madelyn peeked out from behind the guests at the counter and said, "Good morning, Mr. Dawson. I am so glad you are back."

"Good morning, Mrs. Madelyn," he reciprocated with a genuine smile. "Me too."

Noel forced a grin and kept walking.

Not quite keeping up, Cavin shrugged his shoulders in response to Mrs. Madelyn's quizzical reaction.

Once on the other side of the kitchen door, Noel turned abruptly, and Cavin accidentally bumped into her. He nearly knocked her backward but grabbed her shoulders just in time and held her firmly.

Noel quickly straightened herself and pulled back but not far. "Listen, Mr. Dawson," she started as Cavin studied her green eyes. "While I appreciate what you did out there for the kids, I don't appreciate you teaching them to lie their way out of a challenging situation. You and I both know there is no nonprofit."

Cavin, taken aback by her accusation, offered a swift rebuttal. "An animal nonprofit to be exact," he reminded her, "which, if I recall correctly, were your words."

Noel's nostrils flared. "I went along with you because at that point we were already knee-deep in lies."

"I did not tell any lies," Cavin claimed. "We literally just created a nonprofit out there," he contested while pointing his finger toward the front of the store.

"You don't just create a nonprofit for strangers on a whim."

"You went along with it," Cavin debated, "and I do not consider you all strangers."

"Just because you brought us coffee and hot chocolate, which probably started this whole idea, now that I think of it, doesn't mean we are friends."

The insult stung a bit. "Are we in Atlanta or Beaufort?" Cavin asked.

"What is that supposed to mean?" Noel snarled.

"It means what happened to small-town kindness and hospitality?"

"It sounds like Georgia has already shown you plenty of that."

Cavin couldn't help but smirk at the accusation. "Has anyone ever told you that you are cute when you are mad?"

Noel suddenly felt herself at a loss for words, glaring at Cavin for just a moment before her eyes fell to the floor. That's when the tears began to trickle down her cheek one at a time like a leaky faucet. "Yes," she uttered. "My husband."

The tide shifted, and now Cavin didn't know how to respond. He had never been good at handling crying women. Noel turned away from him, but he could still hear sniffles as she stepped slowly toward the kitchen's island where she slumped over and rested her face in her palms.

"I am sorry I crossed a line," Cavin apologized. "I will be sure not to let that happen again."

Cavin liked women. He dated plenty of them and hit on a lot more. Sometimes they gave him their numbers like Georgia did last night, and other times they laughed at him. However, none ever just started crying like Noel. One thing he didn't do intentionally was flirt with married women. He didn't initiate it or reciprocate it if they started the game; he instead always made sure to walk away from such situations.

Before Noel could gather herself and formulate a response, Cavin hastily showed himself out the kitchen door and down one of the candy shop's aisles as quickly as Noel walked it earlier. He didn't even notice that Mrs. Madelyn gave him the same quizzical look as she shot Noel on their walk through.

When the front door fell shut behind Cavin, he watched the kids hand a fresh cup of hot chocolate to a couple. When those people walked away, Cavin spoke. "Levi, Laney, I shouldn't have lied to Mr. Sam and Ms. Georgia. I was trying to help you guys and maybe it did temporarily, but we should always tell the truth no matter what it costs."

"But you saved our hot chocolate stand," Levi reminded him.

"I should have done it differently. With honesty we might still have saved the stand."

"We like your idea," Laney proclaimed.

"What idea?"

"Raising money to help find lost animals like Scout."

"Who is Scout?" Cavin asked.

Levi pointed. "The missing dog on the poster. But we can't donate money to help find other animals until we make enough to help Mom keep the candy shop open."

Cavin's brow furrowed. "What do you mean?"

Laney punched Levi's arm. "You're not supposed to tell," she whispered harshly.

"Cavin's our friend," Levi contested.

Cavin smirked. *Not according to your mother*, he thought.

"We're giving all the money to the candy shop," Laney confessed. "But no one knows we know about the candy shop closing after Christmas."

"Yeah so thanks for lying for us," Levi said seriously.

"No," Cavin responded. "Don't thank me for lying. In fact I am going to straighten all of this out with Ms. Georgia."

Disappointment filled Levi's and Laney's faces. "Does that mean we are going to get shut down again?" Levi questioned.

"No," Cavin promised.

"Good. Will you also help us find the dog?"

"Help you find the dog?" Cavin quizzed.

"Yeah, the missing dog," Laney reminded him as she pointed at the poster. "There's a $500 reward," she shared with bulging eyes. "That should be enough to keep the candy shop open and start our dog-finding business."

Cavin stepped closer to the poster. "It is actually a $5,000 reward," he clarified with surprise lining his voice as he studied the photograph of the small, brown Goldendoodle, noticing the patch of white around its nose which complemented his meticulously trimmed curly coat. "Wow, somebody really loves that dog."

"Five thousand dollars," Levi shouted. "We will be rich. We can definitely save the candy store and more dogs."

Cavin's heart warmed at the realization that the kids planned to donate the hot chocolate stand funds all along. "You are both very generous. I will see what I can do," Cavin said, unsure if he was still welcome around Noel's kids and the candy store. "But right now I need to figure out how to fix four flat tires before I can go play golf."

"Four flat tires," Levi declared. "That's all of them."

"I know, right?"

"My daddy is a mechanic; he can help you," Laney offered.

"Really?" Cavin replied.

"Yeah, we can have Mom call him for you," Levi suggested.

Yeah, right, Cavin wanted to say. Slim chance of that happening after the conversation he just walked away from. "That is okay, I will figure it out but thanks for your willingness to help."

Cavin knew he would now have to skip coffee in order to make the tee time, but thankfully, he drank a cup of hot chocolate. "Hey, how about one more cup for the road?" he requested, glancing at his watch.

The kids promptly made him another.

"I know you taught us to be honest, but please don't tell Mom we know about the candy shop closing," Levi requested.

"Is that lying if we don't tell her?" Laney asked while she handed Cavin the hot chocolate as the contents sloshed like a rough sea when her unsteady hand moved across the table.

"No, that is not lying; it is just keeping a secret."

"Good," she replied.

Noticing the level in the urn, Levi suddenly exclaimed, "We're going to need more hot chocolate!"

15

"Have you been crying, dear?" Mrs. Madelyn inquired empathetically, finding Noel in the back during a break between customers.

"Yes, I'm afraid I have been."

Noel shared a synopsis of the conversation near the hot chocolate stand and then followed it with one explaining her private talk with Cavin in the kitchen.

"He asked me if anyone ever told me I was cute when I was mad," Noel grumbled. "Why did he have to say that?" she grunted.

Mrs. Madelyn's eyebrows climbed her forehead. "Honey, that sounds like a compliment to me."

"Yeah, but . . .," Noel trailed off.

"How did you respond?"

"I started crying and then said that Fletcher told me that," Noel explained.

"Oh," Mrs. Madelyn murmured. "Then what?"

"Cavin said something about not crossing boundaries again, and all of a sudden, he was gone."

"He hurried out of here as quickly as he scurried in earlier," Mrs. Madelyn noted.

"Hopefully he won't come back," Noel spewed.

"Sweetie, I think Cavin was simply trying to help."

"You would say that," Noel huffed.

"He stood up for your children," Mrs. Madelyn reminded her.

"You're just saying that because you think he's cute and that I should date him. Well even if I wanted to date him and for the record, I don't; he lives in Atlanta. On top of that, I think Georgia already beat everyone to the punch. Imagine that."

Mrs. Madelyn recalled the memory of Georgia storming into the candy shop demanding they shut down the hot chocolate stand immediately. Once she held everyone's attention, Georgia talked in one of those forceful whispers pretending she didn't want the customers to hear although most took in every word. The woman always seemed to be on a power trip. "That Georgia is a handful," Mrs. Madelyn said.

"Maybe they will fall in love and he will take Georgia back to Georgia with him where her big city thinking would probably fit in a little better. She has been attempting to change everything good since moving here. She's so rigid with her rules. Beaufort is a laid-back town. No one who's from here cares if a couple of kids want to sell hot chocolate on the sidewalk."

"You are right about that, and I'm sorry that Georgia and Cavin upset you, but at least Cavin acknowledged your frustration and apologized. That must say something about his character." Mrs. Madelyn decided not to push the dating issue for the time being. It wasn't simply that she wanted Noel to date Cavin; she understood the hurdles Noel pointed out. She just knew Noel deserved a good man in her life. Someone like her Jack who would always be there for her. Someone like Fletcher who had always been there for Noel although death stole him away far too soon. There would be no replacement for Fletcher, of that she felt certain. However, Mrs. Madelyn was optimistic that other good men were out there, and Cavin just happened to be single and quite handsome. "You are right about Georgia. She has really rubbed a lot of people the wrong way with her agenda. I'm not sure how she got voted into her position."

"Oh, I'll tell you how she got voted into her position. You should have seen the way she walked away from the hot chocolate stand earlier. Georgia draws a lot of attention, and she knows exactly what she is doing. She would probably bring an upscale strip club here if the town would let her."

"I pray Beaufort will stay far too classy for such establishments," Mrs. Madelyn replied.

"Me too," Noel agreed.

The simple sounds of Christmas music mixed with customer's voices reminded Noel and Mrs. Madelyn that they needed to put a pin in this emotional conversation and get back to the floor.

As soon as Noel nudged the kitchen door, Levi came hustling through the opening as if it were made for him. "Excuse me," he requested. "We have more hot chocolate to make," he added, passing them by.

Noel dredged up a smile. "I am proud of you two."

"Thanks, Mom. This hot chocolate stand is really a hit," he responded enthusiastically as he washed his hands thoroughly.

Impressed by how well the kids remembered to wash their hands anytime they entered the kitchen, Noel smiled.

"We knew it would be," Mrs. Madelyn encouraged before walking out front to find a handful of cheerful customers wandering the store with cups in hand. A few hovered near the counter, and Mrs. Madelyn rushed to ring up their selections.

"Levi, make another batch of the hot chocolate mix and put the milk in the pot on the warmer while I help Mrs. Madelyn on the floor quickly. Then, I will pour everything into a large thermos and help you transition the product to your table."

Noel swiftly returned to provide fudge samples and answer questions about specific candies customers sought without luck. After all the time she spent walking the aisles positioning products in the most optimal places, she knew the store like the back of her hand. Noel couldn't believe the kids already sold three-quarters of the first batch of hot chocolate—she was so proud of their efforts.

Levi read the hot chocolate mix recipe his mother wrote for them earlier, and he made sure to follow it closely while waiting for her to come back. She mentioned consistency being the key ingredient several times, and he recalled her also saying this when he helped make fudge and candy. He loved helping his mom in the kitchen, and he loved even more making things on his own and impressing her and Mrs. Madelyn with his abilities.

The powdered sugar, cocoa powder, powdered milk, vanilla, chocolate chips, and dehydrated marshmallows were all within reach although he used his stool to grab a couple of the items. He and Laney each had a stool for reaching things on shelves and to create a better vantage point during prep time. Measuring everything was the hardest part of this project, but Levi recalled his mom saying that having the perfect amount of each ingredient was what made their homemade hot chocolate so delicious.

Just before Levi finished sifting all the ingredients and mixing them together in a large bowl, his mom returned and helped him stir the mix into the warmed milk. Then he purposefully walked through the store as they each carried a full thermos.

"Take your time so you don't accidentally drop it," Noel suggested as he outpaced her adult steps.

"Customers are probably waiting, Mom," he replied without looking back although he slowed a bit and steadied the thermos with both hands. The contents still churned like an angry sea, but the tight lid kept the chocolatey waves at bay.

As Levi bounced down the aisle, Noel couldn't help but notice his resemblance to a cute little elf with his Santa hat flopping to and fro. The kids were growing up way too fast, and she wished life would slow down just a bit.

Cavin made it back to the house in time to catch the taxi he called after leaving the candy shop. He wasn't sure why he focused so much on getting the rental vehicle's tires fixed. Although still an important issue, paying for a ride was quick and easy and wouldn't bankrupt the company. This way he would be sure to make his tee time and could deal with the tires later.

He decided that rather than visit a local sporting goods store, he would purchase clubs from the pro shop. The set would be more expensive but would make a good impression at the country club.

Cavin circled the rental vehicle once more glaring at each of the four tires while shaking his head in disgust.

When the driver pulled into the driveway, Cavin tossed his duffel bag into the backseat and climbed in next to it. The two exchanged pleasantries, and then the guy made him laugh.

"Who did you piss off?" he inquired, staring at the sunken SUV.

"I know, right! At least this time I am confident it was not an ex."

The man sitting behind the steering wheel chuckled. "Been there, done that."

It didn't take long for them to arrive at the country club where Cavin handed the fellow a cash tip before asking if he would be available to pick him up later this afternoon.

"Just let me know when," the driver offered with an appreciative smile.

It didn't surprise Cavin that he was the first to arrive for the golf outing. He purposely came early to allow plenty of time to pick out a nice set of clubs, and he was grateful for the club pro's expert recommendation leading him to the best set for the occasion.

By the time Cavin swiped the company credit card, the other men began showing up. Jeff and Daniel—one of the gentlemen at

Georgia's table last night—were among the first to arrive, and they introduced him to the friends who accompanied them. Cavin quickly realized that everyone seemed to know each other, regardless of who brought whom.

"Fellows, I have already taken care of today's round as well as the cart fees," Cavin announced. "I also started a tab for us at the register so make sure to grab beverages and snacks to take with you on me," he insisted.

"You're the man, Cavin," the guy who introduced himself as a chiropractor announced.

"You will fit in well in Beaufort," the doctor greeted with a strong handshake.

"I'll get you next time," Jeff offered. "But the rest of you are on your own," he quipped.

A round of laughter filled the pro shop. Each man grabbed a few items, and then they loaded their personal belongings and clubs into the three carts that awaited them under the luxurious awning beyond the front doors.

Cavin climbed into one of the driver's seats, and Walt, the accountant in the group who looked every bit the part with his thick glasses and short, plump stature, plopped down beside him.

"Do you guys want to play individually or split into teams?" Walt asked, digging through a handful of snacks he grabbed in the clubhouse.

"How about three teams of two?" Daniel suggested. "That way Jeff doesn't destroy all of us."

Everyone laughed except Cavin who smiled in response to the information to which he already had insight.

"I will play with Jeff since I am the weakest link," the doctor suggested. "Unless Cavin thinks he can challenge me for the title."

Laughter erupted again, and all eyes turned to Cavin.

"Cavin might challenge me for the pedestal you clowns put me on," Jeff inserted.

Cavin held his hands up in submission. "I am average," he claimed.

"That settles it then. Just play with the person in your cart," the chiropractor mentioned realizing the teams seemed evenly split.

Cavin would have been content to ride or play with any of the five men, but being closest to the accountant throughout the day might prove helpful. How many accountants could there be in a town the size of Beaufort? Walt probably knew the figures line by line for nearly every business in town. Although client confidentiality would keep him from sharing details, Cavin felt sure he could still garner some valuable information, especially if the guy had a few more drinks like the one currently in his hand.

A well-manicured asphalted path led them away from the clubhouse toward the course where after a couple of turns beneath gorgeous live oak trees, they parked at the first tee box. Neatly trimmed grass stretched across a wide-open area, and the guys pointed out a rather obvious flag on the lavish greens where the cup for hole one rested.

Cavin hoped to tee off after everyone else in order to gauge each player's skill level. He figured Jeff, the pro in the group, would either want to go first or last, so once Jeff offered to start the round, Cavin quickly made the next request.

"Since I just picked up this new set of clubs in the pro shop this morning, I would like a few warm-up swings with my new driver," Cavin mentioned. "So I will follow the rest of you guys if that is okay."

"You should have told us you had new clubs," the chiropractor mentioned. "We could have hit a couple baskets of balls at the driving range so you could break them in."

"We should have done that anyway," Daniel commented.

"Oh, it is not that serious, guys," Cavin remarked.

"That's a nice set," Jeff observed.

The others chimed in with similar responses as they looked

closer at the shiny clubs, each one's neck sticking out of the brand new bag and begging to be swung. Cavin also picked up a box of top-of-the-line golf balls, and the club pro threw in a couple of complimentary bags of tees, a divot tool, ball markers, and a towel featuring the country club's logo since he spent all that money. When Cavin selected a left-handed glove to wear, the pro told him the story about golf gloves being invented in the late 1800s but added it took a while for them to become popular.

"Well, we are here now so start us off, Jeff," the doctor encouraged.

A slight breeze blew left to right as Jeff set a pristine white ball on a tall blue tee and readied his stance. Cavin noticed the man's athletic form from head to toe and watched how he maneuvered the club with ease starting with a slow and steady back swing before coming forward and ending with a picture-perfect note. As expected, he crushed the ball down the center of the fairway. Cavin guesstimated the drive at around 275 yards which was impressive.

The guy who claimed the weak link title stepped up next. His stance showcased several noticeable flaws, and his swing looked a bit erratic. It didn't shock Cavin when his ball traveled about half the distance of Jeff's, curving into a wooded area out of bounds.

"I warned you," he laughed.

"You won't be the last person to hit a tree today," Daniel reminded him with a courtesy chuckle.

The next three guys hit decent shots, each ball landing within a hundred or so feet of one another. And as Cavin stepped into the tee box, all eyes fell on him, and the chatter grew silent. Everyone always wanted to know what the new guy brought to the table. Cavin purposely downplayed his approach and stance and even thought about shanking a ball into the woods. Instead he drove the ball a bit right and landed it nearly in the middle of the rest of the group.

"Nice shot, teammate," Walt complimented.

"Not bad," voiced another.

"So Cavin's not the weakest link," the weak link teased, throwing his hands up in defeat.

The next few holes went about the same, and the scorecards clipboarded to the steering wheels showed similar totals for each team. Golf talk soon gave way to social and business conversations, and that's the part Cavin looked forward to the most. He listened intently to the discussions about individuals, businesses, and the town's events. He learned about the Thanksgiving Feast, and Daniel mentioned the mayor's party occurring later this evening.

"His wife is a hoot," Jeff announced.

Cavin figured that out firsthand last night while at the table with Georgia and the group. He brought up Georgia's name to the guys as they putted on the fourth green and received mixed reactions although nearly every one of them made a comment about her attractiveness. She was one of those women who demanded attention with both her personality and looks.

Noel's name popped up during the conversation about the Thanksgiving Feast, and one of the guys told a story about how the mayor's wife tried to guess all the pies Noel baked. Each of the men spoke kind words about Noel, and one suggested she must be a superhero to take on all the responsibilities left to her following the tragic accident. Cavin wanted to ask follow-up questions, but somehow the conversation shifted quickly, and he never found a time to bring up Noel again without it sounding like he was prying.

Once Walt emptied a couple of canned beverages, he began opening up more to Cavin as the two of them rode along the cart path having private conversations.

"I understand some of the downtown shops are struggling to make a profit," Cavin mentioned casually as they cruised along the path heading for the seventh hole. "That's unfortunate."

"You seem like a savvy businessman, so I am sure you noticed that Beaufort is primarily made up of small businesses. We have worked diligently to keep large chains from moving in and taking over because our local family businesses are so important, especially those that provide locally sourced products. However, around fifty percent of small businesses fail within five years."

Cavin could teach a class on the statistics related to small businesses or nearly any size company for that matter although the numbers shifted in different areas of the country and even from one town to the next based on a variety of factors. "Yeah, the numbers are staggering," he agreed.

"There has been a steady turnover rate of businesses outside of the major staples in our community. Ownership and rent in the waterfront district are quite the investment, so maintaining a substantial sales flow is vital."

"What types of businesses seem to struggle most in Beaufort?"

"Restaurants often come and go, which is consistent throughout the United States."

"I believe around seventy-five percent of locally owned restaurants flop within the first five years," Cavin noted although he could quote more precise figures. Startup costs were often lofty due to industry-specific equipment needs, and finding reliable employees often proved to be emotionally and financially exhausting. "Are there any local restaurants you don't think will make it?"

Walt shook his head in agreement in regards to the figure Cavin shared. "For sure," he replied, listing a few that he didn't think would survive much longer. "I imagine we don't have to worry much about Clawson's, Dock House, and some of the others that have showcased staying power."

Earlier, Cavin mentioned that he visited both of those establishments, and Walt nodded approvingly. One of the restaurants Walt suggested might not make it was a couple of buildings over from

Beaufort Candy Company which was music to Cavin's ears since he already listed that line of buildings as a target for buyout.

When the wheels on the cart ahead of Cavin and Walt came to a halt at tee box number seven, the conversation also halted, but Cavin looked forward to picking up where they left off at the next opportunity.

Cavin decided that now would be an opportune time to flex his golf muscles, so he paid special attention to his footing, the proper bending of the knees, and a slow and steady backswing. He let his hands relax until the forward momentum of his long-distance driver forced his fingers to squeeze the handle grip at precisely the right moment.

For a seasoned golfer when the sweet spot on the head of the club struck the ball just right, the sound and feeling was comparable to a professional baseball player knowing a homerun had been hit at the point of contact. Although thousands of people weren't gasping in the stands as the ball flew through the air, the five men gathered nearby immediately turned off the volume of their conversation. With widened eyes and mouths agape, the sounds of nature became present as they silently watched the flight of the ball in awe. The familiar chatter of nearby birds and the little feet of squirrels scampering on pine bark suddenly became apparent, yet none of them really heard that nor the mower in the distance.

When the ball landed, ten eyeballs shifted in unison toward Cavin.

"Holy cow, you drove that ball over 300 yards," Jeff estimated.

"And right down the middle of the fairway," Daniel added.

"That's my teammate," Walt exclaimed as he raised his hands for a double high-five.

Cavin grinned while soaking in the praise of his peers. "That's my lucky shot of the day."

"That's THE shot of the day," the doctor diagnosed.

"Nice one, buddy," the chiropractor added in amazement.

Cavin usually pulled out a drive like this once or twice every time he played with amateurs, and amongst them he chopped it up to happenstance. He grew up playing golf with his dad and his dad's friends. By the age of fifteen, he beat all of them on a regular basis, and by the age of eighteen, he outplayed every man at the country club to which his family belonged. In college he set records and was ultimately invited to play professional golf which he dabbled in on and off during his early twenties.

Cavin's dad set steep professional expectations for him immediately after college and often encouraged him to quit playing golf in hopes of making it big when a lucrative career awaited him in the family business. "Use golf to help the business make more money," his dad often suggested as the two encountered countless arguments over the topic. "Even when you win these amateur tournaments, you only make chump change compared to what you can make for our family in real estate development." Eventually Cavin caved in to his dad's relentless pressure and even went some time without playing golf at all.

As the golfers climbed into their respective carts, all of them were still talking about Cavin's drive. He doubted most of them had ever seen a ball driven that far in person unless they attended a professional event. The others were hitting their third or fourth shots on the hole when they reached Cavin's ball, and his second swing landed him within a few feet of the flag. A few minutes later, he sank the putt on a par five.

The guys encouraged him to frame that ball, and Cavin knew they would talk about how dominantly he played this hole the rest of the round and beyond. When he and Walt settled into their cart, the conversation about the businesses struggling in downtown revived. Walt didn't offer any numbers, but as the day wore on and Walt lost count of how many beverages Cavin bought him, he provided more information than Cavin could have dreamed.

By hole eighteen, Walt confirmed what Levi and Laney shared with Cavin in secret this morning, confessing his intention to buy Noel's building once she had no other option. This man, who spoke kind words about Noel earlier, revealed how he wanted to take advantage of her devotion to her family's business. "My family has owned the adjacent building for ages," Walt explained.

As Cavin received this information, he steadied his poker face, realizing his golf teammate had just become his business opponent.

16

Officer Rainey's broad shoulders filled out his uniform as he smiled proudly and approached the hot chocolate stand. After strapping his duty belt around his waist every morning, he always hoped his wallet would be the only item he would need to reach for. Of course this personal item wasn't part of the heavy belt but tucked just below in the pocket of the black pants he wore.

"Levi, Laney, what do we have here?" He parked his patrol car in the neighboring lot after cruising by and spotting the kids standing behind the table waving at him. Before he could get out though, their excited voices chimed through the radio on his shoulder.

"A hot chocolate stand," Laney answered matter-of-factly.

"Well you know police officers have to stay hydrated too, so I will take a cup."

"One cup of hot chocolate coming right up," Levi announced.

"How much do I owe you?" Rainey asked while glancing at the wallet in his hand.

"We are taking donations," Laney explained.

Since the debacle this morning, the kids changed their pitch and were pretty sure they raised more money this way.

Rainey dropped a wrinkled five-dollar bill into the jar, nearly filled to the brim. "It looks like you two have been busy today."

"We have made six gallons of hot chocolate," Levi shared, his face glowing like a lightbulb.

"Wow, that's amazing. I'm so proud of you both."

"When we saw you, we hoped you weren't coming to shut us down," Laney mentioned.

"What? Why on earth would I do that?"

"Earlier that Georgia lady said she would call the police if we didn't shut down. Then Mr. Kevin and Mr. Sam showed up, and Mom and Georgia came outside, and they let us stay open for now," Laney explained.

Rainey wondered how the adult version of the story might sound, but the perspective the kids offered made him empathetic toward their cause. However, in his line of duty, he learned to control his emotions, especially before drawing conclusions. On a side note he was also curious to know who Mr. Kevin was.

"Maybe I need to arrest Ms. Georgia," Rainey declared in a teasing manner before taking a sip from the cup.

Laney and Levi chuckled erratically.

"Yeah do that," Levi agreed.

The three of them chatted a bit longer while Rainey sipped on the beverage before deciding to step into the candy shop to collect the full scoop. "I am going to run in and talk to your mom and Mrs. Madelyn really quick," he mentioned. "Sell some more hot chocolate while I'm inside."

When Cavin's driver dropped him off at the curb in front of the rental house, Cavin handed him cash, grabbed his bag, and then walked to the trunk to collect his new golf clubs. All the while he heard what sounded like a loud vacuum but couldn't quite figure out the origin of the noise although it sounded close.

Cavin tapped the trunk's lid and then waved to the driver

letting the man know he retrieved everything. The guy drove off, and when Cavin rounded the rear of the sunken SUV on the driver's side, the source of the noise became apparent. Cavin immediately set everything in his hands down, and the man kneeling near the vehicle's front tire looked up. Upon recognizing the person's face, Cavin drew the nine iron from his bag ready to defend himself.

"What are you doing here?" Cavin bellowed attempting to speak above the roar of the air compressor.

The man reached down, flipped a switch, and the tank shut off. "What are you doing here?" he reciprocated.

"I am staying here," Cavin explained while nodding toward the house letting the golf club dangle next to his leg. "But you already knew that because you followed me and Georgia here last night and flattened my tires."

Keaton shot him a perplexed look. "Yeah I flattened all your tires last night, woke up feeling guilty, and came back to put air in them for you," he replied sarcastically, raising an eyebrow.

Although Cavin's thoughts in the moment ran more on adrenaline than logic, he had to admit that the narrative did sound pretty weird. However, what if that was simply the story this guy told because he got caught? What if he came back to do further damage to the tires or maybe even something more extreme?

"How do I know you are not back to steal my tires?" Cavin quizzed.

Keaton glanced at the air compressor, the tires, and then Cavin. "In broad daylight?" he quizzed, raising the second eyebrow.

"It happens in Atlanta all the time," Cavin pointed out.

Keaton chuckled. "We're not in Atlanta, boss. This is Beaufort, North Carolina. You can't get away with stuff like that here."

As if on cue a patrol came cruising down the road, and Cavin waved his hand and golf club in the air to draw attention.

"Oh geez," Keaton murmured. A moment later the blue lights

flashed on and the vehicle pulled to their side of the road. "You see what I mean? I guess I should start running now."

"Sounds like guilt speaking," Cavin projected.

"Now I understand why my sister said you're a troublemaker."

"Excuse me?" Cavin interrupted just as the officer approached them from his vehicle.

"Everything okay here?" the policeman checked.

"This man is messing with my vehicle," Cavin explained. "I am trying to get to the bottom of it and could use your help."

"Rainey, this is all a simple misunderstanding," Keaton declared. "We don't need your help."

"Yes, we do," Cavin disagreed.

Keaton began unscrewing the hose's nozzle from the nearly fully inflated tire's valve stem.

"Keaton, take your hands off the man's vehicle while we discuss this."

"Rainey, my hands are not on the man's vehicle; my hands are on my air compressor's hose and nozzle. I'm taking it off so he can figure out this dilemma on his own."

"Keaton, just stop what you are doing so I can better understand this situation."

Keaton raised his hands in submission but shook his head.

"Sir, can you tell me your side of the story, starting at the beginning?" Rainey asked Cavin.

"Rainey," Keaton butted in. "Since you made me take my hands off this here air compressor weapon, can you have him put down the golf club so that we all feel safe?" he teased sarcastically.

Rainey breathed out a heavy sigh. "Sir, please set down the iron while we all talk," Rainey requested. "Like adults," he added, glaring in Keaton's direction.

Cavin set the club on the nearby grass and then with an outstretched hand slowly reached toward the officer. "My name is Cavin Dawson," he announced.

"Oh brother," Keaton mumbled.

"I am Officer Rainey," he responded while shaking Cavin's hand firmly.

"My name is Keaton," Keaton called out waving his hand.

Both men looked at Keaton, and then he grinned.

Cavin told the story about Keaton harassing him and Georgia last night then shared the news about discovering the flat tires this morning. Lastly, he explained finding Keaton fooling with the tires when he returned from playing golf.

"Is all that true?" Rainey asked Keaton.

"I simply tried to warn this guy about Georgia last night because he looked like innocent prey. I didn't harass them."

"Were you drunk?" Rainey interrogated.

"I had some drinks, but so did they."

"Keaton, how many drinks did you have?"

"I don't remember. Maybe you should do a breathalyzer test now because I may be acting under the influence as a Good Samaritan pumping up four flat tires for this stranger."

Rainey had to admit that a lot of things didn't add up, and he ignored Keaton's comment. "Did you flatten this man's tires last night?"

"No," Keaton answered.

"Did you set foot in this yard at any point last night?"

"Nope."

"Can you confirm this man's tires were flat last night or this morning?"

Keaton laughed. "Nice try, but I can't. I wasn't here."

"So why are you here now?"

"Finally someone poses a sensible question," Keaton acknowledged. "My sister called and asked if I would pump up this man's tires as a favor to her."

Officer Rainey and Cavin both immediately expressed confusion. Cavin, recalling Keaton's earlier comment about

Keaton's sister saying Cavin was trouble, wondered who his sister was while Rainey began connecting the dots.

Officer Rainey quickly determined that Cavin must be the Kevin the kids mentioned earlier although he never got a chance to hear Noel's perspective on the hot chocolate stand dilemma. She and Mrs. Madelyn were busy with customers when he entered the candy shop before departing to head in this direction.

"Do you know Keaton's sister?" Officer Rainey checked. "And do you know why she would ask her brother to inflate your tires other than for obvious reasons?" Rainey added as he studied the tires again. "I've driven by here a couple of times today and couldn't help but wonder who the owner of this vehicle ticked off. Honestly, I've been expecting a call."

"Who is your sister?" Cavin asked Keaton.

Keaton laughed out loud. "Maybe we should play a guessing game to see how many women you have met in this town in your short time here," he posed. "I am beginning to think you are not so innocent after all."

"Keaton," Rainey warned.

"What?" Keaton responded harshly. "This could be evidence. I am helping with your investigation; this information might lead you to the perpetrator who flattened all these tires."

"Is Georgia your sister?" Cavin considered out loud. That would explain why she said this man wasn't a threat last night.

Keaton laughed once more. "Nope, not a chance. Try again."

"Who else have you met?" Rainey asked in order to humor Keaton's curiosity.

"Really? This guy is messing with my tires, and I am the one being interrogated?" Cavin questioned.

"Seriously, dude, what is your hang-up on me having anything to do with your tires going flat? I was here to fix your problem, and now you are creating another one."

Cavin filtered through all the people he met since arriving in

Beaufort, and only one other woman came to mind—Noel. But Laney said her dad was a mechanic, not her uncle. That didn't seem to add up. However, if Noel felt at all sympathetic toward him, she likely wouldn't send her husband after Cavin hit on her. Maybe she sent her brother instead.

"Is your sister Noel?" Cavin asked.

Wide-eyed, Keaton looked at Rainey. "Bingo," he responded by turning his attention to Cavin. "You passed the test."

"Do you know Noel Puckett?" Rainey checked.

"Yes, I do."

"Then you probably know she is a great person with a lot of responsibilities," Keaton said to Cavin. "I'll make you a deal—I'll still pump up your tires if you stay away from my sister."

Cavin didn't care for ultimatums, but he didn't have any intention to have personal contact with Noel moving forward anyway. However, he still wanted to do business with her, so that posed a problem. How could he explain that to her brother? He couldn't, and he didn't need to. "I am not one for being put in a corner, so I am not taking your deal. Although if it makes you feel any better, your sister and I have an understanding based on mutual respect of her situation," Cavin explained. "And I will find someone else to pump up the tires."

"Why don't you two stop trying to be so macho?" Rainey suggested. "Mr. Dawson, I've known Keaton pretty much my whole life, and based on his responses, I don't think he flattened your tires. It appears he has good intentions here, and I can confirm this with Noel if you like. I think it's in your best interest to let him pump up your tires while he's here with an air compressor."

Cavin glanced at Keaton then back at Rainey and once more returned his attention to Keaton.

"You're not going to get another mechanic out here until Monday at the earliest," Keaton mentioned. "If you'd like me to take care of the tires, I'll still do it since my sister asked me to."

Cavin felt confident he could figure out another way to fix this issue whether that meant buying his own air compressor or renting another vehicle for the time being. However, either of those options would be a waste of precious time. "I would appreciate it," Cavin finally agreed although hesitantly.

"I'll hang around just to make sure everything goes smoothly," Rainey offered. "I'll also file a report and see if we can figure out who deflated your tires in the first place. Probably teenagers looking to have some fun on a Friday night."

"Be thankful they didn't slash them," Keaton pointed out.

It didn't take Keaton long to work his way around the vehicle, and suddenly, all evidence of the SUV ever having been sunken drifted away. However, prior to letting Keaton turn on the air pump, Officer Rainey circled the vehicle several times, snapping photographs for the file while looking for anything the perpetrator may have left behind, but he didn't discover any major red flags.

"Where is your car?" Cavin asked Keaton after shaking his hand in appreciation trying to let go of the negative emotions he associated with the man.

"I don't have a car," he shared, glaring at Rainey. "Someone impounded it."

Cavin couldn't help but wonder if that was a red flag. What if Keaton had only come to pump up the tires so he could steal the vehicle?

"How did you get here?" Cavin inquired nonchalantly.

"I walked."

"You walked all the way here with that heavy compressor?" Cavin queried while wondering why Officer Rainey wasn't asking these questions.

"I did," he answered simply. "From the shop where I work."

"Keaton has a big heart," Rainey shared, having a good feeling where Cavin's mind was headed. "I'll give you a ride back,

Keaton," he added, trying to avoid any further accusations.

"Let me," Cavin offered. "I owe you," he said to Keaton.

"You don't owe me anything, but you're welcome to drive me back to the shop if you like." Keaton didn't really want to ride with either of the men standing before him, but his arms already felt worn out from carrying the heavy air compressor all the way here, and he hated riding in police vehicles.

A few minutes later Cavin let the man whom he thought flattened his tires last night hop into the SUV. Knowing now that Keaton was Noel's brother, coupled with the fact that Officer Rainey vouched for him, said something about his character although his interactions with the officer indicated Keaton probably had some underlying issues.

"Do you know why Noel asked you to inflate my tires?" Cavin wondered aloud after reversing out of the driveway. Considering the earlier scene at the candy shop, the request from Noel didn't seem to add up. The only thing he could think of was maybe the kids begged her to send someone to help.

"She said you protected our kids."

Our kids?

Cavin considered the best response as he pieced together all the information he gathered from the moment he met Noel until this conversation with Keaton. Was this guy actually Noel's husband? Because Laney told him that her father was a mechanic. Why lie about being Noel's brother though? Maybe this man was a pathological liar; he definitely remained the top suspect in Cavin's mind when it came to the tires.

"Levi and Laney must have told Noel about my tires because I did not mention to her that they were flat."

"I'm not sure how she knew about the tires," Keaton answered, shrugging his shoulders before showing Cavin where to turn.

Cavin cringed inwardly as he broached the next subject, and he was pretty sure he could feel sweat beads forming along his pristine hairline. "You introduced yourself earlier as Noel's brother, but then you just said *our kids*. Are you really Noel's brother or are you her husband?" he asked directly. "Because Laney told me that her father is a mechanic, the signs seem to point to the latter."

Keaton chuckled at Cavin's confusion. "Man, it's a good thing you didn't decide to go into law enforcement, you would make a horrible detective," Keaton joked. "Laney is my daughter."

Cavin's mind raced. He knew that good detectives asked probing questions, and he always believed that there were no dumb questions, only dumb answers, since there was only one way to learn the unknown. "Is Levi your son?"

Keaton laughed again even harder. "Your mind is traveling in the wrong direction," Keaton ascertained. "Levi is my nephew; he's Noel's son. Laney spends a lot of time with Noel and Levi. People who don't know better often think the kids are brother and sister."

Cavin assumed all along that both children belonged to Noel, but he realized he never asked. He should have. However, that didn't really matter, and it didn't change her marital status. He should have asked that question as well before flirting with her. "I see."

"I am Noel's brother," Keaton clarified just in case this man's mind failed to connect all the dots.

"What is Noel's husband's story? If he is not a mechanic like I initially thought, what does he do for work?"

Cavin wanted to learn as much as possible about this family, and he figured it would be a lot easier to ask Keaton this question although it seemed they were still on the fence about each other.

"Man, that's a sad story."

Cavin's brow furrowed as they passed through a neighborhood filled with older restored homes. This marked the second time he heard similar words about this family. He wanted to ask a follow-up question but decided to wait and see if Keaton would reveal more.

Keaton anxiously rubbed his pant leg just above the knees as he peered out the passenger window watching a man with his dog pass by on the sidewalk. Maintaining his gaze, he revealed softly, "Noel's husband died last year" as if talking instead to the stranger on the sidewalk.

17

It suddenly made sense to Cavin why Noel cried when he asked if anyone ever told her she was cute when she was mad.

"What happened?" Cavin asked Keaton who seemed to be in another world.

"You should ask Noel," Keaton mumbled, his gaze on the picket fences draped with flowing greenery.

"I thought you did not want me to talk to Noel."

"I don't want you to hurt Noel," he reasoned, suddenly turning to Cavin with a focused intensity, "or the kids."

"What do you mean?" Cavin questioned as his foot held the brake pedal at a four-way stop.

"Noel likes you."

Of all the words Keaton could have offered in response, Cavin expected those the least. "I doubt that," Cavin instantly debated with a scoff.

"You can take it or leave it," Keaton offered.

"You did not see how mad Noel was at me the last time we spoke."

"Do you know anything about women?" Keaton questioned.

"I am not sure any of us do," Cavin admitted with a serious look.

"I know this about my sister—if Noel asked me to pump up your tires even though she was mad at you, that means she likes you more than I thought," Keaton presumed.

A car horn suddenly startled both Cavin and Keaton causing their eyes to dart to the mirrors, and that's when Cavin realized they lingered at the stop sign way too long.

Cavin quickly stepped on the gas pedal but didn't know what to say. Thankfully Keaton spoke up again telling him where to turn next, and a moment later they pulled into the parking lot of an old battered shop. Cavin steered the wheel vigorously dodging potholes in the asphalt and hoping one wouldn't pop his freshly inflated tires although he guessed such a thing couldn't happen at a better place. As he pulled the vehicle to a stop near the building, he noticed how the paint on the white cinder block walls peeled haphazardly and two glass garage doors stood dulled by years of grease and grime.

"I appreciate your honesty," Cavin shared as Keaton climbed out of the vehicle. Then the two of them walked to the back hatch to retrieve Keaton's air compressor.

"I cannot believe you walked all that way to inflate my tires," Cavin said once he realized the trek must have been around a mile.

"That's what people from Beaufort do, my friend."

"Southern hospitality at its finest," Cavin claimed with a genuine smile. "Did you know who you were coming to help?"

"Are you asking if I knew I was coming to help the guy who took Georgia home with him?"

"Yes," Cavin clarified.

"No, I didn't know that."

"Last night you said you knew my name," Cavin pointed out, interested to see how Keaton would respond.

The tank bobbed slightly in Keaton's arms as he belly laughed. "I was so drunk I wouldn't have remembered your name even if I did know it."

Cavin chuckled and wondered if Keaton liked Georgia as he suspected previously. "Would you still have come if you knew who I was?" he checked.

"It wouldn't have changed a thing," Keaton promised as his face grew serious. "Just don't string my sister along if Georgia is the one you want."

Cavin nodded his head in understanding as Keaton walked toward the station. "Okay."

"Thanks for the ride," Keaton called out over his shoulder.

"You are welcome."

Cavin sat in silence in the driver's seat for a few moments mulling over the conversation he just shared with Keaton. Last night he wouldn't have guessed in a million years that the man was Noel's brother and Laney's dad. It also came as a surprise that Noel's husband was dead. Someone at their age should never have to know what being a widow felt like. He couldn't even begin to fathom what that could do to a person. He also couldn't help but wonder why Keaton didn't want to reveal what happened to Noel's husband.

Cavin felt a pit in his stomach as he considered his options. He felt like he owed Noel an apology—a different apology than the one given yesterday. Of course he couldn't have known that she would associate the comment about her being cute while mad to her deceased husband, yet Cavin's thoughts still recoiled from the emotional blow.

Only one good option came to mind, Cavin thought as he drove toward the candy store hoping to see the doors still open for the day. Then another thought entered his head, and he quickly punched a phrase into his GPS and took a detour. He nearly forgot about this idea during the busy day filled with so much adventure. The errand took longer than expected, but eventually, when Cavin rolled past Beaufort Candy Company looking closely for an open sign or interior lights, he noticed that the kid's hot chocolate stand no longer sat in front of the shop. He prayed Georgia didn't find a way to shut them down.

Even from the street, Cavin saw the Christmas lights glowing from the inside, and the window displays still looked elegant at this distance. At first this seemed to answer his question, but then he wondered if Noel left the place lit up at night during the holidays.

Once parked in the prime real estate lot, Cavin scurried to the entrance having no idea what he was going to say if and when he came face to face with Noel. The large box in his hands would be an obstruction, and he never expected it to be so enormous and oddly shaped. It reminded him of one of those boxes that an outdoor basketball goal came packaged in at the sporting goods stores. Thankfully the weight of these contents paled in comparison.

Cavin held the box awkwardly in one hand while using his knee to help balance it as the door handle gave way, and suddenly chocolate, Small Business Saturday shoppers, and Mrs. Madelyn's curious face surrounded him.

"Let me help you with the door," a random customer offered.

Another person asked if Cavin needed help carrying the package.

"No, thank you, it is far less heavy than it looks," he replied surveying the store for Noel.

A moment later Levi and Laney came running in his direction with excitement flooding their faces. "What is in that huge box?" Levi asked, emphasizing the word *huge*.

"Is it a Christmas present?" Laney wondered.

Levi's eyes bulged. "It won't fit under the tree."

As Levi's tree remark caused all of them to glance at the enormous Eastern Red Cedar at the back of the store, the kitchen door suddenly swung open, and Noel walked out from where Cavin left her standing this morning.

Upon spotting Cavin, Noel stopped dead in her tracks. Not just because he held an oversized box, but because she never expected to see him again. After taking a moment to gather herself, Noel walked toward her children and the man everyone watched cautiously maneuver through the aisles wondering what he might knock over.

Cavin carefully managed not to break anything as he toted the cardboard box toward the rear of the store. He wasn't sure why he headed in that direction other than it being the last place he saw Noel, and upon stepping inside the candy shop, he failed to notice her anywhere else.

With his eyes locked on Noel's, Cavin realized he never responded to the kids. "I must admit this box is not quite as exciting as it may seem, but hopefully you all will find the contents useful," he said to all three of them.

"Thank you," Noel offered when she reached Cavin.

Cavin's brow furrowed. "You do not even know what is in the box," he proclaimed with a grin.

"Yes, I do," she replied confidently. "Because I brought a box exactly like that in through the back door earlier today."

"We have two of these?" Laney spouted like a water fountain suddenly pressed to the max.

"The other box has already been broken down," Noel revealed. "That's where your gallon jugs came from."

So she did know what was inside, and now Cavin understood how. "I am sorry; I had no idea you already got some."

"That's okay, it means just as much," Noel promised. "Follow me, I'll show you where to put it."

The four of them paraded through the store and into the kitchen where Noel made a spot for the oversized cardboard box. The kids wanted to open it, so Noel and Cavin let them.

"Wow, that's so cool," Levi said as he examined the twenty jugs pressed against each other inside the dark box.

"Was there that many in the other box, Aunt Noel?"

Cavin let out a silent sigh—now Laney decided to call Noel her aunt.

"Yep," Noel answered.

"Let's go tell Mrs. Madelyn what Kevin brought," Levi suggested.

And just like that, Cavin and Noel found themselves alone in the kitchen once again standing in nearly the same spot they occupied early this morning.

"I didn't expect to see you again," Noel mentioned honestly.

"I kind of owed the kids these jugs," Cavin insisted, "and I owe you another apology."

"Cavin, you don't owe me anything," Noel claimed, raising a hand as she spoke. "When you said what you said this morning, it triggered a memory. A good memory, just a sad one," she explained.

"I know," Cavin responded.

"I doubt you can know this," she said.

"I know your husband passed away, and I am terribly sorry to hear it and that I hurt you, Noel."

"You didn't hurt me," Noel replied. "But how do you know about Fletcher?" she questioned and frowned slightly.

"Your brother showed up at the house to pump up my tires."

"What?"

"Wait, you did not send him?" Cavin asked, instantly assuming Keaton tricked him into thinking she did. He should have known the guy only showed up to cause more damage.

"Well, yes, I sent him," Noel replied, trailing off for a moment. "But he told you . . . about Fletcher?" she checked.

"Yes," Cavin answered. "Well, kind of," he rephrased.

"I can't believe it," Noel remarked unable to hide the puzzle pieces trying to come together on her face.

"Did you not want me to know?" Cavin asked.

"It's not that," Noel answered. "It's just that Keaton never talks about what happened to Fletcher, Lexi, and our parents."

"Your parents?" Cavin questioned. "Lexi?"

"I guess he didn't mention those details, huh?" Noel asked not surprised.

"Honestly, Keaton did not divulge much at all. He told me to ask you what happened."

"It's a long story," Noel insisted, biting a fingernail. She gnawed on her nails more in the past year than in her whole life, and it wasn't because she liked the taste of them. "And this isn't the place or the time to tell it."

"Will you share the story with me over dinner?" Cavin asked tenderly somewhat surprised by himself.

Noel's bottom lip quivered as she felt a wall of tears pooling behind her green eyes. She never shared this story with anyone she didn't know, and she wasn't sure if she was ready to do that quite yet or if she could ever reach that point.

18

Noel wanted to say no to Cavin. Why did he need to know how Fletcher and her parents died? Why would she even consider telling him? She didn't know this man. He didn't live here; he lived in Atlanta—500 miles from Beaufort. However, as these thoughts circled through her mind, something deep within Cavin's caramel-colored eyes struck her in a way she hadn't experienced since the accident.

Most people wanted to avoid the topic or they waited for her to bring it up, but Cavin asked her—with sincerity and empathy lining his voice—to share the story. He could have asked pretty much anyone who lived here, and they would have given him at least a synopsis of the story. Everyone talked about the accident for months, or at least she heard as much from friends and witnessed the whispers at the grocery store, the bank, and everywhere else she went in order to survive. Mrs. Madelyn ran errands for her for a while, but eventually she encouraged Noel to ease back into the public. She convinced Noel that both she and the kids needed to live their lives even though it was difficult.

Noel figured Cavin was intelligent enough to realize he could ask anyone he met in Beaufort about the accident, yet he showed up here with the courage to look her in the eyes after thinking he hurt her.

"When?" Noel uttered her shaky voice lined with uncertainty. "I have two kids and a candy shop to take care of around the clock; I can't imagine when I would have time to have dinner with you."

Mrs. Madelyn pushed back the door just in time to hear that last line Noel spoke to Cavin whose back faced her as she stood quietly hoping not to interrupt such a serious-sounding conversation. She came looking for Noel to let her know it was time to close the store, but customers were still shopping, and she didn't want to hurry them out knowing Noel desperately needed every penny. Standing there, she thought for a moment about easing her way out, but then she thought better.

"Tonight? Tomorrow night? Next week? Anytime that works for you," Cavin answered leaving the opportunity wide open.

"Tonight," Mrs. Madelyn interrupted, knowing if Noel had time to think through the idea of going on a date, if in fact that was the case, she would back out. "Jack and I will watch the children. He would love to have them over since he rarely gets out anymore."

Noel glanced over Cavin's right shoulder at the sound of Mrs. Madelyn's chipper voice, but Cavin didn't turn; he kept his eyes locked on Noel's as if no one else existed.

"Alright then," Noel responded to both Mrs. Madelyn and Cavin at the same time, and then she suddenly felt the lump in her throat drop to the pit of her stomach upon the realization of what she just agreed to on a whim.

Noel watched the edges of Cavin's lips lift as hers pursed together fought something between a smile and a grimace. The mixture of emotions playing out within her mind and body outlined her face.

"Noel will need about an hour to get ready," Mrs. Madelyn informed Cavin as if Noel were her daughter and going on her very first date. However, she just wanted to do everything in her power to keep this ball rolling in the right direction. Cavin may not end up being Noel's knight in shining armor, but this was another first her friend needed to experience, and if nothing else, time alone with another adult and no children around should be therapeutic. "I will take care of closing the store and making sure the children have everything they need," she insisted.

Cavin positioned his body so that he could look back and forth between Noel and Mrs. Madelyn. "That works perfectly for me since I am still wearing the clothes I played golf in," he acknowledged as he looked down at his outfit thankful that no sweat showed through the carefully selected material. "I never made it back inside the house to take a shower because your brother was there pumping up my tires when I arrived," Cavin explained. "By the way, thank you for sending him."

"You're welcome," Noel replied sheepishly.

Mrs. Madelyn stepped fully into the kitchen and grabbed both of them by an arm like a kindergarten teacher. "You two can talk about all of this at dinner," she encouraged. "Right now, you both need showers and new outfits, and I need to tend to these patient customers," she added, eyeing the half dozen people remaining in the store, mostly near the checkout counter where Levi and Laney seemed to be doing a fine job of entertaining them.

Noel felt a trance-like state come over her as her feet climbed the steps one at a time as her right hand slid along the aged handrail. The jingling door didn't even register after Cavin said his goodbyes to Laney and Levi. Noel sighed. Leaving Mrs. Madelyn and the kids downstairs to tend to the store while she did something for herself seemed wrong for some reason.

When Noel closed the door at the top of the stairs, she let her back collapse against it, and her body slowly oozed downward like tree sap inching toward the ground until her backside met the wooden floorboards. She wrapped her arms around her knees, plucked the Santa hat from her head, and dropped her face into her hands. All of a sudden, she felt completely alone and overwhelmed.

"What am I doing?" she whispered into thin air. Scratch that, thick air.

Noel let that thought linger for a moment as a fresh batch of tears rolled from her eyes. With her lips pressed tightly together, she smeared the moisture on her face with the backs of her hands.

"Fletcher," she called out. "What should I do?" The idea of spending time alone with another man seemed inappropriate. "I love you. I committed my life to you."

Suddenly the *until death do us part* line in the vows she recited at their wedding ceremony slid across her mind. "No, Fletcher; no, God; whichever of you put that thought there," she hedged. "Death wasn't supposed to do us part," she cried. "We were supposed to live a long and happy life together. I need you. I need to go out to dinner with you tonight—not some man I don't know. That doesn't seem fair to you or to me."

With tears streaming down her cheeks making miniature puddles on the floor, Noel sat with her thoughts. She wasn't sure how much time went by, but eventually she remembered she only had an hour to get ready. Several times she considered cancelling the plans she made or rather the plans Mrs. Madelyn made for her. She knew what her friend was trying to do, and while she appreciated it, she didn't feel ready.

We'll never be ready. We just have to be brave.

"No, Fletcher, no," she murmured authoritatively as the words he spoke to her just before Levi came into this world fluttered through her mind like an injured bird.

The two of them were speeding toward the hospital, Fletcher holding her hand firmly as they breathed in unison like they learned in Lamaze class. They had so much fun prepping and planning for little Levi's arrival beginning with all the times they made love—Fletcher teasingly called it *practice*—followed by Noel usually punching him in the arm then either ripping his clothes off or snuggling into his naked body depending on whether he said it before or after the act. She cherished every moment including choosing names, assembling the crib, and babyproofing their home. However, Noel never quite felt ready to be a mother, and as the contractions grew closer and so did the hospital, she screamed, "I'm not ready for this."

We. Fletcher always approached every challenge in their lives with a *we*. With Fletcher she never felt alone. But now, she did. Noel wasn't sure how she made it through the past year and however many months she had been an *I*.

"I'll do it, Fletcher," she muttered. "I'll be brave," she cried. "God and Fletcher, you two better be with me."

Somehow Noel picked herself up off the floor and made it to the bathroom where she stepped into the shower and turned the nozzle to cold.

"If you want to feel sorry for yourself, take a hot shower," Fletcher used to say. "If you want to rejuvenate yourself, take the path less traveled and turn the nozzle in the opposite direction."

How he took cold showers, Noel never quite understood. Fletcher was a man of the sea though. He would drop anchor in the middle of the ocean, sound, river, or lake in the middle of summer, winter, spring, or fall, and jump right in with all the fish. Shirtless he would tread water and call up to her on the boat, "Join me, babe. The water feels so refreshing today."

If the water was above seventy degrees, she would hop in, and the two of them would swim like dolphins. When they were miles away from other human beings in the vast and mysterious Atlantic Ocean, playfulness often turned into intimacy. Through trial and error, they learned how to make love while treading water which proved to be one of the most intense full-body exercises either ever experienced. The profound pleasure made the extreme challenge exciting beyond explanation.

Wrapped in one another's naked bodies, they danced together like synchronized swimmers. Sometimes their lips came together above the surface, and other times they let their bodies sink below until they had to come up for air. Sex in the sea was different, and the resistance of the water forced them to slow down, providing a tantric-like quality every time.

As thousands of freezing droplets traveled down through the maze of goose bumps on Noel's skin, she reveled in these memories of Fletcher. With her eyes closed, she breathed heavily as the water circled in the drain near her feet. She never imagined having sex with another man. She was one of the rare women who could say she lost her virginity to her husband, and although that happened before they married, she took pride in knowing they only experienced such an intimate and bonding act together.

Starting over with someone new seemed impossible, especially as a mother. How could she hold another man's hand? Kiss his lips? Tell him her secrets? Maybe time would allow it, but the idea seemed too complex. It would take so much effort, and she just didn't know if she had the time or the energy for any of it.

Noel toweled off realizing no one had knocked on or opened the unlocked bathroom door. With kids in the house around the clock, that only happened if she showered after their bedtime or in the early morning hours. A surprising sense of relaxation settled into her shoulders during an otherwise tense time. She wrapped the towel around her body and ventured to her bedroom where she slipped on a pair of jeans and a white sweater with navy blue pinstripes.

Noel spent the next twenty minutes blow-drying her hair and applying a thin coat of makeup. Then she climbed into a pair of light brown boots and grabbed her gray parka jacket.

"Mom, you look beautiful," Levi claimed with enthusiasm when Noel walked downstairs.

"You sure do, Aunt Noel."

Mrs. Madelyn smiled proudly in the background as she finished running the numbers at the register.

"Thank you both," Noel replied, hugging each of the kids individually.

When Noel recognized the data on the screen in front of Mrs. Madelyn, she scurried behind the counter to check the Small Business Saturday sales total. She couldn't believe she forgot about this until now. The numbers could have even been pulled up on her phone at any point while upstairs, but she had been so preoccupied with getting ready. Looking now at the figures, she experienced a sharp pang of disappointment in her heart.

She exchanged glances with Mrs. Madelyn, but neither wanted to say anything in front of the children. The numbers weren't bad; they just weren't good enough. Similar to yesterday, the customer count was solid, but the overall sales weren't. Mrs. Madelyn hoped Noel could get this off her mind tonight. She needed a way to escape the pressures of business, and she prayed Cavin could offer that opportunity.

"Mrs. Madelyn said we get to spend the evening at her house with her and Mr. Jack," Laney mentioned with her chin resting in her folded arms atop the wooden counter as she studied them from the customer's side.

Noel smiled. Mrs. Madelyn always made things fun, and she remembered that from when she was young.

"She said we might get ice cream, too," Levi added.

"Mr. Jack's special homemade Christmas ice cream," Mrs. Madelyn clarified.

"It's red and green," Laney informed Noel.

"That's amazing," Noel exclaimed remembering the ice cream. "You will love helping Mr. Jack make it. He will let you add Christmas sprinkles, too."

"Really?" Levi checked looking at Mrs. Madelyn for confirmation.

Mrs. Madelyn's whole face smiled. "Of course."

"Why aren't you coming, Mommy?"

While upstairs earlier, Noel thought about how to answer this anticipated question. Unfortunately, she hadn't come up with a worthy answer, and she turned to glance at the cuckoo clock hoping Mrs. Madelyn would leave with the children before Cavin arrived. In eight short minutes, an hour would have passed since he left. She should have told him she would meet him somewhere else. She also should have told him she didn't want to eat out in Beaufort.

"Mommy has some things to take care of," Noel finally replied.

Levi frowned, and Laney's brow furrowed as her lips puckered.

Mrs. Madelyn recognized and understood Noel's avoidance tactic. "Let's go surprise Mr. Jack," she suggested quickly.

The kids jumped at the idea, but as they made it to the front door and Noel reached hurriedly to unlock it for them, Cavin appeared on the other side dressed in dark blue jeans, a navy blue sport coat, and a button-up shirt looking like a GQ magazine cover model.

"Oh my," Mrs. Madelyn whispered as she turned and fanned herself where only Noel could see the gesture.

"What are you doing here, Kevin?" Levi asked inquisitively.

Noel had no idea how Cavin would respond, so she beat him to the punch with the first thing that popped into her mind. "Mommy is having a business meeting with Mr. Cavin," she concocted.

Cavin's eyelids fluttered a little as his gaze locked onto Noel's, and then he smiled as he turned his attention to the kids.

"Where are you two going?" Cavin asked, realizing Noel's desire to change the subject.

"To see Mr. Jack and make homemade ice cream," Laney announced excitedly.

"That is no fair, I want to do that," Cavin exclaimed with a pouty face. "Ice cream sounds much better than a business meeting," he replied, glancing at Noel with a smirk.

"You can come if you want," Levi invited.

"Maybe next time," Cavin responded, touching the little guy on the shoulder.

Mrs. Madelyn winked at Cavin and then herded the kids toward her vehicle while Noel let Cavin into the candy shop to provide adequate time for them to pull away so Levi and Laney didn't spot her and Cavin leaving together.

"Would you like to choose the place we have dinner, or would you like me to suggest one?" Cavin asked. Earlier he researched the fine dining options in Beaufort preparing to make a choice.

"I would prefer to eat somewhere other than Beaufort," Noel requested. "To be fully transparent, I am not ready for all the questions and comments that are going to come from people seeing me in public with another man." As soon as she spoke the words *another man*, she wished she chose different terminology. The phrase made it sound like she was either cheating on Fletcher or that people saw her out with lots of men.

"I respect that," Cavin accepted his facial expression showing understanding.

"Thank you," Noel responded, but she had no idea what to suggest. None of this had been thought out, and she hated that she kept running into snags at every corner.

"We can go to the grocery store and pick out ingredients, and I can cook a meal for you at my place," Cavin offered.

"No," Noel responded promptly and more harshly than intended. "I mean that's nice of you to offer, but I definitely am not ready for that either." Being together in public with a man seemed scary enough; she couldn't fathom being alone with Cavin at his house.

"I am open to any suggestions," Cavin replied. Too bad his family didn't have a private jet yet. He could fly Noel anywhere she wanted—somewhere she wouldn't know anyone.

"Let's go to Swansboro."

"Sure," Cavin replied although he had no idea how far away

this town could be. He didn't remember driving through the place on his trip from the airport. It didn't matter; he didn't have anything else going on tonight.

The neighboring towns like Morehead City and Atlantic Beach would be too close, Noel decided. The chances of them running into someone there that she knew seemed likely.

"There's a nice Italian restaurant on the Swansboro waterfront. How does that sound to you?" Noel inquired.

"Absolutely perfect."

Noel figured the time she and Cavin spent figuring out where to have dinner should have given Mrs. Madelyn ample opportunity to get the kids settled in the car and off to their destination.

"Where is your Santa hat?" Cavin asked with a grin. He never saw Noel without it until now, and he wasn't sure which look he liked better. The chin-length wavy bob seemed to fit her face just right. Of course he previously noticed the rich brown color spilling out from beneath the white puffy rim of the hat, but in a way it was as though he was seeing Noel Puckett for the first time all over again. While she looked super cute wearing the Santa hat, this Noel, with her hair fixed and a smidge more makeup than he remembered, was absolutely stunning.

19

oel thought she and Cavin would escape to Swansboro without a hitch, but she failed to consider the walk from the candy shop to the adjacent lot where Cavin parked his vehicle. It just so happened that as Cavin opened the passenger door for her like a gentleman which ironically made her feel a bit uneasy, Chelsea and Rainey pulled in one space over and quickly hopped out of their car.

"Hello there, Noel," Chelsea greeted with her eyes dancing from across the roof of her car.

Cavin couldn't see Chelsea from his vantage point, but at the sound of her voice, he turned and spotted Officer Rainey dressed in plain clothes and then the source of the voice, a blonde-haired woman on the other side of the vehicle.

"Hey, guys," Noel replied, trying to play it cool.

"Good evening, Officer Rainey," Cavin said while extending his hand.

"You can call me Rainey," Rainey responded, since Cavin was with his friend Noel.

Noel suddenly looked perplexed. "Do you know everyone in Beaufort?" she questioned without even thinking.

"I have not met Rainey's wife," Cavin teased. However, earlier today he noticed the ring on the officer's finger.

"I am Chelsea," she introduced herself as she hurried around the front end of the vehicle to extend her hand to the handsome man opening his vehicle's door for her best friend.

"It is a pleasure to meet you, Chelsea," Cavin remarked. "I am Cavin Dawson."

Chelsea studied him from head to toe, none too discreetly. "How do you two know each other, and where are you heading?" Chelsea inquired her eyes darting between Cavin and Noel impatiently waiting for an answer. She tightly clutched the purse dangling at her side.

"Business," Cavin answered quickly while recalling Noel's words from earlier. "We have a business meeting this evening."

Rainey's eyes widened, and he couldn't help but smirk while studying Noel's facial expression.

"Right," Chelsea laughed. "I am not the police officer here, but I can see straight through that lie."

Cavin's face turned a light shade of red and Noel's a noticeable amount darker.

"Would the two of you like to join us for a 'business meeting' at Clawson's?" Rainey invited holding up air quotes for the words *business meeting*.

Cavin looked to Noel for a response, and Rainey and Chelsea followed suit.

"Thanks, but I am not ready for that," Noel insisted, accepting the fact that misdirecting her friends didn't work like it had with the kids. *Nor am I ready for this*, she kept to herself feeling precarious in this conversation.

Chelsea wrapped an arm around her husband's and tugged him slightly in the direction of the restaurant. "Okay, then we will let you two get to your meeting," she announced with a mischievous smile. "It was great to meet you, Cavin Dawson."

"You as well, Chelsea Rainey," Cavin responded casually

heading for the driver's side door to allow Noel a moment with her friends. "Nice to see you again, Rainey," Cavin concluded before disappearing behind the vehicle.

Chelsea took full advantage of the time it took Cavin to walk around the large SUV. "Call me tonight after your business meeting-or in the morning or whenever it adjourns—and give me all the details," she requested while fluttering her eyebrows and biting her lip.

"It's not like that," Noel insisted, reaching for the door.

Rainey smiled and pulled on his wife's arm. "Just have fun," he remarked, "but not too much fun," he added like the second big brother he always was.

In middle and high school, he and Keaton kept away the boys who creeped her out and even some of the ones she liked but they knew were trouble. Noel never considered that it would persist into adulthood, but it all of a sudden became a reality, and she figured Rainey and Keaton would probably be even more protective now because of the current state of her fragile heart.

A minute later Noel's head fell against the headrest, and her eyelids closed as Cavin cranked the engine and reached for the navigation system.

"What is the name of the restaurant?" he inquired.

"Let's just go," Noel urged a little louder than intended.

"Okay."

Cavin shifted the gear into reverse and glanced in the rearview mirror.

"I can tell you how to get there," Noel explained, deliberately calming her tone and wishing she could backtrack in order to offer this response as her first.

Cavin backed out of the parking space, and neither he nor Noel said anything until they crossed the bridge leading out of the Beaufort waterfront district. He could tell she needed some time to breathe, and he wondered what was going through her mind.

As they left the parking lot, she placed her elbow on the window frame and rested the right side of her face in her palm, and it remained that way even now.

"If you would rather people not see you with me, we do not have to go out for dinner," Cavin surprised her with his bluntness.

Noel closed her eyes for about the fifth time and then spoke slowly as she opened them and gazed out the window at the small private airport runway they passed. "It's not about you," she revealed. "This is one of the hardest things I have ever done."

The air grew silent for a few moments as they traveled over a high-rise bridge with a magnificent view of land merging with water.

"What do you mean by that?" Cavin eventually asked respectfully.

"This is the first time I have been anywhere with another man since Fletcher died," Noel explained hesitantly.

Cavin sighed realizing the conversation that initiated this outing, or date, or business meeting, or whatever the title involved the story of how her husband died which meant he didn't know the details: how, when, where, and all the rest. Nor did he know what had or hadn't transpired between then and now. He noted the name Fletcher knowing he didn't want to avoid it like one might the name of an ex.

"I want you to be comfortable," Cavin insisted. "This does not have to be a date. We can be two friends enjoying dinner together or professionals having a business meeting. I will not try to hold your hand or kiss you or do anything else that might make you feel awkward."

The words Cavin chose surprised himself and not just because he said them but because he meant them. Usually on a first date, he hoped for more than just conversation, and although the goal at the end of the night wasn't intimacy, he longed for some type of physical connection even if just flirty touching.

"I appreciate you saying that," Noel acknowledged although

everything about this evening already felt way more awkward than she could even begin to explain. However, Cavin wasn't at fault. She remembered how at ease she felt after her shower, but the tension began to increase again when she and Cavin started talking to the kids and Mrs. Madelyn and even more so when met unexpectedly by Chelsea and Rainey. Now her shoulders felt tighter than the lines Fletcher used to tug on once a giant fish took the bait.

As she breathed in slowly considering Cavin's thoughtful words, Noel felt a sudden release like a fish set free back in the water. She previously decided there would be no handholding, kissing, cuddling, or anything else physical with him tonight, but something about his reassuring words liberated her mind and body.

They traveled in silent contemplation during the remainder of the drive to Swansboro which took about forty-five minutes in total. Noel appreciated the time Cavin gave her to decompress after such a challenging day.

Cavin admired the beauty of the landscape as they crossed a small bridge that led to the town of Swansboro. At first sight the place resembled a small fishing village. Docks lined the left side of the bridge with an array of boats jutting into the water while the back sides of the shops and restaurants that lined Main Street came into view. Many offered balconies for sitting while eating or drinking coffee. To the right the water view was more expansive, but Cavin could see the tree line on the opposite shore. Noel informed him that the Italian restaurant was just over the bridge on the right.

They parked in a gravel lot, and then Cavin shared an idea with Noel that she didn't know how much she would appreciate until he offered it as an option.

"Would you like to walk along the waterfront and talk about your story," he asked, "rather than sit in a restaurant filled with patrons while staring at each other from across the table?"

"Walking and talking sounds much nicer," Noel acknowledged, especially after sitting in the vehicle for some time. "However, I do want to have dinner with you like we agreed."

Cavin grinned. "Mrs. Madelyn kind of did the agreeing for you," he pointed out with a smile.

Noel laughed. "You noticed that, huh?" she replied, experiencing the relief of shared laughter.

"I was okay with it," he reported, chuckling easily.

Absentmindedly, Noel punched Cavin in the arm playfully just like she used to with Fletcher. "Sorry about that," she quickly noted.

"I am okay with being a punching bag if you need one," Cavin offered. "As long as you do not hit much harder than that," he teased.

Noel realized she probably would have benefited from a punching bag this past year although not a human one. As they approached the walkway along the waterfront, she turned to Cavin. "The truth is I do and don't know exactly how Fletcher, Lexi, and my parents died," she revealed in a voice not much louder than a whisper.

Cavin's facial features initially showed a surprised and then puzzled expression. "Who is Lexi?" he asked softly, remembering hearing Noel reference that name earlier and wanting to place that piece first.

"Keaton's wife . . . and Laney's mom," Noel offered in explanation.

Upon reflection Cavin suddenly felt terrible for his prior treatment of Keaton. The man irritated him on the night of their introduction, but Cavin had no idea what the guy had been through. Now he understood why Georgia called Keaton's story a sad one.

Georgia. The mere thought of Georgia instantly brought a

cascade of plans back into the forefront of Cavin's mind and at a time when he would rather not have them. He suddenly recalled the mayor's and his wife's invitation to their party this evening. He also indicated to Georgia that he would probably see her there. Thankfully, they never made formal plans to attend the event together nor had he officially committed to joining her for tomorrow morning's church service when she suggested it. Nonetheless after all of today's excitement, the invitations completely slipped his mind.

Considering this dilemma, Cavin nearly glanced at his watch to see if time allowed for a late appearance at the party, but he quickly dismissed the idea, deciding it would be rude to interrupt such a serious conversation.

Cavin reached into his pocket and muted his phone, choosing instead to give Noel his full attention for the remainder of the evening.

"All four of our family members died in a tragic boating accident," Noel explained, instantly bringing Cavin's mind back to the present. "Levi, Laney, and I were also supposed to be on that boat," she added with a sniff.

They walked about twenty steps in silence as little waves pressed against the seawall repetitively reminding the structure that it stood in the way of nature. A man fishing on a kayak tossed his hand up in the air acknowledging their presence, and Cavin waved back. Lost in thought Noel never saw the fisherman nor did she hear the hum of the vehicles passing over the very bridge she and Cavin drove over just a short while ago.

The words *supposed to be* echoed in Cavin's mind as they walked below the bridge. "I am so sorry," he uttered cautiously. After another moment passed, he inquired, "Where were you instead?"

"Levi and Laney spent the night together at our house the night before our planned weekend camping trip to Shackelford Banks which is an island not far from Beaufort but only accessible by boat," she explained. "In the early morning hours on the day we were scheduled to leave for the excursion, the three of us became ill with some sort of stomach bug that hit me first. I am pretty sure I picked it up from Rainey and Chelsea because they both became sick right after I'd been at their house a couple of days prior." Noel paused for a moment, and Cavin could see her jawline tightening visibly. "Fletcher had been away most of the week captaining a fishing trip, so once the kids and I experienced symptoms, I encouraged him not to come home to get us. Rather than cancelling the last planned trip of the season that everyone was looking forward to, I offered to stay home with the kids and ride out our ailments." She closed her eyes remembering how Fletcher had come home to grab a few things anyway, and before leaving it surprised her when he kissed her. She got aggravated at him and told him he might get sick, but he said the reward outweighed the risk. At the time Noel found it careless, but she would remember that kiss—their last kiss—for the rest of her life. Their lips moved slowly and passionately as if they might never touch again, but Fletcher always kissed her that way.

"Oh my goodness, I bet the kids were bummed," Cavin replied, not yet fully realizing the weight of the happenstance. "Thank God the three of you did not go," he added suddenly comprehending the long-term benefit of their temporary sickness.

Feeling tears form around her eyes, Noel stuffed her hands into her pockets. "I sometimes wish we had gone," she admitted for the first time to anyone other than herself. On several occasions she almost voiced her thoughts to Mrs. Madelyn and Chelsea but then stopped herself because they sounded morbid and might cause unnecessary worry. Why she just disclosed her unsettling thoughts to Cavin, she was unsure but maybe because soon he would be gone, too, like the family members she missed so much.

"Do you think maybe you could have done something to help if you were there?" Cavin asked curiously.

Noel shrugged her chilly shoulders. "I doubt it. Fletcher was a professional fishing boat captain. He knew those waters like the back of his hand. He frequently drove to and from Shackelford even in the dark without incident. He grew up navigating the waters around Beaufort, and there is no one I would trust captaining a boat more than my husband."

"Then why do you wish you had gone?" Cavin asked, and suddenly the answer struck him like a lightning bolt. "Oh, I understand what you are implying," he added, not wanting Noel to have to admit the words aloud.

"It's hard knowing we should have been there," Noel confessed.

"I imagine. Where was Keaton?" Cavin asked, immediately assuming that since he apparently pawned Laney off on Noel these days, maybe he did the same then to get drunk whenever he wanted.

Noel grew silent, and then the tears pushed their way down her cheeks.

Cavin knew he promised to refrain from physical touch this evening, but he suddenly felt compelled to rub Noel's shoulder blade gently. They dodged a couple who walked by them holding hands, and Cavin saw the woman look at Noel disapprovingly while whispering something to the man as if crying in public were frowned upon. He considered glaring in their direction but decided to ignore them instead.

When Noel caught her breath, she swiped away the tears with the sleeve of her jacket. "Keaton was driving the boat," she revealed.

Cavin waited a few seconds considering whether or not to verbalize the thought that immediately came to mind. "Oh, based on what you said a minute ago, I assumed Fletcher was manning the boat."

"That's one of the odd things about the accident," Noel admitted. "Fletcher never let anyone else drive the boat."

The wheels turned in Cavin's investigative mind, but he waited for her to continue.

"Keaton won't tell anyone why he was driving instead of Fletcher," Noel explained. "The police almost arrested him for withholding evidence."

"My goodness," Cavin replied, then another question floated into his mind like a balloon. "How did the police know Fletcher always drove the boat?" he inquired wondering if Noel told them but doubting she would have any reason to have that discussion with the authorities, maybe with her brother but not an investigator. At least not unless there was more to this story or if she suspected foul play was involved. "I hate to ask this but was Keaton drinking?"

"The answer to your first question came up later in the investigation in a meeting with detectives when Rainey mentioned that Fletcher never allowed anyone to drive his boat," Noel explained, and then she somehow let out a hint of a laugh while crying sounding like a bull snorting although Cavin couldn't imagine why she found humor in the question nor the answer. Then her answer to his second question cleared things up. "Prior to the accident, Keaton wouldn't touch alcohol. He hated everything about it—the smell, the taste, and the effect it has on the brain," she explained.

"Really?" Cavin responded surprisingly although he could see why a man who felt responsible for the death of loved ones might turn to alcohol. Now he felt bad about making an assumption about Keaton once again. Maybe he should stop doing that, he realized.

"Regardless of what happened out there, Keaton holds himself responsible," Noel shared.

"What did he say happened?" Cavin came right out and asked.

"Keaton said they hit a sandbar."

"How did he survive when no one else did?"

"Keaton said everyone except him went flying because he saw the sandbar at the last second, and only had enough time to brace himself and hold onto the steering wheel for dear life. He said he tried to scream, but by the time it came out of his mouth, it was too late."

"Oh God," Cavin sighed.

"The actual causes of each person's death varied slightly. My mom and Lexi were sitting in the back of the boat, and my dad and Fletcher were at the front." Noel paused for a moment realizing she never shared the details with anyone. The autopilot response had always been that her family members died in a tragic boating accident, and after hearing that, people didn't ask questions. "Mom and Lexi both flew forward toward Keaton, hitting their heads on unforgiving parts of the boat," she mentioned first, not wanting to explain further although certain Cavin understood. "My dad flew out and landed on the sandbar— the impact was too great for any chance of survival." Noel stopped there for a moment trying not to visualize the accident for the millionth time, but she never could push away the imagery. "Fletcher was near the bow. His head rammed into something that knocked him unconscious but didn't kill him, and he flew completely over the sandbar. His cause of death was listed as drowning."

Cavin let the silence linger in the air for a long while, and then Noel's quiet tears erupted into muffled sobs as she covered her face with her hands and eventually her jacket. Nonetheless she kept pacing instinctively knowing that if she stopped she would fall to the ground. Cavin's insistence on walking along the waterfront brought Noel relief because she would have never made it through this conversation in a restaurant, but for some reason she didn't fully understand, she needed to get this out.

"I am so sorry, Noel," Cavin finally uttered, reaching for her shoulder again, but she didn't even seem to notice the gesture. "I am sorry this happened to your mom, dad, Lexi, Fletcher, and to you." Cavin felt the need to name them all. They were real people. Even though he didn't know them, they were as real to Noel as he was standing beside her right now, and he knew she loved each of them unconditionally. That was evident.

Noel eventually pulled her face out of her jacket, and for a split second she locked eyes with Cavin. "Thank you," she mumbled simply.

They reached the end of the waterfront area and started walking down random streets passing historic homes full of charm and character. Cavin had no idea where they were headed, but as long as Noel continued he would keep walking beside her. He would walk all the way back to Beaufort if she wanted. They didn't even have to eat; he would be fine with going hungry.

"I cannot fathom going through what you have been through," Cavin admitted.

"I wouldn't wish it on my worst enemy," Noel asserted. "Not that I really have any," she added, thinking that Walter, who had been trying to force her to sell her family's building at a fraction of the value, might be the person she liked the least. Oh, and Georgia—she didn't really care for Georgia, and even more so after the lady threatened the children and tried to flaunt the connection she made with Cavin. Some women were way too skilled at stabbing each other in the back.

"I am sure," Cavin replied. "Can I ask you another question about the accident? And if you would rather not answer or if I am asking too many personal questions, you can tell me it is none of my business."

"Believe it or not, I actually appreciate your questions. No one ever asks any questions; they just tell me over and over how sorry they are, and they look at me like I am the most pitiful thing they have ever laid eyes on," Noel explained.

"I understand all of that," Cavin reasoned. "Was Fletcher wearing a life vest?" he wondered aloud after receiving permission.

"Not at the time which is another red flag. Fletcher always wore a vest, and he made every person in his boat buckle one on, no matter what; otherwise, he wouldn't leave shore."

"Did Keaton say why Fletcher was not wearing a life jacket?"

Noel shook her head. "He just said Fletcher took it off. He won't explain more, not even when the police interrogated him over and over. I've asked him many times, too," Noel explained still shaking her head. "I've even questioned him when he was drunk, hoping he would spill the beans, but he won't."

"Geez, Noel. You are so strong to have made it to this point in your recovery after experiencing this tragic accident."

Cavin was the first person to acknowledge Noel's direct connection with the accident; even though she was not physically present on that boat, she always felt like she had been right there with her loved ones.

"Thank you," Noel replied gratefully.

"It is also so brave of you to share this story with me," Cavin acknowledged.

At the mention of the word *brave*, Noel felt her whole body shudder—not just because she couldn't seem to escape that term but because she couldn't deny that the moment he spoke it, she saw Fletcher in Cavin Dawson's eyes.

20

oel figured that she and Cavin must have walked for nearly an hour. Not once did they discuss which direction to go while wandering through the maze of downtown streets—decorated festively for the Christmas season—ultimately ending up back at the waterfront. The two of them simply went with the flow letting the cold breeze guide them wherever it might as the welcoming glow of nighttime in Swansboro surrounded them.

Noel felt much better now than when they left Beaufort, better than she had in a while, in fact. She never realized quite how heavy all the details of the accident weighed on her even after a year passed. So many questions still loomed in her mind; some similar to the ones Cavin posed. If only Keaton would reveal what happened out there on the water, maybe then she could close another chapter of the horror story.

During dinner Cavin and Noel barely spoke another word about the accident. The fluffy Christmas tree in the corner of the room twinkled with white lights, and candles on the windowsills and tables created a warm, flickering luminosity throughout the restaurant—a welcome distraction from the chilly November weather awaiting them outside. The conversation felt much lighter as Cavin and Noel learned more details about each other.

Cavin told Noel about the prestigious private school he attended in Atlanta, and Noel shared stories about the three typical public school levels she climbed. She described how she met Chelsea, Rainey, and Lexi at a young age and mentioned other elementary school playmates; some of whom they hung out with as they grew up wandering the waterfront district and exploring the waterways in boats during their teenage years.

Not many families moved in and out of Beaufort which usually proved to be a perk because friends stuck around for the long haul. The student population at Cavin's school often changed due to parents moving in or away for better opportunities which made having close friends a challenge. Noel felt bad for him, especially when he revealed he didn't even have a best friend now.

"I have always only had acquaintances," he explained. "Nowadays I travel so much that it is hard to have close friends. I am rarely around long enough to get together with anyone on a regular basis."

"My closest friends these days are Chelsea, whom you just met, and Mrs. Madelyn."

"Chelsea seems friendly, and I love Mrs. Madelyn's personality. She appears to be a lot of fun."

"They are both great women," Noel guaranteed. "Where did you meet Rainey?" she inquired curiously.

Cavin chuckled and then told her the story, all of it, knowing if he didn't, her brother or Rainey certainly would. He still felt bad about judging Keaton so harshly. Noel took the opportunity to fill Cavin in on the history between Keaton and Rainey by explaining that they became adversaries soon after the accident.

Cavin wondered what it would be like to settle somewhere and make real friends, and the thought brought a tentative smile to his face. "What are your hobbies?" he asked ready to start a new topic.

"Does taking care of Levi, Laney, and the candy shop count?" Noel asked. "That's about all I do these days."

"Those sound more like fun responsibilities than hobbies," Cavin appealed.

"Fair enough. How about you? What are your hobbies?" Noel inquired. "You said you played golf this morning; is that one of them?"

Cavin described growing up playing golf at the country club and playing in college before eventually earning the opportunity to play professionally.

"Wow, I have never met a professional golfer . . . however, I have drunk an Arnold Palmer," she teased.

Cavin laughed louder than intended and nearly spat out his beverage, interrupting the conversation at a few nearby tables as people glanced over at the commotion.

"Well, I am not really a professional golfer," he admitted, unaware of the random stares from nearby strangers as his eyes returned directly to Noel's which sparkled in the dim romantic glow of the restaurant. "However, I must say I am impressed that you know the name of a former great."

"I know more than one name," Noel declared confidently. "I know Tiger Woods, Nancy Lopez, Phil Mickelson, Jack Nicklaus, Annika Sorenstam, Lee Trevino, Rory McIlroy—" she trailed off trying to think of others but couldn't recall anyone further on the fly.

With each name mentioned, Cavin's eyebrows climbed a little higher on his forehead. "Impressive. How do you know of all those golfers?"

"My dad watched golf, and when I was little, I liked to sit in his lap—so I watched golf, too," she clarified with a smile brought on by a flash of delightful memories.

"Did he play?" Cavin asked, unable to recall a time when he ever sat in his mom's or dad's lap.

"A little."

"How about you?" Cavin checked.

"I played piano," Noel replied, suddenly remembering one of her hobbies.

Cavin instantly glanced at her fingers. "Did you know long fingers can be an advantage for piano players and golfers?"

Noel glanced at her thin spaghetti noodle fingers and then at Cavin's which looked more like fettuccine compared to hers. Both appeared longer than average, but neither was abnormal. "Of course I knew that about piano players but not golfers."

"It is certainly not as much of a factor for golfers, but some studies have shown it can be helpful."

Noel nodded her head. "Makes sense."

"Do you still play piano?" Cavin asked.

"I used to play at church and sing, but it's been a while."

"You should play," Cavin encouraged. "If you still love it, that is."

"I do love both."

"I want to hear you sing and play," Cavin insisted.

"You do?" Noel questioned not expecting him to show interest.

"Of course."

"Maybe one day," she replied, shrugging her shoulders noncommittally.

"I will let you watch me play golf if you let me watch you play the piano," Cavin teased, although somewhat seriously.

"That doesn't sound like a fair trade," Noel contested.

"Why not?"

"Golf takes a long time, so I would be doing a lot of watching," she pointed out with a wink, her head tilted ever so slightly. "I would want to play, too."

Cavin's ears perked up. "Really? You would play golf with me?"

"Sure, why not?" Noel offered before realizing what that meant. A second date was what that meant, she quickly understood if this was a first date although an official label didn't exist. It did and didn't seem like a date even though that made no sense.

As Cavin peered into Noel Puckett's emerald green eyes, he wondered what thoughts traveled through her mind. Of all the women he dated over the years, not one ever offered to play golf with him. They didn't even play when invited. One did drive the golf cart once and drank a lot of booze, but the country club nearly kicked him out for that incident.

"I am going to hold you to it," Cavin declared.

Noel thought through the idea a bit more and decided to add a disclaimer. "If I play golf with you, you have to sing with me while I play piano," she insisted, and then a voice in her head reminded her: *that's three dates.*

"Wait a minute, you should have made that arrangement before agreeing to golf," Cavin pointed out grinning.

Noel chuckled. "I won't hold you to it, but if you are the gentleman I think you might be, I imagine you will oblige."

"What makes you think I am a gentleman?" he asked curiously.

"Let's see. You opened every door for me this evening, you rubbed my back when I was crying, and I noticed some other things that will remain unsaid."

"Like what?" he queried.

Like you not turning to check out Georgia's strut as she walked away this morning. "There are some things a lady doesn't share," she contended, batting her eyelashes.

"Fair enough, but I will warn you that I may be a terrible singer."

"I might be a terrible golfer," she countered.

Cavin encountered his fair share of those over the years, and many athletes claimed the sport to be the most difficult. "Once we are out there, if you grow tired of chasing balls, you can always just drive the cart. Most people enjoy that aspect of golf," he inserted. "However, you aren't allowed to get drunk."

"Oh yeah, how come?" she asked, playing along.

Cavin communicated the PG-13 version of the story that

popped into his mind earlier, and as their conversation shifted amongst other topics, it didn't take Noel long to decipher that Cavin's family was relatively wealthy although she didn't ask or comment about it specifically. Within the stories he told, Cavin randomly mentioned limousines, maids, butlers, and even a helicopter his dad once wanted to buy. On the other hand, Noel grew up having all her needs met, but looking back she realized Cavin had a lot of opportunities she didn't. At the same time she could tell his parents focused far more on success than spending time together as a family.

The dinner table discussion never ceased nor did their dialogue during the entire ride home. Cavin talked more than she did, but Noel held her own and surprised herself with some of the details she opened up about, like how sales had been lower than she hoped these last two days. For some reason, being in Cavin's presence felt easy which came as somewhat of a surprise since Noel initially labeled him as an arrogant businessman.

Somehow they didn't talk in depth about what Cavin did for work, and Noel was admittedly relieved that job-related conversations didn't dominate their *business meeting*—she laughed privately every time she recalled her description to Chelsea and Rainey. Once inside her house in the dark, Noel chuckled again at the thought of those two words. The night never seemed like a business meeting at all, she considered as her back slid down the same door at the top of the steps.

"Thanks, God," she whispered. She thought about saying thanks to Fletcher, too, but for some reason that didn't feel quite right as a few tears of gratitude trickled down her face reaching the corners of her lips—somewhat forming a smile. Noel felt a twinge of guilt for having such a nice time with Cavin. Honestly the whole experience surprised her. She anticipated coming home much earlier and wishing she never agreed, or let Mrs. Madelyn agree on her behalf, to have dinner with a man who felt like a stranger a handful of hours before. She imagined it would be one big mistake that she might beat herself up about for days or possibly weeks or months.

However, Cavin proved to be a gentleman and true to his word. Other than consoling her with a few gentle, harmless back rubs, he never attempted to touch her although he assisted her with her coat after dinner and escorted her to the door at the end of the night. Even though the evening went well, when they said goodbye, it came as somewhat of a surprise to her when she found herself wondering when she would see him again.

During the ride home from Swansboro, she called Mrs. Madelyn to let her know their evening ran later than expected, and she could hear Mrs. Madelyn's smile through the phone.

"You deserved a night where you lost track of time," her dear friend said quietly knowing Cavin sat on the other side of the vehicle.

A smile spread onto Noel's face, and out of the corner of her eye, she looked over at Cavin as he stared straight ahead at the road. Mrs. Madelyn was right—he was handsome.

"The kids are fast asleep on a makeshift cot on the living room floor," Mrs. Madelyn revealed. "Why don't you let them stay the night here with me and Mr. Jack? He said he will sleep in the recliner in case they wake up wondering where they are."

Noel nearly cried, but she already cried enough for one evening. Having a night alone of completely uninterrupted sleep would be a blessing, especially this night she decided.

However, after climbing into bed, Noel spent the next hour with her eyes wide open in the dark reliving the new memories she made with Cavin Dawson that evening. No one could or would ever take the place of Fletcher Puckett, but with her entire body relaxed and enveloped in the soft covers, Noel closed her eyes realizing that one day at a time she could move forward. She believed she took the first step today although not alone as the piano-playing fingers on her right hand stretched wide over Fletcher's spot on the bed.

"Thank you, Fletcher," Noel whispered, remembering how they often fell asleep holding hands. "I love you."

21

"Are you coming?" the first message from Georgia asked as Cavin checked his phone in the parking lot about ten minutes after dropping off Noel. "Where are you? I thought you were going to be at the mayor's party?" the second message, sent an hour later, accused. "I guess you are not going to make it," the last one concluded. "I kind of feel stood up."

Once Cavin silenced his phone when he and Noel started walking along the Swansboro waterfront, he never glanced at it the remainder of the evening. Prior to reading these messages from Georgia, he spent ten minutes in complete silence gazing out over the creek absorbing his thoughts following a spectacular evening with Noel Puckett. In all honesty the night started off rocky, and he nearly spun the vehicle around and took Noel home before making it out of Beaufort but thank God he hadn't. At some point everything shifted between them. Noel loosened up and became a different person—a woman like none other. Something about her changed him, too; being with Noel made Cavin want to be a different man, a better man.

Cavin hadn't purposely avoided the texts from Georgia, as well as other business-related messages, all evening. He usually kept a close eye on his phone constantly working on business deals, checking the stock market, and being available to address other important matters instantly during business hours and his personal time. However, something about the depth of the conversations with Noel captivated his attention compelling him to silence the ringer and notifications.

As the stars twinkled above the shimmering lake, Cavin felt zero remorse for missing these messages and calls or for not responding. His dad sent as many texts as Georgia asking for updates, and he even called around eight o'clock. He insisted on knowing how the rental vehicle ended up with four flat tires. Apparently their administrative assistant forwarded the news although Cavin wished she kept it to herself. He should have asked for her discretion about it, but he didn't even think of that when she returned his call on the fifth hole earlier today. Afterward they texted back and forth, and she secured a replacement vehicle, but once he returned to the house and everything ensued with Keaton, Cavin cancelled it. He gathered from the messages that his dad clearly wasn't happy about the situation or about not receiving an update on the potential business development opportunities.

Cavin thought about messaging Georgia and his father, but at this late hour he really didn't want to shift out of the state of bliss he felt after spending an unforgettable evening with Noel Puckett. He didn't want to go to bed with anyone or anything on his mind other than the woman who owned the candy shop.

After the relatively late night, Cavin slept an extra hour on Sunday morning, the first day of December. He texted Georgia while sipping a cup of coffee, letting her know his plans changed abruptly yesterday evening and that he had no phone access. He wasn't sure how else to word it, but he did apologize even though they never had specific plans. He also explained that he wouldn't be able to make the church service this morning but mentioned perhaps he could attend next Sunday.

Although most people took Sundays off, neither Cavin nor his father did. Therefore Cavin spent a good part of the morning on the phone updating his dad on the groundwork laid during his first two days in Beaufort. He filled him in on the many influential people he met and explained that business development opportunities were already presenting themselves. He shared details about the identified locations of interest and mentioned meeting the owners of the top two buildings on his radar and told him about spending time with them outside of typical business functions. *Wining and dining*, his father called the dance, and Cavin could hear him smiling through the phone.

Cavin also briefed him on the waterfront parking lot which the town of Beaufort owned. When he explained making friends with Georgia—being sure to highlight her positions as a real estate attorney and town councilwoman—as well as the mayor and other local dignitaries, his dad verbally applauded his efforts.

"Keep up the great work, Son," his father encouraged. "I planned on giving you a hard time about the flat tires and all the hassle my administrative assistant went through on her day off to secure the second vehicle you never required, but I will let it go since you have hit the ground running. As you know, weekends are either used for getting ahead or falling behind."

Cavin knew his father didn't care if the administrative assistant put in a few extra hours on a Saturday, but he let that comment slip into the salty Beaufort air even as the two of them worked on a Sunday. "Thanks, Dad."

The line grew silent for a moment.

"At least tell me what happened with the tires," his father asserted.

Cavin should have known the man couldn't actually let it go. "I think some teenagers were just out on a Friday night having fun," Cavin assumed because honestly he didn't have anyone else to blame. "A local mechanic pumped up the tires for me on his day off, so it all worked out."

"That is good because I thought you did something stupid," his dad chastised. "I hope you gave that fellow a good tip and showed him how much his business revenue would increase if he opened on Saturdays."

After all that transpired yesterday, Cavin realized he never even thought about paying Keaton, let alone giving him a tip. He should have. Later he would have to make it up to him; Cavin not only felt indebted to Noel's brother for the work but also for underestimating him.

Once Cavin hung up with his father, he replayed all the details of their conversation in his mind. This made him think of Noel and how much her candy store meant to her and her family. However, Cavin knew if he brought up that point to his dad, he would have heard, "Business is not personal."

Cavin spent the next few hours crunching numbers and drafting preliminary proposals for the properties he briefed his dad about although these offers wouldn't be formally presented until weeks later. A lot of research still lay ahead, and he needed to get to know decision makers personally, individually tailoring each proposition to meet the specific needs of the business owners and the community.

Each property presented its own unique challenges. Cavin needed to remain in the good graces of Georgia, the mayor, and the other town council members. Ultimately, since these matters usually came to a vote, he would need to convince the majority of the key players that selling the parking lot would benefit Beaufort as a whole. He could back up his proposal with sales figures and tax revenue data, but experience reminded him that he also needed to demonstrate that the loss of prime waterfront parking access would ultimately be a valuable tradeoff from the community's perspective.

Walt's interest in Noel's property posed a dilemma in regards to Cavin's interest in both his and Noel's buildings; however,

Cavin already determined the man's love of dollar signs and imagined he could make an offer Walt couldn't refuse. Walt's focus on purchasing Noel's property at a fraction of the value, and likely splitting the building into several smaller shops as well as renting the home above the store actually played to Cavin's advantage. Walt might also want to divide the home into a couple of small apartments.

While the revenue in Walt's plan appeared lucrative, Cavin's lens stretched much wider as did the budget at Cavin's disposal. Walt, an accountant who dabbled in real estate, understood money, but Cavin spotted red flags that revealed the man didn't have as much as he pretended.

As for Noel, Cavin knew he could offer her a more competitive deal than Walt and ultimately a fair value for the property. However, the idea of buying her family's building which happened to be smack dab in the middle of the other two properties stung him the most. Noel didn't seem to care about the money aside from having sufficient funds to meet the needs of her family and run the candy shop. Cavin hoped that time would lead him in the best direction.

After eating a salad for lunch, Cavin wandered onto the porch to stretch his legs and decided to walk across the street to the creek. The timing couldn't have been more perfect. As he neared the sidewalk, Cavin spotted Noel, Levi, and Laney walking in his direction, all three donning their Santa hats.

"Kevin," Levi shouted a moment later, noticing him before the others.

Levi came running up to greet him, and Laney followed behind while Noel continued to walk at a leisurely pace. Cavin couldn't help but notice a smile sprout on Noel's face as quickly as a wildflower bloomed in the spring nor could he contain his excitement to see the three of them, especially Noel. Truth be told he wanted to kick himself for not asking for her number last night at the end of their date. Fear hadn't held him back; he had simply been wrapped up in their conversations until the moment he walked her to the front doors of the candy shop which had to be the most interesting place he'd ever dropped a woman off following a first date or any date for that matter.

"Is this your house, Kevin?" Laney asked as her eyes widened to match the following statement. "It's big."

"For now it is," Cavin answered. "I figured you all would be working at the candy store today, maybe even managing the hot chocolate stand," he added as Noel came within earshot.

"Beaufort Candy Company is closed on Sundays," Noel revealed. "A lot of the shops close so that the owners and employees can enjoy a day of rest, attend church, or spend the time with their families. Some of the others close on Mondays or Tuesdays instead since those days are typically slower."

Cavin previously considered walking down there at some point today, and the idea struck him once more as he descended the steps a few moments ago. He would have been bummed to find the shop closed. "What are you all up to?" he inquired.

"Looking for Scout," Levi announced with excitement lining his little voice.

"The lost dog?" Cavin checked.

"Yep," Levi answered.

"Come help us," Laney requested.

Cavin looked to Noel for approval.

"You should come," Noel encouraged, stuffing her hands into the back pockets of her jeans. "It would be nice to have another set of eyes."

Cavin considered the alternative—working on the proposals. "If everyone else is taking the day off, I guess I should, too," he announced while imagining his father's ears burning right now.

"We need all the help we can get," Levi suggested, raising his walkie-talkie as high in the air as his arms allowed. "The police are on the case also," he announced proudly.

"We are junior officers," Laney explained, showing Cavin her walkie-talkie.

"That is awesome and impressive," Cavin replied. "Do you all have time for me to run inside and grab a couple of things?"

The kids shook their heads up and down, and Noel answered, "Of course."

When Cavin returned, Levi pulled a folded and crumpled sheet of paper from his pocket and handed it to Cavin.

"What is this?" Cavin asked.

"Open it. It's one of the fliers for the missing dog," Levi explained. "Scout's owner got hot chocolate from Laney and me yesterday. We didn't know it was him until he pointed to the flier on the nearby pole and asked if we'd seen his dog. Then when we told him we were going to find Scout for him, he brought back extra fliers for us to hand out and put up."

"He also gave us a twenty-dollar tip," Laney shared with bulging eyes.

Noel smiled almost as broadly as when the kids told her the story this morning before church. She loved their excitement about helping others, especially strangers.

Cavin nodded his head, showing his understanding. "That is amazing, you guys. What would you like me to do with the flier?"

"You like to talk to people so ask anyone who walks by if they've seen Scout," Levi instructed.

Noel hastily pulled a hand from her back pocket to cover the erupting giggle, and her shy demeanor caused Cavin's cheeks and brows to rise as he shot her a little grin in response.

"Yeah, and show them the picture," Laney added.

The four of them wandered the streets of Beaufort, specifically the neighborhoods surrounding Cavin's rental, for nearly two hours. The kids called out, "Here, Scout, here, boy," a hundred times as they surveyed every place a dog could possibly hide:

behind bushes, fences, cars, porches, and all kinds of other spots. They ran in and out of people's yards and knocked on front doors asking homeowners if they saw the dog on the poster.

Cavin and Noel often found themselves left behind, and they took full advantage of the opportunities to learn more about each other and engage in the occasional flirtation. When their eyes weren't on one another, they remained focused on the mission although the kids reprimanded them several times for being distracted. Noel and Cavin smiled obligingly but then carried on as the December sun moved high across the sky.

"Do the people here not mind the kids running through their yards?" Cavin asked knowing that where he came from they would be constantly scolded by residents.

"I love that you say what is on your mind," Noel complimented. "Pretty much everyone in Beaufort encourages the local kids around Levi's and Laney's age and above to run around and have fun. We adopted the *it takes a village* philosophy many moons ago. Most of the children are super respectful, and being able to roam freely is a perk of growing up in a small, safe town where everyone knows one another. We all have each other's numbers and know where one another lives and works. Those of us who are now parents and grandparents grew up the same way when we were kids, so we know firsthand how much fun it is to have the freedom to explore this place," Noel explained. "Plus, as you have witnessed today with these two communicating on the radios with the police, these two junior officers have a key to the city," she laughed.

Unfortunately they didn't find Scout on day one of searching. However, Noel was grateful they ran into Cavin after wondering when she would see him again. Not being accustomed to this dating thing, she never even thought about giving him her phone number. She supposed she would need to get used to it again because she liked him even more after spending the afternoon with him and the kids. She appreciated his silly banter with Levi and Laney, and the way he approached them on their level.

When Laney asked the next question, Noel realized she might not ever have to make plans with Cavin again; it seemed the kids and Mrs. Madelyn would do her bidding for her.

"Mr. Cavin," Laney started then paused as her investigative mind turned. "I think that's your name, Cavin, not Kevin. I keep hearing people say it differently than Kevin," she observed rather wisely for a youngster. "Aunt Noel is helping us make Christmas cookies to decorate tonight, and she is going to play the piano, and we're all going to sing Christmas carols. I was thinking since you took the day off from your work, maybe you have time to make cookies and sing songs with us."

Noel cringed a little wanting Cavin to say yes while also thinking it might be best if he said no. Then she thought about saying *maybe another night*, but he studied her with those eyes, and something in them told her that he needed time away from work with others as much as she did.

"You are right. My name is Cavin," he clarified, "but you two can call me Cavin or Kevin." As Cavin spoke, he glanced from the kids to Noel and back a couple of times attempting to gauge Noel's body language in response to Laney's question, but he couldn't quite read her.

"Yeah, you should come, Kevin, that way we have two boys and two girls," Levi pointed out. "And I think I want to keep calling you Kevin."

"Since you put it that way, I guess I could swing by for a little bit if it's okay with Noel."

"While the kids have you on the hook to sing with us, I guess I better not let you off since you did kind of agree to that yesterday," Noel teased and shrugged her shoulders.

Cavin laughed. "Did you put these two up to this?" he checked.

"I wish I could take credit for such a genius plan," Noel admitted.

A few minutes later the four of them climbed into Cavin's SUV, and he drove them to the parking lot next to the candy shop where Noel guided him to one of the spaces near the building designated solely for her residence. Then Levi and Laney excitedly led Cavin around back to a staircase on the waterfront side of the building. When they reached a quaint cast-iron balcony with a table and chairs for four overlooking Taylor Creek, Cavin took in the view with awe.

"This is the best view I have seen in Beaufort yet," Cavin declared to Noel. "And I have discovered some really nice ones."

"It never gets old," Noel guaranteed as she paused to appreciate the sounds of the waves and the salty breeze that blew in their direction.

Cavin could have lingered in that spot taking in the scene for hours, but the kids were eager to drag him through the door. With each of them holding one of his hands, he entered Noel's house for the very first time.

Inside he discovered antique furniture, a worn couch, a dated television, and carpet just begging to be replaced. However, the place smelled like candy rather than old flooring, and Cavin could tell that people well loved this home over the years. Toys scattered here and there along with drawings displayed on the fridge and cartoon character blankets draped unceremoniously over chairs reminded him that two children lived here with a hard-working single mom.

Cavin remembered Noel saying this house once belonged to her parents, and he realized she probably never found the time or energy to update anything or really even make it hers even if she wanted. He wished he could fly his family's staff here to spruce up the place for Noel and the kids. They would have it looking pristine in no time. However, all those thoughts drifted away as the cookies went into the oven because the aroma soon filled the air with another sweet smell.

While waiting for the dough to bake, Noel wiped a layer of dust from the piano in the corner of the room and opened the lid slowly. Lost in thought she pulled the bench from beneath the instrument and slid her body into place. Cavin watched her eyelids collapse as she felt the keys for the first time since losing her family members, and when she started playing a familiar tune, her face gradually pinkened as if the morning sun slowly rose on her cheeks.

When Noel sang the first line of Silent Night, the kids nestled in next to her one on each side and began singing along. Cavin, initially embarrassed to join in, soon realized he felt more comfortable here than at his own family's home. Together they sang three more songs while the cookies baked, only pausing to decorate the treats with icing along with red, gold, green, and silver sprinkles. Laughter filled the air as they made messes, but no one seemed to mind.

"You lied to me, Cavin Dawson," Noel scolded him playfully as the kids scurried off to their rooms to collect their favorite toys for show and tell with Cavin.

"What?" he asked dumbfounded. "When?"

"You can sing," Noel asserted.

Cavin grinned boyishly. "My mom may have insisted I join the school chorus when I was a kid," he revealed. "However, I did not lie to you; I clearly remember saying that I *may* be a terrible singer."

"The cat is out of the bag now," Noel stated matter-of-factly.

"I think it is pretty obvious which of us is the professional," Cavin complimented. "And considering the way your fingers danced across that antique piano, I can only imagine what your talent would bring on a newer, tuned instrument."

"Thank you," Noel replied shyly. "It has been a while since I tuned the piano."

"You are welcome," Cavin responded. "By the way I like how

you conned me into singing before playing golf with me."

Noel bit her lip through a smile. "I will still play golf with you, but I may be terrible," she reminded him with a playful wink.

Cavin chuckled heartily, and Noel joined in. They all proceeded to enjoy a fun-filled night packed with music, laughter, and cookies. After Levi and Laney put on their pajamas, they excitedly relayed to Cavin how Noel had them write down all of the Christmas activities they hoped to enjoy from now until the big day. Two seconds later they invited Cavin to participate in every single one of them.

Cavin, Noel, and the kids ended up spending every evening together for the rest of the week. In the mornings Cavin went to the gym around six o'clock and then worked tirelessly the rest of the day so that he allowed plenty of time in the evenings for the scheduled adventures. He researched, met people, visited businesses, and ate lunch with Jeff, Gerald, Walt, and others keeping his friends close and the competition even closer. He happened into Georgia at the gym nearly every morning which only came as a slight surprise since she recommended the place. They chatted, and Cavin slowly made it known that he only wanted a friendship. She didn't seem to mind all that much but still flirted and asked him to have drinks and go to lunch, but he declined respectfully. Georgia realized Cavin spent his leisure time with Noel as did everyone else in town.

Levi and Laney continued taking turns flipping the Days Until Christmas signs each morning when they woke up for school. When the bell rang, they hurried home to open their hot chocolate stand for an hour and then spent the remaining sixty minutes of daylight each day searching for Scout. Cavin and Noel helped them some, and Mrs. Madelyn watched the store while they went out looking equipped with posters and walkie-talkies.

Rudy bought a cup of hot chocolate from the kids every day that week, and they gave him updates on their search for Scout. It didn't take very long at all for them to make some progress. The first time they spotted the dog, Levi and Laney were ecstatic.

"He's so adorable," Laney avowed.

"He looks like a real-life stuffed animal," Levi added with a tickled grin.

They all just knew they would be able to pick up the little brown dog with the white splotch around his nose and take him home right away. However, Scout wouldn't come to them, and they ended up chasing him like a cat pursues a mouse.

That's when Cavin came up with the idea to bring treats along moving forward. Rudy told Levi and Laney that Scout always shied away from strangers, probably from spending so much time isolated on the boat, but he promised if they caught the dog, Scout would only lick them to death. They saw him a couple of days later but still couldn't get their hands on him, and at least one of them thought they spotted him in the distance on a few other occasions.

Georgia gave Noel and the kids a hard time about the sidewalk stand again on Monday after she learned no one filed an application for a permit, but Noel pulled her aside and told her if she spoke another discouraging word to her children, they would file a harassment lawsuit. As a seasoned attorney, the threat of being sued didn't scare Georgia one bit. However, Cavin spent part of his time on Monday researching the town rules on storefront selling, and he printed the document showing that owners had a right to the space in front of their businesses. Noel hugged him tightly that morning after he brought the document to her along with a cup of her favorite coffee. Of course he remembered to bring one for Mrs. Madelyn as well. With the kids back at school, he couldn't bring them hot chocolate, so he ordered hot chocolate from them every evening, providing a generous tip.

"The language in this document is open to interpretation," Georgia told Noel. "We can't have peddlers on the streets hawking their goods."

"Try me," Noel barked.

Noel spent her days making and selling candy, serving fudge, restocking the shelves, maintaining the display windows, and sharing the Christmas spirit with all who crossed through her threshold. She wore her Santa hat without fail even when out with Cavin and the kids. They picked out a Christmas tree from the local tree farm and decorated it at home while watching *Rudolph the Red-Nosed Reindeer*; they made gingerbread houses, sang Christmas carols at the local retirement home, went on a Christmas lights scavenger hunt, and even painted homemade ornaments.

Near the end of the week, Mrs. Madelyn asked Noel what she wanted for Christmas this year. Noel listed all the normal things, including the kids.

"I mean what do you want that you don't already have?" Mrs. Madelyn clarified.

Noel closed her eyes and let her mind drift to the thoughts that occupied it all week. "Someone to experience the magic of Christmas with," Noel shared with a telling grin. "Someone to hold and kiss and do all the things with that Fletcher and I used to do, but in our own way building new traditions with the kids that also include keeping Fletcher's memory alive in our hearts."

This week for the first time, Noel felt hope again while enjoying a healthy balance between her home and work life. Feeling inspired she stopped working after closing time, and she gave the fate of the candy shop to God during her quiet time each morning and at night while lying in bed following her unforgettable evenings with Cavin and the children.

"Might that someone be Cavin?" Mrs. Madelyn asked with twinkles in her eyes.

"I would really like that," Noel revealed. "I am just afraid that

I am going to fall in love with Cavin and then he's going to head back to Atlanta where he's lived his whole life and where his family's business is. He has no reason to stay in Beaufort."

Mrs. Madelyn placed her hands on Noel's shoulders as they stood in the kitchen alone. "I believe he has three reasons to stay here," she claimed. "I have been watching you two this week. I see the way you look at each other, and the way the kids adore Cavin, and the joy you all spark in his eyes."

"You actually think he might stay?" Noel inquired doubtfully.

"I told you I have been praying for a Christmas miracle," Mrs. Madelyn reminded her. "Talk to him about it, sweetie. That's the only way you will ever know."

Knowing Noel and Cavin needed some alone time together to sort out where things might be leading, Mrs. Madelyn offered to let the kids stay with her and Jack again on Saturday night so that Noel and Cavin could spend an evening without distractions.

Noel subsequently asked Cavin if she could surprise him with something special on Saturday evening, and he agreed. She then got permission from the elderly couple who owned the home he was renting to decorate it for Christmas. They said they planned on doing it themselves after Thanksgiving, but getting the month-long rental request at the last minute left no time.

Noel took Cavin out for dinner at Clawson's, and then they went to the Christmas tree farm for a second time to pick out a tree. She found out his favorite Christmas song, "Mary Did You Know," and invited him to attend church with her the following day. Noel actually talked him into getting two trees—one for the living room and another for the spacious front porch. The two of them decorated both, draped live green garland across the railing, and wrapped the trunks and low-lying branches of the live oaks in the front yard with thousands of white lights.

When they finally plugged in the cords, everything lit up at once. The yard resembled a Christmas paradise. Standing there wearing long coats and thick toboggans, Cavin wrapped his arms around Noel and kissed her lips for the very first time. He wanted to kiss her every day that week, but the timing wasn't quite right. The kids were almost always around, and Cavin also didn't want to rush Noel's first kiss since losing Fletcher. She talked about him a lot, sometimes like he was still there. Cavin wanted to allow her all the time and space she needed before things turned romantic.

The tender way Cavin kissed Noel made her melt on that cold December night in Beaufort, North Carolina. With glove-covered hands she held his face as their mouths moved together and their bodies became flush. Noel felt a warmth she longed for this last year, and she was glad Cavin waited until this very moment to kiss her. As he held her close, kissing her passionately under the moonlight, she felt certain that he granted her Christmas wish.

But then beneath the glow of all the bulbs when Noel asked Cavin if he could see himself staying in Beaufort long term, she watched his gaze fall to the ground between their boots. The conversation fell silent for an awkward moment, and it wasn't what Cavin said next that scared Noel but what he didn't say—yes.

Cavin told her that he loved spending time with her and the kids and wanted to continue seeing her while in Beaufort through Christmas but implied he wasn't certain where life would take him beyond that. He brought up his family and the family business as Noel expected, but for some reason he didn't seem to share the same hope as her.

22

As Cavin walked toward a crowd of people huddling near two large doors that led to a sanctuary, he realized he couldn't recall the last time he stepped into a church. However, when Noel invited him last night to hear her sing a solo Christmas carol this morning, he couldn't say no. She said her song would open the service, and afterward she would find and sit with him.

This past week Cavin silently wrestled with the connections he formed with Noel and the kids, and that's why her question about the future caught him off guard. He usually enjoyed time with women on his extended business trips—several weeks, maybe a month, but he never spent time with any of their children. He found something uniquely authentic about this woman who, rather than letting him into her bedroom, allowed him into her life, her whole life. Cavin didn't need to make love to Noel to know he was falling for her in a way he never fell for anyone. However, he knew that when Christmas came, this project would soon be over, and he wasn't sure what that meant about the bond forming between them.

During his drive, Cavin's mind bounced back and forth between fear of disappointing his family and missing out on this new budding romance when he slowly became aware that every house in the neighborhood was painted white, and the church he now stood in front of wore the same distinctive resemblance. He imagined there must be a significant reason, and most likely the historical society required the paint color. The well-preserved historic homes with a matching white aesthetic and beautifully lined by trees held a charming effect overall.

In a way the crowd congregating at the church reminded Cavin of the variety of people he saw at the restaurant where the band played the night he met Georgia. Some dressed in suits and ties while others donned jeans and sneakers, and the rest of the people fell somewhere in between. No one seemed bothered by the choices in apparel of the others as evident in the intermingling of each group. Of course Cavin wore a suitcoat, buttoned-up shirt, and tie because he learned that dressing nicely demanded attention and respect.

Cavin shook hands with strangers introducing himself to as many people as possible. He ran into the chiropractor with whom he played golf, and the man introduced him to his family and the pastor. Cavin spoke to the latter near the entrance and came across a few other familiar faces from his short time spent in Beaufort. Everyone seemed to remember him, and he knew his dad would be proud.

"Make a strong first impression," his father insisted, "and people will remember you the rest of their lives." As the years passed, Cavin realized his dad's words rang true.

Once Cavin made it into the sanctuary where old wooden pews lined a dated yet pristine worship area, he glanced around contemplating where to sit. Surveying his options Cavin knew the front row would make it easier for Noel to find him, but he didn't really want to park himself in the spitting section in case the preacher was one of those types. Nor did he want to hunker down near the exit appearing like he wanted to be prepared to make a break for it, plus Noel would have a hard time locating him there.

That left the middle in a space that probably held a couple of hundred people, and Cavin chose the only entirely empty pew in sight, closer to the front than back. Sitting down he began reading the bulletin the greeter handed him with a smile and a warm welcome. Over the next few minutes while studying the words on the bifold brochure, Cavin's peripheral vision caught a glimpse of people filling in the seats on his left and right. He peered up to say hello to those who sat nearby and waved at some of the others, and eventually he set the bulletin on the hardwood bench beside him to save a seat for Noel which felt really nice.

Cavin's and everyone else's attention suddenly turned to the stage when a woman stepped up to the podium and spoke into the microphone welcoming everyone to the service. She then encouraged the congregation to greet those around them and welcome the guests. Cavin shook hands with a handful of people who thanked him for joining them, and then the lady's voice chimed again.

"I want to welcome to the stage for the first time in far too long our beloved Noel Puckett who will be playing the piano and singing 'Mary Did You Know.'"

The crowd applauded, and a couple of people even let out big whistles surprising Cavin in a good way. The atmosphere then began to settle as the congregation took their seats. Cavin's heart skipped a beat when Noel, who looked like an angel as the heavenly rays of light shone down on her through the stained-glass window, floated onto the stage wearing an elegant yellow dress, black heels, and her patented Santa hat. She was absolutely radiant.

As Noel sat down at the piano and her fingers began to slow dance along the familiar ebony and ivory keys, Cavin realized he was among the few people still standing. The person next to him, whose presence he suddenly felt in the space he saved for Noel, was also upright. When Cavin sat, the woman with the sweet-smelling perfume he couldn't ignore also sat, but he didn't even look her way because he was so mesmerized by Noel and grateful she chose to play his favorite song.

Playing the intro, Noel couldn't help but notice two of the last people standing in a packed sanctuary. She peered directly into Cavin's eyes. Cavin immediately spotted the seriousness in her glare as her eyes darted back and forth between him and the person sitting next to him. It always amazed him how direct eye contact could be recognized from such a distance, but he knew without a doubt that Noel saw him. When he followed her eyes toward the figure beside him, the woman spoke.

"Hello, Cavin," Georgia greeted. "I am so glad you decided to take me up on the invitation to come to church," she whispered into his ear making their faces only inches apart.

Cavin wondered if his mouth fell agape as widely as it seemed in his mind. When he felt Georgia's arm slip around his shoulder letting her fingers dangle on his bicep, he found himself somewhere between cussing in church and passing out in the pew.

Noel, somehow still managing to stroke the keys, more out of rote habit than purpose, suddenly wanted to be anywhere else but here. The situation was upsetting, and as she tried to calm her emotions, the number of thoughts flashing through her mind in a blink became overwhelming. Why was she so upset—Cavin wasn't her boyfriend? They weren't officially dating, but she liked him and thought he liked her. They spent every evening together this week. She let the kids get close to him. The two of them shared a kiss, a magical kiss. She should be the one sitting next to him.

Georgia, wearing a painted smile and an expensive designer dress, kept her eyes peeled on Noel whose stature visibly shrank behind the piano as discomfort overtook her.

Cavin quickly realized that although he was in church, he wasn't anywhere near heaven; he was in the middle of two women whose attention suddenly turned to one another. As Cavin read Noel's and Georgia's faces, he quickly realized something climactic was about to occur. He felt caught in the middle of a duel between two gunslinging adversaries and expected to see desert sand swirling and tumbleweed drifting in the distance at any moment.

What were the chances that Noel and Georgia attended the same church? Actually probably pretty good in a small town like Beaufort, Cavin determined a bit too late. He knew Georgia was already on edge with him, and he didn't want to drive a wedge even further between them nor did he want to risk losing the connection he formed with Noel this week. However, Georgia went too far this time. She could have asked, *Is anyone sitting here?* or *May I sit with you?* But she hadn't, and she hadn't on purpose. Cavin's opportunity to do something about it quickly fell through his fingertips like a slippery fish desperate for water.

Noel knew this was her last chance to avoid this mess without looking any sillier than she already did. She felt like a teenager wanting to sit beside a boy who belonged to another girl. Maybe Cavin liked her, maybe he liked Georgia, or maybe he liked them both. Regardless Noel didn't want to play this game not at church, not anywhere. Rather than singing the opening lyrics of the song, Noel sat frozen in place stilled by overwhelming emotion. When the piano keys suddenly fell silent, Noel huffed a sigh into the microphone with tears streaming down her face. She never wanted to cause a scene, but she couldn't play a moment longer. She knew her vocal chords wouldn't make it through the song, so why even start?

"Oops," Georgia scoffed as the crowd began to whisper.

Noel exited the stage racing down the aisle like a runaway bride. The majority of the congregation possibly chalked it up to the emotional toll of her first public performance since her family's tragedy, but then Cavin stood abruptly, excusing himself all the way down the pew and drawing attention as people were forced to turn their knees or stand to allow him to pass.

When Cavin stepped over Georgia without a word, he heard

her say, "Cavin, where are you going?" loud enough for others to hear.

He thought about turning to answer but didn't. He spent his whole life being diplomatic trying to straddle the fence between his business and personal relationships. But now something told him to follow his heart—to follow Noel Puckett, no matter what Georgia or anyone else in the church thought.

As these thoughts rumbled through Cavin's mind like a stampede of wild horses, he realized he was the only person standing in the entire sanctuary and more eyes were on him than on the pastor who stepped up to the podium attempting to calm the worried crowd.

Cavin followed Noel's path even though he realized he, Noel, and Georgia would be the talk of the town after this situation.

When Cavin reached the massive sanctuary doors, they already closed behind Noel, and the gentleman who gave him the bulletin kindly pushed one open for him.

"I'm praying for you, my friend," the man offered in a sincere tone.

Cavin wasn't sure whether the guy chose those words because he realized Cavin was chasing after Noel or if he thought Cavin was leaving the service for an emergency or some other reason. Regardless he was thankful the greeter never asked why nor pressured him to stay.

When Cavin made it to the concrete platform leading to steps and eventually down a sidewalk paralleled by a cast iron fence and the downtown road where cars lined the street on both sides, he surveyed the area for Noel. Unfortunately he didn't see her anywhere. He hurried to either side of the building checking to see if she headed into another part of the church, possibly to get Levi and Laney who rode to church with Mrs. Madelyn and Jack after staying the night with them.

Cavin quickly decided he shouldn't venture into any other part of the church building in search of Noel. As badly as he wanted to talk to her right now, he didn't want to raise any red flags, especially in areas where children may be present. At that conclusion he began looking for Noel's vehicle which led him up and down the street and through an adjacent parking lot searching for her. He kept expecting to find her locked in her car with her head resting on her arms draped across the steering wheel like a blanket.

Two blocks down he noticed Noel's sedan pull out of a parking spot rather quickly, although not dangerously, and speed down the road away from the church. An instant later he glimpsed the unmistakable Santa hat—not on her head but sitting on the roof of her vehicle. When it blew off like a leaf in the fall, Cavin hurried in that direction hoping she would stop for it, but if Noel noticed, it appeared she didn't care enough to recover the beloved item.

Cavin jogged to the middle of the street to retrieve the hat Noel told him she wore for as long as she could remember. He held it high in the air hoping she would see him standing there from her rearview mirror, but the car kept moving away from him, its taillights fading quickly in the distance.

23

Cavin wasn't sure why he returned to the sanctuary after placing Noel's Santa hat into the passenger seat of his vehicle. He guessed he didn't know what else to do after the following text showed up on his phone while his head rested against the headrest: *Please don't come by, call, or text.* Five minutes later, Cavin tiptoed to an empty seat in the back row and halfway tuned in to the pastor's message about loving others regardless of how they looked or acted.

The preacher pointed out the uniqueness of their congregation made up of individuals from all walks of life—some wealthy, some poor, some middle class, some enjoying a joyful season of life and others experiencing loss or sadness. He finished with a note about the beauty of Christmastime while also bringing to light the loneliness it brings certain people. He reminded everyone to focus on giving this holiday season rather than receiving, and then the congregation sang "Joy to the World."

As Cavin softly joined in on the memorable words, he couldn't help but wonder if, after this morning, he would ever again have the opportunity to hear Noel play the piano and sing. After the service ended, he tried to sneak out the door quietly but got trapped by the pastor and all the questions the new person gets.

Ordinarily he wouldn't have minded, and the guy's calm and sincere demeanor made it hard to be annoyed by the conversation. Then the chiropractor and his family stopped to chat with him for a few minutes followed by the doctor who also played golf with them. The two men started bragging to others about Cavin's golf skills, and then Georgia once again surprised him in front of everyone.

"Lose my number," she politely whispered into his ear, and then with a grin followed by a snicker, she kissed him on the cheek.

Cavin's face turned a shade of red nobody had seen since summer sunburns went out of style. Not only did everyone witness what occurred, and Cavin didn't know how anyone would interpret the whispered words and the kiss, but then two seconds later, Mrs. Madelyn and Mr. Jack appeared with Levi and Laney in tow.

"Hello, Cavin," Mrs. Madelyn greeted while pretending nothing happened. "I want you to meet my husband, Jack," she added, gesturing to the man in the wheelchair she pushed.

Before Cavin could reach out to shake the gentleman's hand, Levi and Laney latched themselves to his legs like ankle weights. "Nice to meet you, Jack. I am Cavin Dawson," Cavin announced as he bent down to hug the kids. On one knee he found himself at eye level with the children and Jack whose wrinkly skin reminded him of his grandfather's.

"Hey, Kevin Dawson," Levi spouted, "I didn't know you had a last name."

"Everyone has a last name," Laney clarified, shaking her head profusely.

Jack and Mrs. Madelyn laughed.

"My last name is Brown," Jack inserted, chuckling. "Jack Brown."

"We are going to walk the streets looking for the lost dog," Laney shared. "Want to come with us?"

"We could use your help," Levi pleaded.

Cavin didn't have plans although he initially anticipated spending more time with Noel and the kids. At least the kids wanted to be around him. Regardless he thought about declining the invitation and preoccupying himself instead with work. That's what he usually did, and after all the time spent with Noel, Levi, and Laney this week, he probably had some catching up to do.

"Is your mom coming?" Cavin asked while he wondered if Mrs. Madelyn knew what happened earlier. He never saw her or Jack in church although he could have missed them. He figured maybe they helped in the children's area.

"She's sick," Levi declared.

Mrs. Madelyn explained further. "Noel messaged me not long after service started and said she wasn't feeling well. She asked if Jack and I would bring the kids home after church."

Cavin found himself wondering if Mrs. Madelyn knew the real reason Noel left church; however, Cavin knew she would find out sooner rather than later.

"These kids talked about finding that missing dog all night last night," Jack mentioned, "so we are extending our sleepover event and going on a hunt for him."

"If you don't have anything else going on, I could use your help pushing this old man," Mrs. Madelyn claimed with a laugh.

"Who are you calling old?" Jack contested with a grin. "I'm younger than you even though you are better looking."

"Older by a month," she acknowledged, whacking him on the shoulder with her rolled-up bulletin.

The gesture reminded Cavin of when Noel playfully punched him, and he wondered if Mrs. Madelyn having a bulletin meant she was in the service.

"But I act a lot younger; don't I, Levi and Laney?" Jack checked.

"You act like a kid," Laney claimed.

"And you're silly like a kid," Levi declared then giggled.

"The jury has decided," Jack teased.

Cavin laughed although he felt uneasy about the whole situation knowing that Noel wasn't happy with him right now. "Sure, I would love to come along," Cavin agreed anyway. What did he have to lose? This was all a simple misunderstanding anyway.

The five of them spent the next hour walking the downtown streets of Beaufort, North Carolina. The kids once again called out, "Here, Scout, here, boy," over and over while all of them looked in every nook and cranny possible. They radioed in to Rainey and some of the other officers giving them their coordinates and requesting assistance.

Cavin particularly appreciated the historical tour that Jack and Mrs. Madelyn provided. They shared a story about nearly every house or business they passed, and Jack explained that the white siding Cavin noticed earlier not only held historical significance but also was practical.

"Whitewashing with lime paint offered an inexpensive and protective option to coat houses and buildings in the South historically," Jack shared. "The lime paint repelled insects, prevented mildew, and reflected the sun keeping the temperature indoors milder during the hot summers when the only way to cool a house was to open the windows. Homes then came fans in the windows, followed by air conditioning units, and eventually professionally installed central heat and air took over. Folks also used to spend a lot of time with neighbors on porches which also stayed cooler thanks to the white paint and the shelter on top."

"Why is it still that way?" Cavin asked.

"Tradition, practicality, timeless character," Jack mentioned as slowly as he moved. "Around here we appreciate the history of our small town, and people like to keep as many things as possible true to their humble beginnings. Whitewashing is classic; the look never seems to go out of style which is the essence of this charming town with its simple coastal ambiance."

"I find all of this information fascinating," Cavin replied, appreciating Jack taking the time to explain everything in detail.

As the group moved along, the kids thought every dog they saw might be Scout, and they even ran through yards chasing pooches that ended up belonging to someone else. Eventually they realized the features didn't match the picture on the poster or the images in their heads from seeing Scout firsthand.

Early on in their search while Mrs. Madelyn and Jack talked to someone they knew on one of the porches, Levi pulled a folded and crumpled paper from his pocket and handed it to Cavin.

"What is this?" Cavin asked. "Something you made at church?"

Levi shook his head side to side. "It's a flyer of the missing dog for you to carry since you didn't bring yours," he explained. "Mom says you are our spokesperson."

"Remember to show them the picture," Laney added with a grin.

"You two don't miss much, do you?"

"What do you mean?" Laney asked.

"You notice things that happen around you, like realizing how I like to talk to people."

"I saw that Georgia lady kiss you today," Levi uttered with a scowl.

"Me too," Laney shared, snarling a bit.

Cavin wished he could crawl under the rocks that mirrored the sidewalk to the foot of the porch where Mrs. Madelyn and Jack were talking to friends. Any chance of Noel missing the town gossip today just went out the window. "I think she was just trying to be nice," Cavin explained, hoping they would buy that and forget what they saw.

"I wanted you to like my mom," Levi announced.

"Yeah, we wanted her to kiss you," Laney mentioned. "Not Georgia."

Cavin almost said, *Me too,* but then realized the conversation was with children, one of them being Noel's and the other basically belonging to her as well.

"But you can't kiss her until I say you can," Levi declared.

Cavin grinned. "Yes, sir," he replied, rubbing Levi's head while wondering if he would ever have the chance to kiss Noel Puckett again. "For now, let's find Scout," Cavin added, changing the subject before the Browns made their way back to the main sidewalk.

Unfortunately, the five of them didn't find the dog on their walk after church, and when Jack invited Cavin to join them for lunch, he declined respectfully, not wanting to push his luck. He knew how protective Noel was over these kids, and she was probably already going to be mad at him although maybe that would give him another chance to see her.

For now Cavin managed to irritate the two most important women he knew in this town, and both made it clear that they didn't want to hear from him. He knew how much influence Georgia held in the local politics, and he still hoped he could figure out a way to acquire Noel's building. However, he made that challenge more difficult by losing Noel's trust even though none of what happened with Georgia had been of his doing.

Cavin wheeled Jack back to the vehicle, and once all four passengers settled in, Levi rolled down the window and pointed at a man walking on the sidewalk in their direction.

"That's Scout's owner," Levi shouted.

"Hey," Laney greeted by waving proudly.

Cavin quickly realized it was the man who looked more like Santa Claus than any other person he ever laid eyes on. He remembered inviting this guy to the candy shop for a cinnamon roll on his first morning in town.

With his thin-framed glasses resting on the tip of his nose, the gentleman stopped near Cavin and enthusiastically waved at the kids.

"If it isn't my little elves," he noted with a chuckle, pulling at the black suspenders holding up the green trousers with his thick white sweater tucked in neatly. "Have you been keeping an eye out for my Scout?"

"Yes, sir," Laney vocalized from the opposite side of the vehicle.

"We just looked for him after church," Levi confirmed.

The man glanced at his gold watch. "You have been looking for a long time."

"We search for Scout every day," Laney announced.

Cavin smiled and extended his hand. "Hello, sir, I am Cavin Dawson."

"Hi there, Mr. Dawson," the man greeted, shaking Cavin's hand. "I am Rudy."

"Nice to meet you, Rudy," Cavin acknowledged.

"Kevin has been helping us look for Scout," Levi declared.

"Yeah, and he is helping us start a non-profit dog finding business," Laney added.

"Is that right?" Rudy said, obviously impressed.

Jack rolled down the passenger side window a few moments ago, and he and Mrs. Madelyn enjoyed listening to the conversation before joining.

"I don't believe I've met you before, Rudy," Jack stated. "I am Jack Brown, and this is my better half, Madelyn."

"It's an honor to meet you, Mr. and Mrs. Brown."

"You too, sir. Do you live here in Beaufort?" Jack asked. "We used to know everyone here, but I don't get out as much these days because of my age."

"I have seen you in the candy store," Mrs. Madelyn announced.

The man rubbed his belly. "You found my weakness," he laughed jollily. "Now that you mention it, I remember you from there as well, and there is also another really nice lady who's always there."

"That's my mom," Levi announced proudly.

"Her name is Noel," Laney informed the man.

"I met these two kiddos in front of the candy shop while they were selling hot chocolate, and I have been by for more several times this week," Rudy explained to all of the adults. "I am a sucker for little entrepreneurs and delicious chocolate."

"They're the best helpers," Mrs. Madelyn claimed.

"I imagine," Rudy accepted with a wink. "Are you two the lucky grandparents?"

"Family friends," Jack explained, "but we like to spoil these two, so we are kind of like grandparents."

"How about you, Mr. Dawson? Are you related to any of these wonderful people?"

Cavin grinned. "I must say I am merely a victim of the candy shop and hot chocolate stand just like you," he teased. "I am visiting the area for a while and made quick friends with this crew."

"Quick friends are often the best kind," Rudy announced. "You fine folks are welcome aboard my boat anytime," he invited, reminding Jack of the way strangers used to invite one another to sit on those porches he told Cavin about and talk until they became friends.

"You have a boat?" Laney asked as her eyes widened.

"My daddy had a boat," Levi shared. "But it crashed," he added solemnly.

"I am sorry to hear that," Rudy replied, frowning.

Everyone's faces told the story, and Rudy's expression dampened at the realization.

"It happened about a year ago," Jack shared. "We miss them dearly and ask that you keep the family in your prayers."

"I pray every day, morning and night, and as much as possible in between. I will gladly add you all to my list," Rudy promised with sincerity. "And to answer your question, Laney, as well as yours from earlier, Mr. Brown, I live on a boat."

"You do?" Laney questioned enthusiastically.

"I sure do. I travel all over the world," Rudy explained. "But I am not going anywhere else until I find my Scout." He reached into his pocket and handed a generic business card to both Cavin and Jack. "You all please call me if you see or find the little guy," he requested. "And do come visit me on the boat, it gets lonely out there."

"I sure will," Cavin guaranteed. He found this man fascinating and wanted to learn more about him. When Rudy first walked up, he almost expected him to announce himself as Santa Claus or Kris Kringle or maybe just Nick or Chris.

After the Brown's pulled away from the curb with the kids waving their arms out the back windows as if in a parade, Cavin continued conversing with Rudy.

"You should come out on the boat for lunch," Rudy suggested. "The crew caught fresh fish, and they're waiting for a reason to cook them."

The crew? Maybe that's what Rudy called his family. "Sure," Cavin accepted, thinking this opportunity could help keep his mind off Noel. "My vehicle is right over there," Cavin announced while pointing at the SUV. "I can drive us to wherever your boat is docked."

Five minutes later Rudy led Cavin onto the very boat Cavin and everyone else in Beaufort admired each time they walked along the waterfront—the largest superyacht he'd ever seen.

24

A day could make such a difference, Noel thought as she washed her face. Knowing the kids would be home any minute, she didn't want them to see her upset. This past week she felt on top of the world and appreciated the time spent with Cavin with and without the kids. She actually convinced herself she was ready to balance her life out once again by letting someone in. Now Noel didn't know if she ever wanted to see Cavin Dawson again.

When Mrs. Madelyn called to ask about taking the kids out to lunch, Noel almost said no, especially when she mentioned that Cavin walked around with them helping look for the missing dog. *How dare he* she wanted to shout into the phone, but she waited until she pressed the end button and then screamed into the thick air in her bedroom while pounding her fists on the mattress where Fletcher used to sleep beside her.

"Why didn't you warn me?" she yelled to her husband as if he might answer.

Noel wasn't sure how long she kicked and screamed and cried, but she knew she had to compose herself before Levi and Laney returned although she didn't know what to reveal to Mrs. Madelyn if anything. The woman knew her well enough to realize the difference between sickness and sadness. In fact Mrs. Madelyn probably already knew the real reason she left church if they stuck around after service even though she and Jack had been in the back helping with the children. All the kids loved hearing Mr. Jack tell Bible stories.

Noel wished she were working today to help keep her mind off Cavin, but the candy shop along with some of the other retail businesses in Beaufort closed on Sundays. Amid the hustle and bustle of a workday, she would feel more comfortable talking to her friend about this dilemma because if at any time emotions ran high, she could find an excuse to walk away. However, she didn't want to have that conversation at home, especially in front of the kids when Mrs. Madelyn dropped them off.

Maybe she would call Chelsea later after the kids fell asleep. Chelsea had been checking in all week by phone, texts, and visits just to hear the latest scoop on her and Cavin. "Tell me more about your business meeting," a text from her read late that Friday night after Chelsea and Rainey ran into her and Cavin escaping to Swansboro. She messaged back and forth with Chelsea all giddy like a schoolgirl. Now with the tide turning unexpectedly, she knew her friend would be there for her. The nice thing about tides related to the waterways was predictability; however, with people things often proved differently which Cavin had reminded her.

Perhaps Noel would beg Chelsea to have Rainey arrest Cavin or better yet run him out of town like the authorities did with troublemakers back in the day. That's what Cavin deserved for showing up here and turning her world upside down as if it wasn't already a hot mess.

By the time the kids burst through the door wanting hugs and kisses, Noel pulled herself together as much as possible, and their excitement elevated her spirits. Mrs. Madelyn walked in not far behind carrying some of their belongings while Jack stayed behind in the car for obvious reasons. Not only was taking the wheelchair in and out of the vehicle a chore in addition to getting him in and out of it, but also Noel didn't have a ramp, lift, or elevator that led upstairs.

Once the kids ran off to one of their rooms, Mrs. Madelyn's hug to Noel told her everything she needed to know.

"I am praying you feel better, sweetie," her dear friend uttered.

Noel knew exactly what it meant or at least thought she did. Then after Mrs. Madelyn told the children goodbye and the kids rambled for fifteen minutes straight about all they did with the Browns and Cavin, Noel's heart sank even deeper.

"We saw Georgia kiss Cavin," Laney spouted.

Noel's face contorted as she fought to stifle her emotions. "You did?" she double checked. "When? Where?" She didn't want to drag them into this adult nonsense, but the words just flew out of her mouth.

"At church," Laney answered as if Noel should know the answer.

Noel suppressed her desire to ask further questions. If the kids saw Georgia kiss Cavin, that most likely meant Mrs. Madelyn and Jack did as well. This news only further verified her suspicions. Cavin, the slick businessman, doubled as a ladies' man. He might get away with his shenanigans in a big city like Atlanta, but in Beaufort hiding secrets didn't come easy. A man couldn't string two women along without soon getting caught. The good-hearted people here would rat out the scoundrel without thinking twice about it.

By sunset Noel received four phone calls from friends asking about what happened at church, all but one mentioning Cavin and Georgia. Two of those friends weren't even at the service. Suddenly it felt like high school all over again, especially when Keaton called.

"I'll take care of him," Keaton promised.

"Keaton, stay out of it," Noel begged while hiding out in the bathroom and whispering. "You don't need any more trouble with the law."

"No one hurts my sister and gets away with it."

Not long after that Chelsea called to console Noel, and Noel could hear Rainey in the background sounding a lot like her brother, only a bit more diplomatic. Eventually Rainey asked Chelsea to put Noel on speaker.

"I will have a talk with Mr. Cavin Dawson about the way men are expected to treat women in Beaufort, North Carolina," he insisted.

"Rainey, you don't have to come to my defense," Noel replied, although having the same idea earlier with Keaton. "I am a big girl now, and I can take care of myself."

"I know you can, but I think this guy will benefit more from an outsider's perspective."

"Rainey, don't get yourself in trouble with the police department."

"I'm not going over there in uniform or on police business," Rainey clarified. "This is personal."

Chelsea chimed in. "Yeah, and I am in a good mind to slap Georgia across her pretty little face in the name of Jesus next time I see her. I can't believe the two of them kissed at church of all places, especially after Cavin saw how much he upset you by sitting beside her."

Noel sniffled. "I can't believe he had the nerve to do all that after acting like such a gentleman all week. I guess my conversation with him last night must have pushed him over the edge, and he just didn't care to hide whatever he and Georgia have going on anymore."

"That makes it even worse," Rainey exclaimed. "If anyone asks, we never had this conversation."

"Rainey, don't put your hands on him or threaten him," Noel pleaded.

"Yeah, Rainey," Chelsea agreed, glaring at her husband all the while wanting him to knock the guy out.

They all talked for a few more minutes before the kids knocked on Noel's bedroom door.

"Why is your door locked, Mommy?"

"Chelsea, I'll call you later," Noel uttered, using the backs of her hands like windshield wipers to clear her cheeks after ending the call and before opening the door.

"I was on the phone with Chelsea," Noel answered simply. "Where's Laney?"

"She's in the living room watching TV. We want to watch a Christmas movie."

"That's a great idea," Noel agreed, pulling Levi onto the bed and giving him a giant teddy bear–style hug.

They rolled around on the mattress for a few minutes having a hugging competition as they liked to do in the mornings when he jumped into bed with her.

Ten minutes later they were watching *Frosty the Snowman* while sipping on hot cocoa and munching on popcorn. Noel decided she would spend the rest of the evening with them not answering any more phone calls or responding to messages.

Cavin pulled into the driveway at the rental house about an hour after dark. He couldn't believe how much time he spent with Rudy today, who he found out was actually Rudolph Emerson, owner of one of the largest candy makers in the United States. The two of them talked business, golf, fine dining, and all kinds of other topics. The man seemed more down to earth than any billionaire he ever met. On second thought Cavin wasn't sure how many billionaires he'd met, but Rudy didn't act like the millionaires he frequently spent time around.

The man surprisingly shed a few tears in his presence. Losing his dog tore up Rudy like a child.

"Scout was a gift from my late wife, Eleanor," Rudy explained.

"Now I understand even better why Scout is so important to you," Cavin shared. "When did you lose your wife?" he asked sympathetically.

"About a year ago. Eleanor was my world. We did everything together. We traveled; we worked; we raised kids; we played golf; and we ate way too much," he confessed while patting his belly.

Cavin chuckled with the man in the midst of a sensitive topic. "Eleanor sounds like an amazing woman."

A gentle smile appeared on his ruby face, and Rudy nodded his head in affirmation. "The best."

The two of them talked about Levi and Laney, and Rudy told Cavin again how much he appreciated him helping the children.

"You like their mother, Noel, huh?" Rudy speculated.

Cavin thought about answering politically but then spent the next thirty minutes telling Rudy everything that happened between him and Noel from the first moment he laid eyes on her at Beaufort Candy Company until she drove away after church.

"Son, do you want some advice from an old man who has learned a thing or two over the years?"

Cavin found it ironic that Rudy called him son because his father would never have this conversation with him. Even if Cavin attempted to share his feelings, his father wouldn't sit still long enough to listen. In fact Cavin wasn't sure he ever talked about a woman to any man for thirty minutes.

"Sure," Cavin agreed, shaking his head.

"Cavin Dawson, you are a businessman, but you aren't your father," he postulated.

Cavin's brow furrowed. While they talked business earlier, Cavin told him about his family's company without revealing the details of why he came to Beaufort. He could tell Rudy saw straight through the "I am visiting Beaufort" line. The man was a genius that much became evident from spending the day talking to him, not to mention the fortune he made in his lifetime.

"What do you mean?" Cavin asked.

"My father was a lot like yours. I loved him and he loved me, and he meant well, but I couldn't be myself until I stepped out from under his wings."

"Was your father in the candy industry?"

Rudy chuckled. "Absolutely not. He owned a designer brand of clothing and became quite wealthy. He wanted to pass the business down to me, but it wasn't my passion."

"Making candy was your passion?" Cavin inquired.

"Living my own life was my passion," Rudy shared. "Eleanor was my passion. My kids were and are my passion. And, yes, being a candy maker is also my passion," he added. "Spend your time on the people and things that light you on fire, son."

"What does this have to do with Noel?" Cavin asked.

Rudy laughed so loudly his belly jiggled. "Everything. I used to be like you, and then I met Eleanor. She stopped me in my tracks. I believe there is a woman out there for every man who will stop him in his tracks, and he has to decide then and there if he is willing to make a sacrifice for her, or if he wants to look back five, ten, twenty years down the road and wish he had. Women like Eleanor and Noel are a once-in-a-lifetime kind of catch, and if you release her, the next man with his wits about him will swoop her up in a heartbeat," Rudy guaranteed. "It doesn't take a rocket scientist to realize that this Noel Puckett has stopped you in your tracks, but you have to decide which is more important to you—your business life or personal life."

"They are both important," Cavin attested.

"Of course they are," Rudy agreed as he pointed to the superyacht surrounding them. "I have made more money than I know what to do with, but the people I love are more important than this yacht, my houses, my airplane, and every other material object I own. It's not that you can't take any of it with you; it's that you would give it all up to have the people you love with you. Or at least I would," he shared, settling back in his recliner to think about Eleanor.

"You would give up all your possessions to have Eleanor back?"

"That's not really a fair question to ask a grieving man," Rudy rebuked him gently with a chuckle. "But yes, I would. I would paddle out of here on that dinghy you saw on the back of the yacht and live in the smallest house in Beaufort to have another life with my Eleanor."

"That is humbling, sir, but I cannot just walk away from my family's business. How am I going to make a living?"

"You can make a living doing what you love, or you can take advantage of struggling small business owners like Noel by buying their buildings to turn them into high-rise apartments and fancy restaurants. It's up to you."

For one of the first times in his life, Cavin was nearly speechless. "How do you know so much?"

"Are you asking how I know your father wants that building?"

"My father has never seen that building," Cavin pointed out.

"You don't want that building, Cavin Dawson, you want a relationship with the woman who owns it."

"Maybe I can have both," Cavin offered.

"You can't have both; the world Noel Puckett lives in doesn't work that way."

"Why not? Why can't my family's company buy that building and help move the candy shop somewhere down the road, or maybe even find a space for them in the newly renovated structure?"

"I like that you have thought about helping keep the candy store alive, but you can dig deeper, my friend."

Cavin sensed that Rudy meant something more than simply walking away from the deal. "If we do not buy the candy store, someone else will."

"Possibly but not if you dig deeper."

"What are you talking about?" Cavin investigated. "And how do I know you are not planning to buy the candy store? Maybe you are just trying to outsmart me with all this talk about following my heart and giving up my family's business for a woman I barely know."

Rudy nodded approvingly. "You are wise to consider all the possibilities and to rule me out as an adversary."

"How can I rule you out as competition? That candy store does not currently sell your candy. It is all homemade by Noel, Mrs. Madelyn, and those children," Cavin pointed out. "Do you even know why those children are selling hot chocolate and trying to find your dog?"

"Yes, I know exactly why."

"They told you?" Cavin questioned.

"They don't have to tell me. It's obvious," Rudy declared.

Was the man really that wise?

"They are doing those things out of the goodness of their hearts," Rudy acknowledged. "That's all I need to know. Their mother and those who came before her taught them how to do that, how to be a family. Because of that, the candy store will find a way to survive. It doesn't need me or you or anyone else."

"While I agree that the kids have good hearts, I am not sure I agree that the candy shop will survive."

"What makes you say that?" Rudy checked.

"I know things, and like I said, I am not the only one interested in buying that building."

"That doesn't surprise me. You know real estate like I know candy although differently because I don't think it's your passion. However, you still know to examine all the ingredients. If you dig deep enough, Mr. Dawson, you will understand that something doesn't taste right in this recipe."

The man mentioned digging deeper three times. Cavin knew he was pointing to something, but he wasn't sure what. He doubted Rudy was going to come right out and tell him. "Explain what you mean by digging deeper," Cavin requested bluntly.

"I would rather you be the one to find the opportunity to save the candy store," Rudy insisted, and their day together concluded soon afterward.

These thoughts and others about Noel and the candy shop ran through Cavin's mind the entire drive home, and now he couldn't wait to get inside and open his laptop. If there was something out there that he didn't know about Noel's business or building, he wanted to find out as badly as Rudy, Levi, and Laney wanted to find Scout.

As Cavin walked toward the door, however, a startling voice called out to him through the dark from the other end of the porch near the Christmas tree he and Noel decorated last night.

25

Cavin stood at the door as frozen as the top layer of the ice-skating pond he visited last December around this time. He wished he could teleport back there right now as the shadowy figure moved through the darkness toward him. Cavin thought about running even though all the person said so far was, "Hey, Cavin." The tone of voice used, however, instantly made him realize the intention behind this surprise visit didn't seem in his best interest.

Cavin recognized the individual immediately. "Hey," he replied sheepishly.

"I want you to see my face and hear my voice, so that you won't have to wonder who did this to you," the person scowled.

"Did what?" Cavin questioned.

At that moment a fist flew through the air at Cavin's face. He didn't have time to duck or dodge or even step back. Four hard knuckles connected with his left eye socket, the force of the punch sending him backward into an unforgiving porch wall. His whole face immediately began to throb, and he figured blood must be rushing to the site of impact although he wasn't yet sure whether it would pour out of a cut or fill a bruise.

Cavin instinctively braced himself for what might come next.

He wished he felt ready to strike, but he had never been in a fight nor been punched. Geez, his face hurt although the adrenaline running through him temporarily camouflaged the extent of the pain. Golfers and tennis players didn't usually run into these situations nor did businessmen, at least not until today for Cavin. Nonetheless he felt his defenses rise and after a moment considered swinging back at the perpetrator as he raised his hands to guard his face from another blow.

"I do not want to fight you," Cavin announced, his voice as shaky as the rest of his body.

"I just came here to give you a one punch warning."

"What?" Cavin asked, somewhat relieved yet still on edge.

"You need to leave Beaufort, or there will be more," the individual promised before walking down the steps nonchalantly.

On Monday morning with an unmistakably swollen black and blue eye, Cavin walked into Beaufort Candy Company with a Santa hat in his hand. He iced the eye last night and this morning, and although it helped the swelling go down some and tempered the pain, neither vanished. He also took over-the-counter pain medication from the local pharmacy he visited after the incident. The pharmacist warned him he would probably wake up in the middle of the night to a throbbing sensation requiring more treatment, and he had.

Surprisingly Noel was behind the front counter rather than Mrs. Madelyn, and while part of Cavin hoped he would see Noel here, another part of him hoped to avoid her because looking into her eyes only reminded him of whom he was walking away from.

Noel never saw Cavin walk in although she heard the bell jingle. When she finished ringing up the customer in front of her, Cavin stood across from her. Noel's mouth immediately gaped open as he began to speak.

"I thought you might want this," Cavin uttered, placing the Santa hat her parents gave her when she was a kid onto the counter.

"Oh my God, Cavin," Noel stammered, noticing the hat but not looking down at it. "What happened?"

Cavin grinned, let out a faint huff, and shook his head. He thought about saying, *I got what you thought I deserved* or *you won't ever have to see me again* or maybe even the truth: *I only wanted you, Noel.* Instead, he turned and walked out the door, thankful that neither the kids nor Mrs. Madelyn were anywhere in sight.

Cavin's feet moved quickly as he passed Noel's display window without looking in. He marched toward the parking lot where his rental vehicle sat fully packed although he had no idea where he was going when he left Beaufort.

Without thinking twice Noel raced around the tall counter with customers watching her just as intently as the congregation at church watched her storm out yesterday. She wasn't sure why she chased after Cavin Dawson—maybe because she felt responsible for his black eye or perhaps because she appreciated him bringing back an item that meant as much to her as nearly any material possession this world offered. With all that happened yesterday, she couldn't figure out where she left it. However, in the short time she had to process her thoughts, she figured that in addition to both of those considerations something about the genuine look on his face spoke volumes to her, saying, *If you let me leave Beaufort, you will never see me again.*

"Cavin," Noel shouted, his back to her as he turned the corner and disappeared behind the brick building.

Noel knew he heard her, but he never looked back. She jogged past the gingerbread house display window with everyone inside still watching her. She cut the same corner as Cavin, and just before he made it to his vehicle, she caught up with him, close enough to tag him if they were playing the game. But this wasn't a game; this was real life, and real life was messy sometimes.

"Cavin," she called out again trying to catch her breath as she reached for his arm.

"What?" he replied somewhat harshly as her momentum twisted him harder than intended. "Do you want to punch my other eye?" he barked.

Noel instantly let go of his bicep and took a couple of steps back. "No."

"Then just let me go, Noel, so you can go back to your life the way it was before I showed up in Beaufort."

Noel ignored the comment. "Who did this to you?" she questioned, staring at his eye.

"Why don't you ask around?" he snapped. "I am sure you can figure it out pretty quickly since you seem to be so good at coming to conclusions."

"What does that mean?" she retorted.

"It means I am leaving Beaufort," he informed her, "just like you and everyone else wants."

"Did you call the police?" Noel asked.

"Did I call the police?" Cavin quizzed with a furrowed brow. "Why?" he questioned. "Why do you want to know? Are you afraid that you or someone you know might get into trouble for this?" he asked, pointing at his aching eye.

"No, because I want whoever did this to you to be held accountable."

"You did this to me, Noel," he declared.

"Me?" she asked with a puzzled face.

"Yes, you. So I am not calling the police. I am just leaving," he reminded her.

"Cavin, I was upset with you yesterday, but I have never punched anyone in the face."

"We both know you did not physically punch me in the face," Cavin clarified.

"I didn't want you to get punched in the face," Noel explained.

"Well, that's kind of a lie, but I quickly came to my senses, and I certainly didn't ask anyone to hit you."

"Well thanks for telling the truth," Cavin retorted. "By the way, I told you the truth, too," he decided to add. "For the record since I now seem to have your undivided attention, I will tell you the whole truth. When I met Georgia and a bunch of her friends at the restaurant the weekend I came to town, she invited me to church, and the mayor and his wife invited me to their party that Saturday night. I told Georgia I would probably see her at both, but neither was ever a date. I was just trying to get to know people in Beaufort. I ended up forgetting all about the party because I spent that Saturday evening with you, and I loved every minute of it," he declared. "Well, that is kind of a lie," he clarified just as she had a few moments ago. "I almost turned around and brought you home by the time we reached the Beaufort line because even though I tried to be as nice as possible to you, you snapped at me several times those first couple of days and blamed me for things that were not my intention."

Noel thought about responding but decided to let Cavin continue because he seemed to have a lot to get off his chest. That's when she noticed that for the first time since she met him, he wasn't dressed up. He was wearing a pair of blue jeans and a hoodie.

"Then things shifted when you were transparent with me that evening when we went to Swansboro, and I am not going to be all cliché and say I started falling in love with you, but I could definitely see why someone would. I can imagine why Fletcher did. I loved every moment I spent with you and the kids this week, and I second-guessed nearly every decision I have ever made to this point in my life."

Noel didn't know exactly when she started crying, but she felt tears sliding down her face one by one as she stood there with her arms crossed while listening to this man pour out his heart.

"Yesterday I went back to the church service, but I did not sit with Georgia. After service, she randomly kissed me on the cheek. I was not even talking to her; I was chatting with some guys I played golf with. I do not like her, Noel. I like you!"

"Stay then, Cavin," Noel demanded surprisingly. "Let's get to the bottom of all of this nonsense like mature adults."

"I cannot stay," Cavin answered, wondering if her comment was an apology. "I quit my job which means between that and this black eye, I no longer have any reason to be here."

"But you work for your dad, for the family business. Why would you quit? It's obvious that you all are doing well."

"There is more to my story, Noel, and you are not going to want to hear it," Cavin acknowledged.

"I do," Noel reassured him calmly.

"I met a man yesterday who rocked my world," Cavin shared. "And you, you have been rocking my world ever since I stepped inside your candy shop. I decided I no longer want to work for my dad; I want to do what I am passionate about."

"Golf?" Noel queried, genuinely interested.

"Maybe, but I do not know for sure," Cavin replied. "I just do not want to do what I came here for anymore."

"What did you come here for?" Noel asked curiously.

"Our family business acquires land, buildings, homes, and pretty much any other type of property we find valuable, and we develop it. I came here to make offers on prime real estate so we could bundle it into a pretty package and make a fortune off of it. That is what I do, or what I did," Cavin explained. "I was working on proposals to buy the parking lot we are standing in, your building, the one beside it, and possibly others."

This news came as a shock to Noel, and she suddenly wished she'd previously asked Cavin more questions about his family business and his purpose in Beaufort.

"Is that why you took me out that first Saturday night to work your magic by getting to know me so you could woo me with some proposal?" Noel questioned. "Was our date really just a business meeting after all?"

"No," Cavin replied. "I took you out because I liked you. You are the one who called our date a business meeting, not me," he reminded her. "And if you choose not to believe me, you are welcome to turn around and walk away or punch me in the other eye or do whatever you would like. Either way, I am leaving Beaufort, and I am not calling the police, so take your shot if you would like."

Noel felt all kinds of emotions coursing through her body from her head to her stomach to her heart, and she decided to listen to the one she felt in her gut, the one Fletcher always told her to trust. Without saying a word, she stepped toward Cavin, raised both of her arms, wrapped them around his shoulders, and kissed him as passionately as she'd ever kissed anyone.

At first Cavin thought Noel intended to choke him, but then when her face moved toward his and their lips touched, he realized what was actually happening. It took him a moment to return her kiss, but it felt right even though part of him still wanted to pull away and drive off as planned. After a moment his shoulders relaxed, and he stretched his arms around her letting his fingers clasp together while he held her at the small of her back as if they were slow dancing.

Cavin wasn't sure if Noel tasted sweet and salty because she tried all the candy she made today, and they were outdoors not far from the beach where salt air made its way onto and into everything, or if it was only in his mind. Regardless, he liked it, and he couldn't stop kissing her.

Cavin's and Noel's lips moved in unison as their bodies flushed together while her hands traveled into his hair. Her nose then poked his black eye, and he pulled back and said, "Ouch."

"I am so sorry," Noel apologized.

It hurt, but Cavin couldn't help but snicker about it. "It is okay," he promised. "I am okay."

Noel's arms remained wrapped around Cavin. "You quit your job because you didn't want to take my family's candy shop?"

Cavin considered the wording. "Getting to know you, Mrs. Madelyn, Jack, Levi, Laney, and Rudy really woke me up," Cavin admitted.

"Who's Rudy?" Noel asked with quizzical eyes.

"He is the man who looks like Santa Claus and owns that giant yacht behind me."

Noel glanced over Cavin's shoulder. "Oh. Rudy owns the mega yacht?"

"Yes, do you know him?" Cavin asked.

"Rudy—Santa Claus's twin—has come into the shop a handful of times," Noel explained. "He's a sweet man. He told me we make the best chocolate he ever tasted."

"Rudolph Emerson told you that you make the best chocolate he ever tasted?"

"I only know him as Rudy, but yeah, if that's his full name."

"I guess you do not know who Rudolph Emerson is?" Cavin queried.

"Should I?"

"He is one of the world's most well-known candy makers," Cavin shared, then mentioned instantly recognizable brand names to further explain.

"You have to be kidding me," Noel replied.

"It is the truth, and Rudy is the one who encouraged me to speak the truth to you, my dad, and everyone else, no matter what it cost me. He said the temporary inconvenience would be well worth the outcome."

"Are you saying you're glad I came running out here and gave you a chance to tell me the truth?"

"I kissed you back, didn't I?" Cavin asked.

"You sure did," Noel remarked, kissing him again. "Is there anything else you need to tell me?"

"I will stay in Beaufort a while longer if you call off your dogs," Cavin offered, "and if you help me find a job."

"If you tell me who my dogs are, I will call them off," Noel promised, wondering if it was Keaton or Rainey who did this to Cavin. "And yes, I will help you find a job."

"Your brother was at my house when I got home from Rudy's last night, and he punched me in the face," Cavin professed.

"Cavin, I am so sorry. I talked to Keaton about what happened at church, but I asked him to let me handle it on my own. I never thought he would show up at your house and hit you."

Cavin looked at Noel like she was crazy. "Everyone in Beaufort knows that you were mad at me and thinks that I was leading both you and Georgia on; and your brother told me last Saturday before I showed up at the candy shop, that I better not hurt you. So, it did not come as a surprise when he showed up on my doorstep and punched me in the face."

"I will talk to him," Noel guaranteed. "All three of us can talk if you like."

"Okay," Cavin agreed.

"You said dogs, is there someone else?" Noel checked.

"Rainey knocked on my front door about an hour after Keaton punched me," Cavin proclaimed.

"Why?" Noel asked hesitantly although relieved to know that Cavin didn't have two black eyes.

"At first I thought Keaton showed up for more, but I turned the porch light on and hollered, 'I am calling the police' through the door, and then Rainey responded, 'I am the police.' When I verified who was on the other side, he took one look at my eye and said he came to ask me to leave you alone and leave Beaufort, but then he said that Keaton must have found me first."

"Do you think Rainey planned on hitting you, too?" Noel

asked, but before letting Cavin answer, she went on to tell him about her phone conversation with Chelsea and Rainey. "I promise I told him not to get involved."

"Rainey seemed calm. I do not think he came for a fight. However, you have some pretty intimidating people on your side."

"They know what I've been through, Cavin, and they don't want to see me get hurt."

"I understand."

"I will talk to Rainey as well. He's a good guy. Keaton is, too, he's just battling a lot of demons right now."

"Thanks, and if you will talk to them sooner rather than later, it might save me another black eye," Cavin requested. "How about that job?" he added.

"Have you ever made candy?" Noel teased but only half-heartedly.

Cavin chuckled. "Only for fun."

"Mrs. Madelyn says she needs to cut back her hours, so while we look for something else more lucrative for you, you could help me out. I know I can't pay you a fraction of what you make, but it might be fun, and I can introduce you to a lot of people in town," she offered. "Wait, you are a social butterfly; you already know nearly everyone," Noel laughed.

Cavin raised his eyebrows. "I am not sure if any of them like me anymore."

"If they see you working at the candy shop with me, they will," Noel reckoned. "And see us celebrating all the Beaufort Christmas traditions together, and walking the streets holding hands, and kissing," she added, kissing him another time.

"You really want to be seen in public with me after I seemingly humiliated you at church?"

Noel kissed him tenderly and then pulled back. "I've kissed you numerous times now in the busiest stretch of the waterfront district; I think everyone is going to know that we are an item."

"As long as you do not tell them we are business partners," Cavin teased.

Noel shrugged her shoulders. "Perhaps we will be both."

"Have you not heard the saying, 'don't mix business with pleasure?'" Cavin asked, grinning.

"When your business is your passion, it's always a pleasure," Noel proclaimed.

"Then maybe you will help me find my passion."

"Maybe you have already found it, and you just don't realize it yet," Noel suggested.

26

Of Cavin Dawson and Noel Puckett weren't already in love, they fell deeply in love one interaction at a time as Christmastime drifted along in Beaufort, North Carolina, much like the seas that surrounded the magical place. The Monday morning when Cavin decided to stay, Noel drove him to Keaton's shop where the three of them discussed the situation that happened on Sunday.

It took some convincing, but Keaton eventually gave Cavin his blessing to stay in town and even apologized for the black eye. Fueled by Keaton's willingness to believe him and trust Noel, Cavin offered to pay Keaton for fixing his tires which he had been meaning to do all week, and he apologized for all the accusations.

"You just treat my sister well, and I'll fix your vehicle any time you need me," Keaton offered, declining Cavin's money. After that Cavin and Noel dropped by Rainey's and Chelsea's house and hashed out the same issue. Rainey didn't seem to need much convincing although he told Cavin he was going to keep his eye on him for Noel.

"Fair enough," Cavin agreed when they shook hands.

"Would you like me to have a conversation with Keaton about punching you in the eye?" Rainey asked. "I'm happy to do that off the clock to avoid legal involvement."

"No thanks," Cavin decided immediately. "It is water under the bridge."

When Mrs. Madelyn showed up for work this morning prior to Cavin's arrival with the Santa hat, she informed Noel of the alarmed expression on Cavin's face when Georgia kissed him on the cheek. That was all the reassurance Noel needed to make an informed decision about her true feelings although she never expected him to hurry out of the store so suddenly. Cavin felt relieved to know that following his resignation from his family's company, he was no longer required to socialize with Georgia or anyone else in town, for that matter, unless he desired to do so.

As soon as Cavin and Noel completed that first order of business, Noel brought Cavin into the candy shop kitchen and began showing him how they made candy from start to finish. The seemingly perfected processes amazed Cavin. Even though Noel previously mentioned making all the candy in-house, the complexity in each recipe which involved combining sugar and other ingredients and flavorings to create a variety of colorful hard candies, gummies, caramels, and chocolates perplexed him. Watching the machines then individually wrap each piece reinforced to Cavin how special the store was to Noel and her family.

The two of them worked together in the back for a week although Noel left him while she helped up front sometimes, and Mrs. Madelyn wandered into the kitchen every now and then to show Cavin a few tricks of the trade as well. Noel made him wear an apron along with another item which caused him to feel silly and special at the same time. On the first day after Cavin agreed to work in the store, Noel asked him to wait in the kitchen while she ran upstairs.

"This Santa hat was my dad's," Noel told Cavin when she returned, wearing the one he brought back to her and holding another out for him. "I want you to wear it."

Cavin studied the noticeably worn red and white garment, and he couldn't help but wonder how many years Noel's father wore it. The white collar-like area remained puffy although slightly yellowed but not enough to warrant replacement. No one made them like this anymore, not with the same quality craftsmanship.

"Noel, this hat is special to you and your family. I can't wear it," Cavin protested. "What if I mess it up or lose it?"

"Cavin, it just sits in a box upstairs. I would rather someone wear it, and it just happens to fit you," she pointed out after pulling it over and messing up his perfectly parted hair for the second time that day. He never seemed to mind when she was kissing him, so she figured it would be okay.

"Are you sure?" Cavin asked, his eyes directed upward toward the hat unable to view it properly now sitting atop his head.

From that moment on Cavin proudly wore the hat knowing full well he could never fill the shoes of the man who once wore it. Something about him wearing it brought comfort to Noel, so it made him feel good, too.

Cavin knew the kids helped in the candy shop, and even though they weren't around much during business hours because of school, their knowledge of everything associated with the family business astonished him. They knew ingredients, recipes, where items were kept, and how things worked. They mastered the hot chocolate process, and each day after school, they continued to run their stand. One day it rained, and they helped Cavin in the kitchen and taught him things beyond his expectations.

Cavin had no idea how Noel, Mrs. Madelyn, and the kids accomplished all this work on their own over the past year. He felt like someone needed to be in the kitchen full time who would benefit from an assistant like himself although perhaps more qualified. He made quite a few mistakes, but everyone always seemed to laugh it off when he burnt a pie, forgot an ingredient, or dropped a whole batch of unwrapped candy on the floor.

Cavin and Noel continued to hang up their aprons at the end of each day to wander around Beaufort with the kids looking for Scout and pinning up more fliers. One evening they finally cornered Scout near the Harvey W. Smith Watercraft Center where onlookers stood on a balcony overlooking boatmakers as they crafted a traditional wooden boat. Cavin remembered wanting to visit the place on his first day in town but never would have imagined it would happen this way. As they slowly moved toward him calling out his name, Scout, suspicious of strangers, evaded them by running right through Levi's legs then darting into the nearby building—featuring large openings on both the street and waterfront side—and through the crafters nearly causing their work of art to collapse.

Thankfully, the seasoned team steadied the vessel as Noel, Cavin, Laney, and Levi chased behind the dog hollering "Sorry." The extra show only excited those standing above who took the time to take in the unique sights, smells, and sounds the facility offered as the crew built boats from start to finish. Scout proved to be quite the elusive animal. Although a missed opportunity to catch him, they still reported it to Rudy who expressed relief just knowing Scout remained safe out there.

"When do I get to work out front?" Cavin asked Noel one afternoon as the two cut fudge together.

Cavin couldn't decide which he liked better working across from Noel gazing into her eyes as they chatted or standing next to her where their arms frequently touched. Mrs. Madelyn caught them kissing in the kitchen several times. On each occasion she either quietly slipped out while grinning to herself, or if they noticed her, she excused herself saying something like "I'll come back later" as they blushed. She often privately expressed to Noel how much joy it brought her to see the two of them so happy.

"We can't have you working in front of the customers with that black eye," Noel teased one day. "If it doesn't heal soon, we might have to get you a pirate patch."

Cavin formed a laugh. "You are so funny."

"Pirates are a big part of Beaufort's culture," Noel insisted. "Blackbeard himself had a house here that still stands to this day. During the warmer months, we have a boat called Beaufort Pirates Revenge that gives tours, and the characters perform reenactments. There are also various events where locals as well as visitors dress like pirates. So, don't be surprised if at any time you see pirates walking the streets."

The next day Cavin showed up for work wearing an eyepatch along with his Santa hat which caused Noel and Mrs. Madelyn to erupt in laughter. The kids loved the look, too—so much that they fell to the floor in a cascade of giggles as the sound of the cane echoed across the shop every time he tapped the wooden boards. In full character, Cavin used a deep, gravely pirate accent which was the icing on the cake, and Noel appreciated the amusement he brought to their lives.

"You may look the part of an experienced pirate, but you have much to learn before you can step onto the floor," Noel teased, although somewhat serious. Her parents always preached that anyone who worked in the candy shop must first learn the ropes in the kitchen in order to explain the processes fully to the customers when out front.

With pirates still in mind later that day after school, Noel and the kids took Cavin to the Old Burying Ground, a popular historic cemetery in Beaufort. Enclosed by a black cast iron fence and covered by a canopy of mature live oaks and other shade trees, dirt paths led through tattered gravesites. The kids were eager to show Cavin the site where a child buried in a keg of rum after dying at sea rested in peace. While the legend of the child's preservation fascinated all who heard it, the many items left to decorate her tombstone included a variety of toys, shells, and all sorts of other trinkets that caused the site to stand out to this day.

Captain Otway Burns and the crew of the *Crissie Wright* also lie buried there after battling a fierce January storm in 1886 which caused their schooner to run aground. This story hit way too close to home causing Noel's eyes to get misty. As Cavin read the placard, Noel held him close as she sniffled trying not to let the kids see or hear her response. Although Captain Fletcher Puckett rested elsewhere, Noel thought of him every time she walked or drove by a cemetery, and this marked the first time she stepped inside the gates of one since her husband died.

By the time they left the grounds, Cavin added the cemetery, of all places, to his top ten favorite spots in Beaufort. After that day Noel decided to face another fear with Cavin Dawson. She walked out on a pier near the end of the Beaufort waterfront, now decorated with strands of Christmas lights streaming from one pylon to the next, and they sat beneath a blanket of stars with their feet dangling above the creek. She told him about her avoidance of all bodies of water since the accident, pointing out that the closest she came to the sea since then was when she and Cavin walked together along the Swansboro waterfront.

The days leading up to Christmastime continued to fly by. The kids brought home all sorts of festive projects from school, and eventually, when Christmas break came around, they were as ecstatic as if they had been given permission to eat all the candy in the entire shop. Finally promoted to work in the front of the store like everyone else Cavin floated from one place to the next arranging candy and pointing people in the right direction. The customers loved him, as Noel knew they would, and she found herself wishing he would stay around, but she knew that things would change soon.

The kids talked Cavin and Noel into going fishing which Cavin called ice fishing because of the bitter cold Sunday afternoon. However, Laney and Levi kept pointing out that no ice topped the water. They caught several fish, and Levi and Laney handled them like pros which impressed Cavin. It was obvious they spent time on the water with Levi's dad of whom they talked highly.

Noel, Cavin, Laney, and Levi continued marking things off their Christmas bucket list including attending the Beaufort Christmas parade, an event the candy shop donated a lot of the treats to that people tossed into the crowd from the antique cars, Christmas character floats, and Santa's sleigh. Somehow Levi and Laney still ran to grab the goodies as if they had never eaten a piece of candy in their whole lives.

Next up was the annual Christmas Flotilla which featured a parade of decorated boats lighting up the waterway as they floated past the balcony attached to Noel's waterfront home above the shop, one of the best views in all of Beaufort. Although the dock across the street from Cavin's rental would have also provided an amazing view, he was grateful not to watch it there. He didn't want to think about losing the place, especially because so far he failed to find another option in Beaufort to fit his budget—a fraction of what used to be at his disposal—even though he saved nearly every penny made at the shop.

The Christmas Candlelight Tour proved quite special, and Cavin cherished the local stories told by those in the historic homes and buildings. The Old Beaufort Jail, constructed around 1829, contained lively ghost stories and was one of Cavin's favorite haunts. He found out the building had been relocated from its original site on Cedar Street to the Beaufort Historic Site to ensure preservation and serve as a museum. At the former location the jailer and his family surprisingly lived on the premises with the prisoners. The Beaufort Historical Association did a fine job maintaining much of the town's history which fascinated Cavin.

On the Saturday evening before Christmas, Cavin, Noel, and the kids walked to the Olde Beaufort Farmers' Market's Olde Fashioned Holiday Market on the courthouse grounds. Winding pathways filled with vendors who decorated their tents festively with Christmas lights, garland, trees, ornaments, and all sorts of other trimmings transformed the area into a magical wonderland cloaked beneath a canopy of live oak trees.

Although neither Noel nor Cavin had much money to spend, and the kids were saving theirs to help save the candy shop, they each purchased a few handmade Christmas gifts. They sipped hot chocolate as they strolled from one vendor's booth to the next, appreciating the amazing stories of how these local artisans handcrafted the unique goods they sold. They enjoyed candy apples made by one of the area farmers as they listened to a hometown musical group sing traditional Christmas carols.

When Cavin left the market, the Christmas spirit warmed his heart more than ever even as the cold crawled up his skin. Spending nearly the whole month with Noel, Levi, and Laney turned out to be more special than he could have imagined even though he had to sacrifice so much. However, peace didn't come with a price tag, and his father tried to remind him of that by sending a proposal to buy Noel's family's building for development. As soon as Noel opened the packet and realized its contents, she handed it to Cavin who stood behind the front counter with her in their matching Santa hats, looking like the perfect couple.

"Right now, I don't even want to know what the offer is," Noel declared as Cavin glared at the documents wanting to rip them to shreds, "but I have to tell you something."

The kids just stepped outside to flip the Christmas countdown sign to a mere two days, a process that always seemed to evolve into other sidewalk fun before the store opened on the "Eve of Christmas Eve," as Noel's mother always used to call it. Mrs. Madelyn was busy in the kitchen baking. Facing her fears with Cavin seemed a little easier to Noel, so as the cuckoo clock sounded behind her, she told him she planned to close the candy shop at the end of the year.

After providing an explanation and shedding several tears while Cavin held her closely, he replied, "Are you telling me I am going to lose a second job in less than a month's time?" Cavin's timely comment made her chuckle and eased the tension if only temporarily.

Cavin lost way more than his job when he walked away from the family business. Within the week of quitting after his father's initial shock wore off and his attempts to talk Cavin out of his decision failed, he retaliated by cutting Cavin off from all the comforts he knew. Cavin instantly felt the impact of the losses. Admittedly, he never previously considered the magnitude of resources that he would lose as a result of his decision.

Cavin had no assets in his name—not a vehicle, house, boat, computer, bed, couch—the list went on and on. He didn't even know if he owned the clothing in his suitcase or those at his apartment in Atlanta or any of the other belongings there. The business owned everything. His dad never paid him a salary; Cavin simply used the business credit cards to buy whatever he wanted within reason. Now his transaction attempts caused an embarrassment when he tried to pay for himself, Noel, and the kids to watch a Christmas play and then again when an employee swiped his card at the general store because his father froze the cards. Cavin had no money in the bank; he didn't even have a personal banking account.

Someone from the car rental company came to pick up the vehicle a couple of weeks ago, and the family who owned the house on Front Street showed up at the front door early one morning and told Cavin that the company renting their home called and terminated the lease agreement. "They didn't ask for any money back; they just said the employee staying in the house should be evicted," the gentleman informed Cavin.

Learning that news hit Cavin hard, but then he experienced small-town hospitality at its finest after he and Noel explained the whole story to the owners later that day. Cavin couldn't contain his tears when the cute elderly couple told him he could live in their home through the end of December without any additional charge. They said they wouldn't say a peep to his family's business if anyone asked. "This deal is all based on a handshake and a hug," the lady promised Cavin.

Both Cavin and Noel shared private details with each other this month that they never trusted with anyone else, and when Noel told Cavin that she planned to meet with Walter Benson, who recently brought in a new proposal of his own for the candy shop building, Cavin asked if he could join them.

"This is the world I have lived in my whole life," Cavin reminded her. "I might be able to help with the negotiation."

Cavin imagined that even under the circumstances or possibly especially because of the circumstances, his dad would pay way more for the building than Walt would offer, so he decided to keep that card in his back pocket. On a positive note if one existed after hearing Noel's sad news, two offers now existed which gave Cavin an advantage during negotiations. In that regard the business development proposition from his father could turn out to be an early Christmas gift in a year when Cavin knew he wouldn't be getting anything else from his parents. He just needed to make sure to frame everything to his dad in monetary terms rather than letting him know that he would be doing Noel a favor on his behalf.

"I would love to have you there when I meet with Walter," Noel answered, relief lining her shaky voice.

The next day the three sat at a long table in Walt's conference room along with Georgia, who Cavin and Noel soon learned represented Walt as his attorney. Thankfully, neither Walt nor Georgia knew of Cavin's prior interest in Noel's building, nor did they know the type of work Cavin did with his family's business. Still both Walt and Georgia appeared nervous with Cavin's presence. On several occasions Walt suggested that he didn't think Noel's father would want an outside party present during the private negotiations.

Those statements waved the second red flag Cavin noticed before their meeting with Walter Benson officially started. The first to climb the pole was Georgia's mere presence. Her being there, especially on short notice, was unusual this early in the game. Nonetheless during the meeting, Cavin remained relatively quiet because he didn't want to play his hand too soon. He did pick up on the way Walt and Georgia carefully selected their words, and even more so he noticed the ones they failed to mention.

Two other major red flags that flapped repeatedly in Cavin's mind occurred near the conclusion of the meeting. First, Walt and Georgia informed Noel that she had until the end of Christmas Day to either accept or decline what they described as a lucrative offer. After that, they said the amount would drop significantly. Following the meeting, Noel told Cavin the latest offer was the highest Walter ever brought to the table even after previously warning her that any subsequent offers would be lower. And the pushy deadline didn't make sense, especially right at Christmastime, with Noel swamped in holiday business at the candy shop.

The final red flag popped up when the potential buyers stated that Noel couldn't take the proposal home with her. They told Noel she could take her time reading over it in the conference room or stop back by to study it at the office anytime at her leisure, but they claimed they didn't want anyone else knowing about the offer because of their top secret plans for the place.

When Cavin realized Noel was about to agree to their ridiculous terms, he demanded that they let Noel take the document home to look over it. He crafted his words carefully, trying not to mention ethical industry-specific business standards, but instead asserted that Noel deserved an opportunity to read through the details and look at the figures without feeling pressured. At that moment when Walt and Georgia locked eyes, Cavin could hear Georgia's silent communication: *The document is too lengthy, and Noel is too busy; she won't take the time to read the fine print, nor will she understand it.*

Later that night after spending time with Noel and the kids checking fun Christmas activities off their list, one by one, Cavin proceeded to read every single word of the lengthy legal proposition Walter and Georgia drafted in addition to the one that arrived from his father.

Over the years Cavin wrote countless rough drafts of such documents, and although his family's company kept attorneys on retainer who were extremely skilled in fine-tuning the proposals, Cavin felt confident analyzing every word. In Walter's pitch the terminology didn't quite add up, and ironically, Cavin was grateful to have his family's business proposition available for side-by-side comparison. Some of the language in Walter's document was deliberately vague, especially early in the proposal, and then near the end as Cavin's eyes grew weary, he discovered the golden nugget.

27

"Noel, I read through the proposals last night," Cavin shared in the kitchen after saying hello to Mrs. Madelyn who let him in the front door of the candy shop thirty minutes prior to his shift.

"The proposals? Both of them?" Noel asked with a deliberate emphasis on her wording. "That huge document Walter and Georgia gave us and the heavy packet your father mailed?"

"Yes, I studied every sentence and dissected the more important ones," Cavin explained.

"You read every page?" she questioned again, astonished. "Every word?"

"Yes," Cavin replied.

"No wonder you look so tired."

Cavin wiped his eyes overlooking the comment. "I think I discovered something we need to look into before you make a decision."

"Okay," she accepted appreciatively, remembering the time on the clock after he kissed her goodnight and realizing he must have barely slept. "What did you find?" she wanted to know.

"Well, I prefer not to get your hopes up, so I need to ask you a few questions and look at some other legal documents and financial statements with your permission," Cavin stated.

"I don't understand. The offers are what the offers are, right? I mean, what else is there to consider?" Noel questioned.

"I need you to trust me," Cavin insisted. "I also need the day off, please," he requested knowing it would take time to dig into the particulars.

"Sure," Noel agreed, assuming she had little to lose at this point.

"I need to see your corporate tax reports from last year and your quarterly reports from this year," Cavin requested.

Noel's face suddenly displayed confusion. "Walter has all of those documents," she explained. "I simply meet him at his office to go through the numbers and then sign the paperwork and write the checks."

"I thought you might say that," Cavin responded. "So, he does not provide copies for your records?"

"No, he says with everything being electronic there is no need for printed copies. Also, he knows how confusing all the business accounting is to me. Dad used to handle all the taxes, so ever since he passed away, Walter took the reins."

A lightbulb began to glow so brightly in Cavin's head that he wondered if golden rays flowed from his ears. "How long has Walter been handling the Beaufort Candy Company's taxes?"

"Well, you see Walter's father passed not long before my family's accident. At the time Walter was working for a large firm in Virginia, but his dad willed the local accounting practice to him, so Walter moved back here to run the business and manage his family's properties."

"That is interesting," Cavin replied, not sure what to think of this news. "Did your dad like Walter?" he asked.

Noel snickered. "Not at all. He loved his dad, but Walter is greedy. Dad talked about switching accountants after Walter took over the company, but he said he had some unfinished business to handle with Walter."

The light in Cavin's head grew even brighter. "Things are starting to make sense," he stated.

"How come?"

"I think I am onto something, but again I want to wait to explain my theory because I could be wrong, and it would take a lot of time which is one thing we do not have. There is a lot going on here, and I am trying to understand all the motives."

Noel wondered what that meant, but like Cavin said it seemed to make sense to wait. "Dad always said Walter seemed more interested in buying his client's buildings than helping them build their businesses," she mentioned. "His family owns a lot of property in town."

"Your dad was a smart man," Cavin concluded. "Do you think Walt will let me look at the tax records?"

Noel shrugged. "I guess if I were with you, he might," she said as she glanced at her watch. "But I have to open the store, and without you here to help in the kitchen, I'll have to spend a little more time prepping today."

"Right, sorry about that," Cavin apologized genuinely.

"I can call Walter and tell him I gave you permission to look at the company's taxes," Noel suggested.

While that sounded like a good idea, Cavin decided he didn't want Walt to see this coming. Cavin already saw how territorial the guy seemed, and if Walt was capable of what he suspected, Cavin didn't want to give the man and his lawyer friend, Georgia, any extra time to cover up the evidence.

"Actually, I have another idea that will give me access to some of the data needed," Cavin mentioned. "You have point of sale software here at the store, correct? With the capability to look at daily, monthly, and yearly sales?" he checked.

"Yes, we do," Noel reported. "I look at it every day. Walter also gives me a document with daily, monthly, and yearly sales goals we need to reach to cover all the expenses."

Cavin furrowed his brow. "Oh, really?" So, he gave Noel access to that printed document but not her tax records. Cavin held his finger to his chin for a moment as the wheels in his mind churned. "Do you ever meet those goals?"

"Rarely," Noel confessed although embarrassed. "That's why I have to sell the building and my equipment so that I don't lose everything."

"Do you know the individual amounts of your expenses?"

Noel shook her head side to side. "No, I place all the orders, and Walter handles the invoices. Everything goes straight to him to save me time. Even though I don't care for him, that's one thing I have been thankful not to have to deal with, and he hasn't gone up on the accounting rates, at least not yet."

Cavin felt all jittery inside, and he hoped that after he cracked this case, Noel's brother would change his mind about his investigative abilities. Something fishy was transpiring here, and Cavin was going to get to the bottom of this murky water.

"Interesting. Do you have time to show me the point-of-sale platform really quickly?" Cavin didn't typically look at data on such interfaces, but ultimately, he often analyzed numbers that came from that very source.

"Yeah, I can actually pull it up on my phone and give you a quick tutorial of the application before we open, and then you can spend however much time you need researching the numbers."

Cavin grinned. "That will be perfect, and I will be right here in the store with you for a while in case you need any help," he mentioned. "I would also like to see the goals Walter created."

Noel spent the next ten minutes reviewing the point-of-sale program with Cavin, ultimately directing him to the numbers of interest. With Noel's permission Cavin snapped photos of the data and of the goals. Like Noel mentioned previously, the mark Walter created often seemed to be missed. However, Cavin previously researched candy store statistics for the purpose of his own proposal for Beaufort Candy Company, and the sales at Noel's store far exceeded the revenue needed to turn a relatively healthy profit in this industry.

"After spending time working in your kitchen and familiarizing myself with your processes, I realize you make everything from scratch in-house using top-quality ingredients, so your costs are probably higher than the average candy store," Cavin pointed out to Noel after digging through the data while she mixed ingredients in the kitchen for a fresh batch of salt water taffy. "Are there any other expenses, especially significant ones, you can think of outside of normal operating business expenditures?"

Noel considered the question as the machine in front of her churned and stretched the taffy, pulling it like extremely elastic rubber bands. "Well, having a waterfront shop causes the insurance to be a bit high due to the threat of flooding from hurricanes," she explained.

"I have already calculated that," Cavin confirmed although hurricanes weren't top of mind at Christmastime.

"We don't pay rent because we own the building," Noel pointed out.

"Right," Cavin noted, *and what you own might be worth way more than you realize*, he thought.

Cavin asked a handful of other questions about expenses and then did more math while studying the numbers on the spreadsheet he created on his laptop. Thankfully he still possessed the computer, but it would probably only be a matter of time before his dad thought about confiscating it.

"I have run all the numbers, and some things are not adding up," Cavin conveyed, wanting to leave it at that for now.

"Do you think we are in a bigger hole than I imagined?" Noel asked. "Do you think that is why Walter's offer is so low?"

Cavin wanted to reveal his suspicions to Noel so badly he could barely contain himself. "No, I do not believe the hole is bigger,"

Cavin assured her with confidence. In fact no hole seemed to exist.

"That's good news," Noel uttered.

Cavin shut his laptop hastily and jumped up from the stool he sat on all week while helping Noel prepare candy. Taking a deep breath, he once again realized how good this kitchen smelled. He never visited a place in all his life that smelled better.

"I need to head over to the register of deeds office," Cavin announced.

"Okay," Noel replied appreciative of his diligent work. She had no idea what he was searching for, but his determination was evident. "I hope you find what you are looking for."

Cavin didn't necessarily want to show up at the local register of deeds office in person because if his theory was correct, he had no idea who else could be in cahoots with Walter and Georgia. However, the property information he previously viewed online, which he double checked again last night, didn't match his conclusion. So, no other option existed.

A cold breeze blew across his cheeks as Cavin made the brief walk from the candy shop to the register of deeds office. Once he arrived, a kind older lady with a monotone voice and gaudy glasses showed him all the same property documents he saw online although it took her ages to dig each one out of a file cabinet and flip through the pages with him. Noel's building showed as deeded to Beaufort Candy Company, Inc. with Noel listed as the sole owner. Cavin expected to see Keaton's name listed as well, but it wasn't although that wasn't a big deal. The records showed the property being passed down from Noel's parents to her. The adjacent building's deed belonged to Walter Benson's family's company with his name listed as the owner. Similar to Noel's, the documents showed the property being handed down from his father.

All of this information didn't add up when it came to the

proposal . . . because the official documents from Walter Benson to Noel Puckett showed Walter Benson as the prospective buyer of a property that included both buildings, and Noel Puckett as the seller who legally owned both buildings. The major red flag was that in the proposition, the title was under Noel's current building's address, but the details showed that such property consisted of both buildings—something that neither she nor anyone not knowing how to decipher the fine print would have ever noticed.

28

Cavin spent the remainder of the day surrounded by documents scattered across the rental's kitchen table which appeared somewhat like a wall collage the FBI might concoct to study a case. He scrutinized each article again, as well as the photos, until his head hurt just trying to gain a better understanding without questioning Walter Benson in person. Getting his hands on the tax returns might confirm part of what Cavin expected, but Walt probably wouldn't offer any insight into the most important piece of the puzzle. Analyzing the tax documents required a conversation with Walt that he wanted to avoid for the time being. The man obviously concocted a well thought out plan leading Cavin to assume the seasoned accountant also formulated a clever backup plan which likely included offering Noel a bigger check for her property.

Eventually Cavin reached a point in his research that prompted him to make a phone call to a person who might be able to help. He remembered some specific spoken words, and even if the individual didn't have the desired answers, a second set of eyes attached to an intelligent brain might prove helpful. However, Cavin made a promise to two little children and a lovely woman to spend Christmas Eve with them. He couldn't do two things at once, and he didn't even know when this person might be available, so he decided to go ahead and quickly dial the number to find out.

When Cavin walked back to the candy shop, he found Levi and Laney serving hot chocolate as expected. Ever since school let out for Christmas break, the two worked the stand a good part of each day, and Cavin decided to assist them for the last thirty minutes before helping close down the sidewalk business. Afterward, the three of them and Noel held their daily search for Scout.

They encountered Scout twice, each time attempting to lure him with food. Even though he came within a dozen feet of their hands, the skittish dog ran off before they could grab him. When they dropped treats and backed away, Scout would eat a bit while keeping his eyes on them the whole time then jet off when anyone approached. The cute Goldendoodle was a smart little fellow. He came up to the candy shop entrance late at night to munch down the food and drink the water Levi and Laney left out for him or other dogs who wanted it which Georgia complained attracted wild animals. She talked to both Cavin and Noel about the issue on separate occasions, but they simply listened and told her they would keep a close eye on the security cameras to see if it became a problem. The footage often showed Scout, but the times when Noel saw it live and scurried down in the middle of the night to attempt to wrangle Scout, he bolted before she could twist the lock on the door.

Even in the December cold, the lows so far stayed above freezing, so Scout managed to survive the elements somehow. However, the overnight Christmas Eve forecast showed lows expected to drop into the twenties and even called for a slight chance of snowfall. As Noel, Cavin, Laney, and Levi left the Christmas Eve candlelight service where Noel delivered the best version of "Mary Did You Know" that Cavin ever heard, she encouraged the kids not to get their hopes up because the area meteorologists often got everyone excited about the possibilities of snow but rarely did Beaufort see any white precipitation.

Early on Christmas morning as the sky began to glow with morning light, everything seemed to fall into place. Rather than being awakened by Santa climbing down the chimney or his reindeer's feet pattering on the rooftop, Levi's and Laney's little ears perked when they heard the sound of barking. Both kids sat straight up from their mattress looking at each other before shouting in unison, "Scout!"

Although still in her room, Noel woke early to wrap presents as Christmas music played softly in the background. She didn't hear Scout's barks, but she couldn't miss the shrill sounds of Levi's and Laney's voices and the commotion they made jumping out of bed and running through the house. Concerned, Noel pounced off the floor as if on a trampoline and met them in the living room not sure what was happening but hoped the kids' excitement was simply related to Christmas morning and opening presents.

However, Noel never expected them up before seven o'clock after their late night pajama party of baking and decorating cookies while watching *A Charlie Brown Christmas*. In fact Cavin promised to arrive on the hour to help with the kids' Christmas presents. Since he had nowhere else to go, Levi and Laney invited him to celebrate Christmas morning with them, and Noel agreed to the idea.

As these thoughts raced through Noel's mind, the children's noises quieted just long enough for her ears to recognize the sound of barking.

"Mom, it's Scout. We hear him barking."

The three of them ran downstairs, their bare feet bouncing on every step. They quickly traversed the candy shop aisles and found Scout looking frigid and fragile barking at the door while peering through the glass at them. Noel's eyes glazed over with awe when just beyond Scout, she spotted a layer of puffy white snow covering the sidewalk, and as she glanced up at the gray sky, she saw little white dots swirling through the air in slow motion.

"Aunt Noel, it's snowing," Laney announced with pure joy lining her tickled voice.

"Wow," Levi replied, seeing the precipitation himself. "That's why Scout wants in, he's freezing."

Praying, Noel twisted the lock slowly as if searching for an exact number on a combination safe. When it clicked, Scout took two steps back but didn't run away like usual.

"When I open the door, don't run out," Noel instructed. "Kneel down and wait for Scout to come to you."

Scout barked as Noel gently pushed the door open, then he stared at the three of them in the open doorway as a blast of cold ran through their bodies like a brain freeze.

"Come here, Scout," Laney uttered as softly as the falling flakes of snow.

"Hey, sweet boy," Levi whispered, holding out his hand as if it held treats.

Suddenly for no apparent reason, Scout turned and raced into the snowy road where street lamps still glowed as daylight began to lift onto the horizon.

"Should we go after him, Mom?"

"If we don't, he's going to freeze to death," Laney anxiously predicted.

Before Noel could make a decision knowing none of them needed to run out in the snow without proper footwear, a figure from across the street ran onto the road and scooped Scout into his arms.

"Mom, it's Cavin," Levi shouted, pronouncing his name the proper way for the first time.

"Cavin caught Scout," Laney exclaimed.

At that moment Noel heard the cuckoo clock sound in the background telling them seven o'clock arrived.

"You showed up right on time," Noel reported enthusiastically, happy to see Cavin with Scout in his arms and the dog's tail wagging. "Come on in," she added. "It's freezing out there."

Levi and Laney lunged toward Scout while Cavin held the animal tightly so he wouldn't escape.

"Hey boy, you are so cute," Levi told the dog as he petted him for the first time.

"You have snow on your fur, little guy," Laney added while rubbing her hand across his back to brush off as much as possible.

"Let me close this door so we can keep Scout in and the cold out," Noel suggested then pushed it shut.

For a moment she wondered how in the world she and Cavin would arrange the kids' Christmas gifts without them noticing. Tradition was to place the presents around the large tree in the back of the candy shop, but with the children already in the store, the tree glowed like an open invitation, only with no real gifts underneath. Fortunately, Scout's surprise appearance and the magic of snowfall in coastal North Carolina occupied their minds while Noel quickly herded everyone upstairs with a promise of drinking hot chocolate, playing on the floor with Scout, and eventually dressing warmly to frolic in the snow. She imagined Cavin with all these options could keep the kids entertained while she played Santa Claus.

Christmas morning went smoothly from there. Noel found a soft, warm blanket to wrap around Scout who, after a short time, decided he wanted to dance across the house as if he lived there his whole life. The kids chased him, and he chased them back, and Cavin watched with a smile while Noel hustled up and down the stairs surrounding the tree with gifts.

Eventually Cavin sent Levi and Laney to their rooms to dress for the snow in the clothes Noel set out for them before disappearing. While the kids climbed into winter gear, Cavin latched a leash they acquired with this very moment in mind on Scout's collar. Then Cavin helped the kids pull on their gloves before leading them outside through the balcony door, making them walk as if on eggshells holding onto the rail tightly while moving down the slippery steps. He let them play in the snow for about fifteen minutes as he held onto Scout's leash like a fisherman gripping a pole with the big one on the other end. Scout played along jumping in excitement while the children threw snowballs, made snow angels, and started rolling body parts to create a snowman.

Noel joined them outside with her camera in hand and whispered, "Everything is ready" into Cavin's ear. They all played in the snow and watched it fall on the creek for a bit longer before heading in to open presents. As Levi and Laney tore the paper off each gift, joy filled Cavin's and Noel's hearts as they watched the children's little faces bubble with excitement. Scout loved playing in the wrapping paper scattered across the floor, and that was the only present he seemed to need. Noel was thankful he never discovered nor started eating the candy.

When the kids finished opening gifts, they ran upstairs and brought Noel a box that Cavin helped them wrap last night.

"What is this?" Noel inquired, smiling with that smile that only a mom is capable of producing.

"We're helping you save the candy shop," Levi announced.

Noel's brow furrowed ever so slightly, but she continued to wear an appreciative grin as she wondered what she would discover inside. What did Levi mean? How did he know? What did he know?

Laney punched Levi in the arm. "Don't tell her, just let her open it."

Noel slowly peeled back the foil wrapping and discovered a small wooden box featuring an ocean wave resin acrylic design handmade by their friend who owned Grace Bell Art. Cavin helped the kids inconspicuously buy the item at the farmers' market, and when Noel lifted the top and pulled back the tissue paper stuffed inside, she discovered a large pile of wrinkled cash and one quarter.

"It's 2,525.25," Laney disclosed.

Levi then punched her in the arm. "You're supposed to let her count it," he reminded his cousin.

"That's a whole lot of money to count," Noel remarked as she looked at both of them before turning her eyes to Cavin. "Where did all this come from?" she asked, wondering if Cavin had something to do with it.

Cavin pointed to the kids. "Your little entrepreneurs."

"We made it at the hot chocolate stand," Levi announced proudly.

"It was Cavin's idea to make all the numbers say twenty-five like Christmas," Laney disclosed. "We even have a little bit of money left over to start the pet finding business."

"You guys are the best," Noel proclaimed, wrapping both of them with big hugs like the greatest gifts ever that they were to her.

Cavin and Noel opened a few small presents from each other that they picked out at the farmers' market event including matching alpaca socks, a book cover journal from Beach Chicken Designs, and a kazoo from Junkman's Crossroads. The kids snickered at many of the vendors' names. Levi was the one who talked Cavin into getting his mom the instrument from the long-haired fellow playing a license plate guitar because he thought he looked like Jesus.

The gift that excited Cavin the most was one he and Noel discovered simultaneously in the Island Accents booth. The seller told them that his wife hand painted the two Santa hats that encompassed six panes of frosted glass on an antique wooden window. The piece exceeded their budget, but as fate would have it, the man secretly whispered into Cavin's ear just before he and Noel walked out of the space, "My wife and I decided to give this artwork to the first couple we saw wearing Santa hats at the

Christmas market. Come back for it when Noel isn't around," he added, "so you can give it to her for Christmas."

Noel's face lit up as she held the art at arm's length with the Christmas tree in the background, and happy tears tickled her cheeks when she set it down and hugged Cavin. "How did you get this?" she asked.

Cavin told her the story, causing more tears of joy to flow from her eyes, and he couldn't help but let the bottom fall out of his as well.

When the kids got bored watching the adults open presents, they ran off to play with Scout some more.

"Did you tell the kids that the candy shop was struggling?" Noel questioned, thinking back to the gift she opened from them and wanting to believe Cavin wouldn't have betrayed her trust.

"Actually, they told me," Cavin reported.

Noel didn't hide her furrowed brow this time. "What?" she asked. "But I told you, just the other day."

"They told me way before that," Cavin shared. "But I was sworn to secrecy, so do not tell on me, please."

"When did they tell you?" Noel asked. "How did they know?"

"One of them accidentally blurted it out the first day I bought hot chocolate from them at the stand," Cavin explained. "That is why they came up with the idea in the first place."

Noel covered her gaping mouth. "How did they know?" she asked again.

"They mentioned they overheard you and Mrs. Madelyn talking one day about the store struggling and possibly having to close it."

"Oh no," Noel sighed. "I feel terrible."

A moment later the kids came running back over.

"Mommy, we have to take Scout to Rudy."

"Yes, we do," Noel agreed, almost forgetting the dog didn't belong to them.

"I am going to miss him," Laney shared.

"I know you will, sweetie, but Mr. Rudy will be very happy to have his dog back."

"I imagine Rudy will let you all play with Scout often," Cavin inserted. "Also surprising Rudy with Scout today will be the best Christmas gift."

As expected, Rudy was tickled pink—or maybe red and green—to have Scout back, safe and secure on the boat.

"You kids just made this old man the happiest person alive," Rudy declared as they oohed and aahed at his fancy boat that Levi and Laney decided looked more like a house on the inside.

"It doesn't even feel like we're in a boat," Laney observed, taking in the size of the rooms and the height of the ceilings.

"It's way bigger than our house," Levi whispered at one point while Rudy gave them the tour.

In the living room area, Rudy opened a checkbook he inconspicuously picked up in the office a few minutes earlier. "I owe you both a finder's fee," he declared, gazing at Levi and Laney with appreciation.

"What's that?" Laney quizzed with a scrunched brow.

"It's the reward I promised on the posters."

"Mr. Emerson, you really don't have to give the kids anything," Noel interjected. "We all had the best time looking for Scout."

"Noel, I am a man of my word," Rudy offered, then turned his attention back to the kids whose eyes shone wide with pleasure. "Since there are two of you, I am writing each of you a check for $5,000. It's up to your mom how you use it, but maybe some of it can go to start your animal non-profit; you could save a portion for college and careers and maybe spend a little on yourselves," he concluded by rubbing their heads.

"We are giving it all to Mom to save the candy shop," Levi announced enthusiastically.

"Yeah, Beaufort Candy Company is more important to our

family than anything," Laney shared.

"You kids have the most amazing hearts," Rudy noted. "However, your mom doesn't need you to save the candy shop."

Noel couldn't hide her sudden confusion, and Cavin, standing on the other side of her and the kids, squinted his eyes a bit wondering what Rudy planned to reveal.

"She doesn't?" Levi questioned.

"But we thought . . .," Laney trailed off.

Noel didn't have the heart to tell the kids that the cash they gave her this morning wouldn't save the candy shop, and she couldn't imagine that an additional $10,000 would quite fill the gap either. It might buy some time, but it would only offer a temporary fix. However, she didn't really want to have this conversation with them, especially here, and she had no idea why Rudy made the comment. She couldn't help but wonder if the kids previously mentioned the fate of the candy shop to him like they did with Cavin. Regardless, why would he make the statement that she didn't need the kids' help?

"Cavin, is it okay if we give Noel and the kids their Christmas present earlier than we planned?" Rudy asked. "The timing seems perfect since you all just brought me my Scout."

Tears of joy swirled in Cavin's eyes like the scene in a snow globe, and somehow as if an imaginary glass existed, they held there rather than falling down his cheeks. "Yes, of course," he agreed, now knowing exactly what was about to happen.

Noel's eyes darted between Rudy and Cavin who both seemed genuinely excited about something.

"I told Cavin this story last night when he came over asking for my thoughts regarding all that's going on with the candy shop, specifically with the proposal and Cavin's research." As Rudy spoke, Noel glanced at Cavin out of the corner of her eye wondering why he chose to share this information with Rudy. She wasn't upset with him, at least not yet, but definitely curious why he would involve someone who was more or less a stranger to her. "You see, the reason I came to Beaufort was because I found out the man who taught me how to make chocolate passed away," Rudy continued. "That man was your grandfather," he offered, looking at the kids with appreciation.

Noel's eyes suddenly swelled with amazement at the announcement that her father taught one of the most well-known chocolatiers in the world how to make chocolate. Rudy went on to share the story of how he ventured to Beaufort many years ago after walking away from his dad's lucrative business to discover his own passion. At the time he thought he wanted to open a restaurant on the waterfront because he dreamed of being a chef. While he explored the idea, he wandered into the candy shop one day where Noel's dad offered him a job on the spot. Needing a steady income while raising money for his restaurant, Rudy took the position because of the kitchen experience opportunity, and the rest proved to be history.

"Dad talked about you a lot," Noel proclaimed as pieces of a puzzle she never thought much about began falling into place. "He told us about giving you a job because you seemed so passionate about being a chef. I vividly remember him saying that within a short period of time, your passion for making chocolate grew into something more than anyone he ever met. Dad said you were successful, but he never told us that we would all know your company's candy if he mentioned the names of the products."

"Your dad was a humble man, Noel, and he didn't just teach me how to make candy; he taught me about what was important in life, things beyond money," Rudy explained. "When I came here this time around, I came to check on you and your brother and the candy shop. I arrived prepared to help financially if needed." Rudy stopped talking for a moment and let his head sink ever so slightly. "I felt terrible because a little over a year ago, your father sent me a document to look over about an investment he wanted to make. He knew that in addition to my chocolate business, I invested heavily in real estate over the years. His letter stated he didn't trust someone involved locally, and he wanted my advice. He said he wasn't hiring an attorney; he wanted to handle everything the old-fashioned way. Somehow that document and the letter got put aside because my wife just passed away, and I didn't rediscover the package until I recently learned of your father's passing."

"What is the document?" Noel asked.

"It's part of your Christmas present, Noel," Rudy offered with a grin fueled with mixed emotions. "I showed it to Cavin last night after he came to me with the results of his investigation. Something wasn't adding up, and I had the piece he needed, and he had the pieces I needed. This document shows your dad purchased the building next to yours which I didn't realize until Cavin pointed that out last night. It wasn't just a proposal; it was a copy of the signed papers. He was simply asking me if he made a good decision because it seems there was still a window to back out because the local businessman who'd taken over wasn't keen on the deal his father, who also passed, agreed to."

"I don't quite understand," Noel commented.

Cavin spoke up. "Yesterday when I went through your numbers, I realized your sales are amazing. Every estimate I ran showed your profits should be much higher than you thought."

"But mom and dad hadn't been able to take a salary for a while because the candy shop was struggling. Nothing has changed. I have barely increased sales," Noel presented.

"That is what your accountant told you," Cavin explained. "The truth is your mom and dad chose not to take a salary because they were making monthly cash payments to Walter's father to buy his building, the one next door to yours. That is what the document Rudy has reveals. Your parents' salaries went to those payments for quite some time. The last payment went through not long before your dad passed making the building his and ultimately, yours. This paperwork provides all the details, but it was never filed at the register of deeds office as legally required."

Noel took a few moments to take in everything. "What if Dad backed out on the deal at the last minute?" Noel considered aloud. "If he sent Rudy the proposal and mentioned that as an option, maybe he was questioning the deal, and when he didn't hear from you, he thought that was a sign?"

Rudy smiled really big. "In that case your accountant should have written you a big fat check," he pointed out.

Cavin chimed in. "Walt would have been legally responsible for returning all of the money your parents paid him and his father."

Noel sighed, suddenly feeling the weight of the world drop from her shoulders. "So that was Dad's big announcement," she realized audibly speaking the words to herself more so than anyone else. "He planned to tell us on the Shackelford Banks trip that he bought the rest of the building he always dreamed of acquiring."

"It appears he did just that," Rudy confirmed.

"And it sounds like telling you all on the trip was probably his plan," Cavin agreed.

"So, if Walter doesn't own the adjacent building anymore and I do, why is he trying to buy my building?" Noel inquired with a scrunched brow.

"He is sneakily trying in one fell swoop to buy the candy shop building along with the one his family used to own but is actually now owned by you," Cavin explained. "I believe he plans to file the paperwork showing your dad's purchase as soon as you agree to the proposal, and then once that is officially documented through the register of deeds, he is going to turn around and buy it right back from under you without you ever realizing what happened."

Noel's nostrils flared. "I've never cared for Walter Benson, but

I never expected he would be capable of doing something so terrible."

"There's even more to it, Noel," Cavin explained, waiting for the smoke to clear from her flared nostrils by the end of this bit of information. "Walter embezzled the salaries your mom and dad should have received once the property was fully paid. When your folks passed away, the timing worked out perfectly for him to shift those funds without you noticing. He obviously knew your dad had not told you about any of this, and even if it ended up that you knew, he realized you would have mentioned it. He probably would have just played dumb and then sorted it all out or offered you some ridiculously low offer for both buildings hoping to capitalize on your state of mind after the accident."

"I bet dad told him it was a secret," Noel imagined. "What are we going to do? Can we prove it?"

"With all the evidence we have, there will be no denying the truth, and I imagine it runs even deeper than we realize," Cavin claimed. "At first I thought Walt was just doing something immoral, but this is illegal. He is a criminal, and so is Georgia who is also directly involved in the coverup."

Grasping the implications of these findings as much as humanly possible at this moment, Noel wrapped her arms around Cavin and squeezed him tightly for nearly a minute. "Thank you so much for saving my family's candy company."

"You saved it," he assured her, "by keeping it going through such a challenging time."

"You're the best," she uttered. "You're trying to be humble, and that reminds me of my dad." Cavin grinned appreciatively, and then Noel turned to Rudy. "Thank you, Rudy. I can never repay you."

Rudy shook his head and hugged Noel. "You repay me," he laughed. "Noel, I owe more to your dad for believing in me than any of us could ever imagine."

"It sounds like we were all lucky to know him," Noel proclaimed, praying her dad could see and hear this conversation, especially after all the tears she cried.

"I wish I had known him," Cavin mentioned.

"You remind me of him every day when you wear his hat," Noel shared. "And now his legacy will continue to live on with Beaufort Candy Company because of you two wonderful men."

"I am proud to wear his hat," Cavin acknowledged with an upward glance. Noel's dedication to the Christmas spirit was contagious; he wore the hat everywhere, matching her.

Noel turned her attention to Levi and Laney who had been patiently trying to take in all of the adult talk. She knew explaining it on their level would be helpful. "Kids, this means that we get to keep the candy shop, and you get to keep all the money you earned at your hot chocolate stand," she explained with a huge smile. "I think we will take Rudy's advice and use that and the reward money to help start your animal finding non-profit, save for your college or careers, and I wholeheartedly believe you two deserve to spend some on yourselves."

Levi's and Laney's response warmed Noel Puckett's heart on this frigid, snowy Christmas Day. The two children instantly grew huge grins and began jumping up and down with their hands in the air dancing all over Rudy's boat. Scout hastily joined in on their celebration as all the adults smiled the smiles that come when realizing that truth always triumphs.

Something told Noel that Levi and Laney would be smart with their spending. She was so proud of their big hearts which they showcased today by being willing to give all their money on a day when they could have been focused on wanting more Christmas gifts. It just showed that even kids could understand that the true meaning of Christmas was about giving rather than receiving.

Cavin and Rudy had also been generous with their time and talents, and Noel knew she would forever be grateful for such a wonderful Christmas gift. It was evident that neither of these gentlemen wanted anything in return; they simply wanted to save Beaufort Candy Company for her and her family, and that was the greatest Christmas present she could have asked for this year or any year.

29

That Christmas turned out to be the most magical Christmas Noel Puckett ever experienced. When they walked off Rudy's mega yacht, she started creating a different type of Christmas list. She checked off the first thing on it when she called Mrs. Madelyn to share the good news about the candy shop with her and Jack, and then the kids sang *We Wish You a Merry Christmas* to them over the phone.

When Noel told Cavin about the second item on the list, he mentioned that she might want to wait to call Keaton.

"Keaton might show up at Walt's door and punch him in the face," Cavin expressed out loud, thankfully able to laugh since his black eye finally faded away.

"You are right, maybe let's skip to number three," Noel agreed.

Noel dialed Rainey's number and gave him the synopsis of what Cavin discovered. He and Chelsea invited them over for Christmas lunch, and then they all looked through the paperwork together.

"I think you are spot on about what Walter is up to," Rainey confirmed. "I will have the office draft the proper documentation, and we will gain access to all your records and more in no time."

"Let's not do that on Christmas though," Chelsea suggested.

"Yeah, I think tomorrow will work fine," Noel conveyed understanding but not wanting to endure the suspense any longer than necessary.

"Do you have copies of these documents?" Rainey checked.

Noel looked to Cavin. "Yes, multiple copies in multiple places," Cavin confirmed. This wasn't his first rodeo although this situation took the cake.

"Have you told anyone about this?" Rainey inquired, and Noel and Cavin shared the names of the people who knew. "Let's keep this quiet, and please make a phone call or visit to urge the others to do the same," he added. "We don't want Walter and Georgia catching wind of this knowledge although I can't imagine how they could possibly wriggle their way out of such a conundrum if all this proves to be true."

"Sounds like a plan," Noel agreed.

"We do need to act fast, however, because I have a feeling if my dad sent a proposal to Noel, he likely plans to send one to Walter if he has not already assuming, like the rest of us, that Walter owns the building adjacent to the candy shop," Cavin advised out loud for the first time. "My father has all the information I gathered, so he will probably also send one to the town of Beaufort. But I think sending a proposal to Noel was his first priority because he knew it would send me a message. That said, his eyes are on money, so he will want all of these properties."

Rainey's, Chelsea's, and Noel's understanding showed on their faces.

"Once we jump on this, I will check with the town of Beaufort to see if they have received a proposal," Rainey assured. "Again I don't think these details are going to change the outcome if everything we believe is true, but if it is all fact, we know Walter and Georgia are intelligent and capable of some crafty schemes, so we don't want to give them time to think of any ways they might elude some of this or run off."

Rainey suggested that the kids not be present for this discussion even though they already knew many of the details. He kept them occupied by sending them into another room to work on a junior investigation that he explained needed their attention. It wasn't the first time the grown-ups used this tactic when engaged in adult conversations, but they had to be careful because these two littles had been trained well as Rainey always liked to remind everyone. "We don't want to stress them out or take the chance that they might slip up and say something to someone," he suggested. "I do want to talk to them though."

A few minutes later, Noel called Levi and Laney into the living room, and Rainey led the discussion.

"You two are the department's best junior officers," he started. "You now know some important information about the candy shop and what the alleged masterminds have been up to," he said, explaining that further in terms they could understand. "Keep in mind that one of the most important parts of being a detective is making sure not to share top secret information. That means we don't talk about this with anyone who is not in this room. Can I count on you two to keep this case quiet?"

"You bet," Levi promised as he pretended to zip his lips.

"Anything for the candy shop," Laney guaranteed.

The rest of Christmas Day was thoroughly enjoyed by all, and Noel's heart swelled with joy when Keaton showed up at her house for Christmas dinner. They celebrated with ham, green beans, squash casserole, macaroni and cheese, and rolls and spent a good amount of the time playing with Levi and Laney as they enjoyed their new Christmas gifts. They also finished the snowman that the kids started on the waterfront side of the building and then created a second one in front of Beaufort Candy Company for all the customers and passersby to enjoy.

No one in Beaufort did much driving on Christmas or the days that followed. Six inches of snow pretty much shut down the town which couldn't have come at a better time of the year, and it sure was nice that everyone lived within walking distance of one another's houses to enjoy family time. Although Noel no longer felt the need to worry about sales and the pressure of being open every day possible to maximize revenue, she still felt anxious about what would happen with the debacle Walter and Georgia created with the buildings. She was grateful that Cavin had been with her the day she met with Walter and Georgia and relieved she rebuffed them pressuring her into signing the papers. If Cavin hadn't been there, she wasn't sure she could have held out. The stress overcame her even more than she realized at the time.

As promised Rainey kicked off the investigation right away after sharing a laugh with Noel and Cavin about a case he just closed where three teenagers received a slap on the wrist for flattening people's tires around town. A search warrant gave the detectives access to Beaufort Candy Company's tax documents and business-related files stored in Walter's computer and file cabinets at his office. Rainey kept Noel and Cavin informed of the findings, and day by day, it turned out that everything Cavin and Rudy suspected was true. One thing Cavin mentioned to Noel later also proved true—Walter was collecting rent from the tenants in the other building by posing as the owner.

This meant Beaufort Candy Company had the means to hire more employees which had been the case all along but the business's crooked accountant covered it up. Noel and Mrs. Madelyn trained two new full-time employees, one who would work in the kitchen and another who would eventually work on the floor. They also brought on a couple of teenagers part-time to fill in some slots so that everyone else's schedules would be a bit more flexible.

"Mrs. Madelyn, you just come in and work anytime you want," Noel told her lifelong friend, "that way you can make spending time with Jack and taking care of him and yourself your primary responsibility."

"Darling, I will be here anytime you need me just like I always have been," Mrs. Madelyn promised.

"I know you will, but I am so relieved to know all the pressure is off your shoulders. I couldn't have kept this store running without you."

"It was a pleasure to overcome so many obstacles with you, Noel," Mrs. Madelyn stated. "We are quite the team."

"Yes, we are," Noel agreed.

"You are part of another team now, too," Mrs. Madelyn stated. "The Noel and Cavin team."

Noel blushed. "Stop it."

"I told you I expected a Christmas miracle," Mrs. Madelyn reminded her. "I just didn't predict all these other Christmas miracles that transpired, but God knew exactly which angels to send our way."

"You were right," Noel acknowledged. "I should have never doubted you."

"Sweet girl, you just needed to figure it out for yourself in your own timing, and you did just that."

"I couldn't have done it without you, Cavin, and the kids," Noel pointed out.

"Speaking of Cavin and the kids, I am excited about spending the weekend with the children next month when you and Cavin go to Florida for his golf tournament."

Once the snow melted, Noel went golfing with Cavin on what turned out to be a relatively warm Sunday. Prior to that, things became so hectic in their lives that she forgot she promised to play golf with him. Once she did, she couldn't believe her eyes. Cavin definitely possessed the talent to play in professional tournaments. She watched enough golf to realize he was a little rusty, but even in that state of being, he was by far the best golfer she ever saw play in person.

Noel surprised Cavin with her own abilities on the greens.

Although she knew she wouldn't be joining the ladies' pro tour, Cavin realized the two of them could likely win some relatively competitive couples tournaments if they wanted. Noel turned out to be pretty good at tennis, too, and they were happy to know they shared athletic interests. Fletcher never participated in golf or tennis, so Noel hadn't played in a long time. His sports were on the water, and Noel loved those also, and that's why the two of them chose that route.

Noel and Cavin talked openly about these things and decided to enjoy some of the water activities as well, especially since the kids loved fishing, tubing, and swimming. Noel had sold Fletcher's boat not long after the accident to help pay for all the unexpected expenses that life insurance would have otherwise covered. Now that both Noel and Cavin were back on their feet, they talked about getting their own boat at some point in the future.

In addition to playing in professional golf tournaments regularly which Cavin expected would bring in a respectable salary and in time possibly a lucrative one, he agreed to handle Beaufort Candy Company's accounting. Noel wanted someone she trusted to fill that role, and she couldn't think of a better person. Cavin would also be in the candy shop helping with business operations on a normal basis.

Noel's former accountant Walter Benson and his attorney Georgia would likely spend time in prison. Their defense lawyers were currently pushing back the criminal trial as far as possible although a judge already quickly ruled that the building adjacent to Beaufort Candy Company legally belonged to Noel Puckett. The court deemed the official papers signed by Noel's and Walter's fathers legal, and the register of deeds office filed them immediately.

This step not only allowed Noel to hire permanently the employees who were working out wonderfully in the shop, but she also carried out her father's dream of making sure local artists and crafters had an opportunity to have a noticeable impact in Beaufort, North Carolina. The Olde Beaufort Farmers' Market, which showcased the area's finest talents, sent a variety of individuals her way to fill some of the spots in the other building that Walter attempted to commercialize.

Cavin found out his dad sent offers to Walter Benson and to the Town of Beaufort; however, as expected, those were not a top priority and showed up after Christmas. Cavin proudly stamped rejected on the offers for both buildings that now belonged to Beaufort Candy Company although legally Cavin knew the one for Walter Benson's supposed building was null and void as soon as the property officially became Noel's. A new draft would be required, but Cavin knew his dad wouldn't bother at that point. He would not want to purchase the parking lot unless he just really wanted to provoke Cavin and realized he could potentially take away parking spots from Beaufort Candy Company and the residences above the buildings. However, the Town of Beaufort, no longer under the influence of Georgia, voted unanimously not to sell the lot.

Once all this transpired, Cavin asked Rudy how long his father held a grudge after Rudy walked away from the family business. "He eventually came around," Rudy revealed, encouraging Cavin to be patient with his dad. "Your mother will talk some sense into him, and they will welcome you back with open arms."

The townhouse above the adjacent building recently became vacant, and Noel offered it to Cavin who happily accepted it while on the verge of moving out of the home the elderly couple so generously let him occupy. Furthermore, Noel and Cavin began to dream of combining her home and the townhouse he quickly settled into knowing it would provide plenty of room for the two of them and Levi while the extra space would even allow for an adjoining apartment for Keaton and Laney.

Perhaps the Christmas miracle that involved Keaton turned out to be the best of all. On Christmas night not only did he come to dinner, but Rainey, Chelsea, Rudy, Scout, Mrs. Madelyn, and Jack also joined in on the celebration of family. By God's grace at the end of the night, Keaton decided to go to rehab. Cavin knew the major turning point occurred when he, Keaton, and Rainey took a walk to Rudy's boat to pick up gifts Rudy had gotten for everyone but couldn't carry by himself.

At the end of the dock before the three of them stepped onto the mega yacht, Keaton fell on his knees and began to sob like a child having a breakdown. Rainey, as if their friendship had never been scarred, joined his lifelong friend on the freezing cold boards to hold him tightly until he could muster the energy to share his emotions audibly.

"The reason the boat hit the sandbar," Keaton began struggling to find the words between gasps for breath, "was because I panicked when Fletcher told me to take over."

The cold December air spitting and swirling snow above Taylor Creek where each flake disappeared upon landing on the surface of the water became silent for a few moments outside of the cries of grown men.

Why did you panic? Both Cavin and Rainey wondered this thought, but each waited for Keaton to speak again in his own time.

"I was standing next to Fletcher at the wheel when he suddenly became sick," Keaton explained. "He mentioned feeling a little off earlier, but all of a sudden, he looked terrible and shouted to me, 'Take the wheel,' and I did, but then he leaned over the side of the boat and began puking into the water." More tears streamed down Keaton's face as he relived the terrifying moments that came next, memories he relentlessly tried to wash away with alcohol, sleep aids, and anything else he could find to take his mind off the reality of what happened on the water that day. "I was trying to steer and keep my eyes on him. Vomit was flying everywhere, and when Fletcher realized it was hitting Mom and Lexi in the back of the boat, he ran to the front and on the way yanked off his lifejacket which throw up covered," Keaton explained while shaking his head. "Fletcher knelt on the opposite side of the bow from Dad, held onto the rail, and stuck his head so far down it looked like he was bobbing for apples."

Rainey rubbed Keaton's back as if sandpapering a piece of wood not even realizing the growing pressure he was asserting, and Keaton didn't seem to notice either. By this time Cavin joined the two men on the frigid dock boards and couldn't hold back his own tears. Although he didn't know any of the others on the boat, he knew Keaton, and he also knew Noel, and as much as humanly possible, he saw the pain in their eyes when they talked about the accident. At this moment the pain pouring down Keaton's face was excruciating—a pain that had been suppressed for far too long.

"I was trying to steer, watch Fletcher, and check on my wife and mother," Keaton cried, shaking his head side to side, visually displaying that he didn't do a good enough job to keep everyone safe. "In the midst of all this, the boat drifted in the wrong direction, and I didn't even notice it," he admitted. "Dusk was settling in, and I just screwed up. At any point I could have steered us in the right direction or just dropped the throttle," he admitted. "In just a few seconds, I could have stopped the boat, and everyone would have lived. We could have all jumped into the water and washed off," he reasoned just as he did in his mind thousands of times. It would have been so simple. He could have prevented the entire accident and saved all their lives.

Finally, hearing all the things Keaton was and wasn't saying, Rainey spoke up. "Keaton, the accident wasn't your fault," he insisted sternly. "You did your best, man. You took the wheel like Fletcher asked, and you were trying to keep an eye on all of your passengers. It was getting dark, and that sandbar you all hit is one of those that is rarely even there," he added vividly remembering intensely examining the accident scene after the incident and throughout the investigation. "No one could have expected you to analyze all these things in just a few seconds."

Cavin wasn't sure what to say; he didn't know anything about the waterways around Beaufort or anywhere for that matter. However, he felt like he needed to say something, and the word brave came to mind as if someone spoke it aloud. "Keaton, it sounds like you were so brave out there," Cavin noted. "Like Rainey said, you tried your best."

Keaton's whole jaw quivered profusely. "It wasn't good enough," he declared, sniffing deeply.

"Man, you are good enough," Rainey proclaimed. "And you deserve to be treated better than you have been treating yourself. It wasn't your fault," he uttered slowly speaking the last sentence one word at a time.

By now the three of them sat basically huddled together in a group hug keeping one another warm and safe and barely feeling the elements all around them.

"You should talk to Noel about all of this," Cavin suggested. "The unknown is causing her to suffer, too. You two need to grieve this together."

"I can't," Keaton retorted. "I can't ever tell Noel about any of this."

"Why not?" Rainey asked. "Noel is your sister; she loves you dearly, man, and she will understand if anybody does. She deserves to know what happened out there."

"That's the problem," Keaton murmured.

"What?" Cavin asked with a furrowed brow.

"Before the trip started, Fletcher went home; he even mentioned kissing Noel," Rainey shared. "Noel will blame herself for getting him sick." It took a few moments for the reality of that conclusion to settle in amongst the group although Keaton vowed to himself that he would never speak a word of this to Noel for as long as he lived. "You guys can't tell Noel," Keaton demanded. "You can't tell anyone," he added. "But I had to tell someone." He paused for a moment as his whole body shivered but not because of the cold surrounding them. "I almost gave up on life today, but something told me to come to Christmas dinner," he shared. "I swear I heard Fletcher's voice saying 'be brave.' He said that all the time."

Rainey's cries suddenly grew a little louder. "I will share this burden with you," he suddenly postulated. "Noel got sick after being at my house," he reminded everyone. "Chelsea and I were sick but didn't realize it in time."

Cavin jumped in. "Rainey, it's not your fault either," he insisted. "Fletcher chose to go home knowing Noel and the kids were sick," he mentioned. "He was a grown man who made that choice, and none of you need to take the blame for his illness."

"Noel will still blame herself," Keaton declared. "I know she will. She might even blame Fletcher for coming home, and I don't want that to happen. At least right now that last kiss has been one of her saving graces. I don't want that special moment transformed into regret."

The depth of that thought, one Keaton experienced over and over, reached Cavin and Rainey instantly.

"Then we tell no one," Rainey offered. "We make a pact right here on the dock to keep this among the three of us. When any of us struggles with what happened out there or why it may have happened, we get together and we talk about it just like we are doing now. We cry if we need to; whatever it takes."

"That's what I want," Keaton acknowledged. "That's what I need."

Rainey studied Cavin's eyes. "Do you agree to those terms?"

"You can't share this secret with Noel," Keaton pleaded before giving Cavin a chance to respond.

"I promised myself never to keep secrets from Noel," Cavin admitted wanting to be true to himself while thinking back about all that led him to the decision to quit his family's company and ultimately remain in Beaufort. As he contemplated what he was being asked to do, he thought about how much he loved Noel and how much she loved Fletcher. "This isn't a secret," Cavin decided. "This is private knowledge amongst three friends, and it doesn't benefit anyone else to know. In fact I agree that it is in Noel's and the kids' best interest not to be privy to this information."

Everyone's shoulders seemed to relax a bit once they reached a consensus although Cavin had a hunch that one day, Keaton would reveal the truth to his sister so that she no longer worried about what led to the accident. He felt certain Noel was strong enough to handle the reality of what happened on that boat. The three men cried at the dock a while longer, nearly frozen before finally climbing aboard Rudy's vessel where they retrieved the awaiting presents.

On the walk home, Rainey teased that the identically wrapped boxes measuring about sixteen by twenty inches, each contained a gigantic chocolate candy bar. Cavin and Keaton burst out in laughter—the kind that heals the soul.

Before the guys returned, Rudy sat with Noel in the candy shop where they sipped hot cocoa. He told her if she and the kids ever wanted to market their hot chocolate mix—now sold in the candy shop by the jar—he would help it quickly become a household brand across the country. But as he predicted, she insisted the whole world could keep coming to Beaufort, North Carolina, to enjoy their family's delicious recipes.

When the guys finally made it back to Noel's place and everybody sat around the living room drinking Laney's and Levi's now-famous hot chocolate, Rudy asked everyone to go ahead and open their gifts at the same time. He watched merrily as red and gold paper fell to the floor and each person discovered a hand-painted representation of Beaufort Candy Company on canvas with the words *A Candy Shop Christmas* written in cursive, Christmasy-looking lettering at the top. Garland hung draped above the store's awning and in the windows, and the beautiful gingerbread house candy displays appeared behind the glass panes featuring the magical Christmas glow inside the shop. The days until Christmas sign stood out front along with the little black table where so many people enjoyed treats from the candy shop, and last but not least, snow blanketed the ground.

"How did you know we would get snow this Christmas?" with tears trickling down her cheeks, Noel asked the man who looked like Santa Claus.

Rudy smiled. "I didn't," he admitted. "I just prayed for a magical Christmas for all of us."

Scout barked, and a round of laughter flooded the room as everyone talked about the beautiful painting while reminiscing about the memories made at the Beaufort Candy Company this Christmas and sharing stories of Christmas's past.

Sitting thigh to thigh with Noel, Cavin turned to her amongst all the chatter and whispered, "I love you, Noel Puckett."

She grinned from ear to ear. "I love you, too, Cavin Dawson."

"You are the best friend I have always wanted," Cavin murmured as he placed a hand on one of her cheeks before drawing his lips close to the other and then whispered softly into her ear, "One day I want to marry you."

Noel closed her eyes silently thanking God that Mrs. Madelyn had been right about Cavin all along. At that moment Levi and Laney jumped into Cavin's and Noel's laps then hugged them tightly. As they all sat together wearing their signature Santa hats, they realized this Christmas was one that none of them would ever forget and one that was going to last forever.

THE END

Photo Credit: Mashal Smith

A Note from the Author

Thank you for reading A CANDY SHOP CHRISTMAS! While Beaufort, North Carolina, is a real town, Beaufort Candy Company came from my imagination as a depiction of my love for candy stores and the magic they bring to our lives, especially at Christmastime. I am grateful that you chose to invest your time in this book. If you haven't read my other novels, A BRIDGE APART, LOSING LONDON, A FIELD OF FIREFLIES, THE DATE NIGHT JAR, WHEN THE RIVERS RISE, WHERE THE RAINBOW FALLS, ALONG THE DUSTY ROAD, and THE ROOTS BENEATH US, I hope you will very soon. If you enjoyed the story you just experienced, please consider helping spread the novel to others in the following ways:

- REVIEW the novel online at Amazon.com, goodreads.com, bn.com, bamm.com, etc.
- RECOMMEND this book to friends (social groups, workplace, book club, church, school, etc.).
- VISIT my website: www.Joey-Jones.com
- SUBSCRIBE to my Email Newsletter for insider information on upcoming novels, behind-the-scenes looks, promotions, charities, and other exciting news.
- CONNECT with me on Social Media, and feel free to post a comment about the novel: "Like" Facebook.com/JoeyJonesWriter and "Follow" me at Instagram.com/JoeyJonesWriter. "Pin" on Pinterest. Write a blog post about the book.
- GIVE a copy of the novel to someone you know who would enjoy the story. Books make great presents (Birthday, Christmas, Teacher's Gifts, etc.).

Sincerely,
Joey Jones

About the Author

The writing style of Joey Jones has been described as a mixture of Nicholas Sparks, Richard Paul Evans, and James Patterson. The ratings and reviews of his novels A BRIDGE APART (2015), LOSING LONDON (2016), A FIELD OF FIREFLIES (2018), THE DATE NIGHT JAR (2019), WHEN THE RIVERS RISE (2020), WHERE THE RAINBOW FALLS (2022), ALONG THE DUSTY ROAD (2023), and THE ROOTS BENEATH US (2024) reflect the comparison to *New York Times* bestselling authors. Prior to becoming a full-time novelist, Joey worked in the marketing field. He holds a Bachelor of Arts in Business Communications from the University of Maryland University College, where he earned a 3.8 GPA.

Fun facts: Joey Jones lives in North Carolina with his family. Christmas is his favorite holiday! In January 2025, Joey underwent successful SI Joint surgery at Mayo Clinic in Rochester, MN. Joey often says he could see himself living in Beaufort, the setting of this novel.

Joey Jones is currently writing his tenth novel and working on various projects pertaining to his published works.

Book Club/Group Discussion Questions

1. Were you immediately engaged in the novel?

2. What emotions did you experience as you read the book?

3. Which character is your favorite? Why?

4. What do you like most about the story as a whole?

5. What is your favorite part/scene in the novel?

6. Do any particular passages from the book stand out to you?

7. As you read, what are some things you thought might happen but didn't?

8. Did the characters make the right choice by not telling Noel how the accident happened?

9. Do you think Keaton will eventually explain the accident to Noel?

10. Is the ending satisfying? If so, why? If not, why not, and how would you change it?

11. Why might the author have chosen to tell the story the way he did?

12. If you could ask the author a question, what would you ask?

13. Have you ever read or heard a story anything like this one?

14. In what ways does this novel relate to your own life?

15. Would you reread this novel?

Also by Joey Jones

A BRIDGE APART

A Bridge Apart, the debut novel by Joey Jones, is a remarkable love story that tests the limits of trust and forgiveness . . .

In the quaint river town of New Bern, North Carolina, at 28 years of age, the pieces of Andrew Callaway's life are all falling into place. His real estate firm is flourishing, and he's engaged to be married in less than two weeks to a beautiful banker named Meredith Hastings. But, when Meredith heads to Tampa, Florida—the wedding location—with her mother, fate, or maybe some human intervention, has it that Andrew happens upon Cooper McKay, the only other woman he's ever loved.

A string of shocking emails lead Andrew to question whether he can trust his fiancée, and in the midst of trying to unravel the mystery, he finds himself spending time with Cooper. When Meredith catches wind of what's going on back at home, she's forced to consider calling off the wedding, which ultimately draws Andrew closer to Cooper. Andrew soon discovers he's making choices he might not be able, or even want, to untangle. As the story unfolds, the decisions made will drastically change the lives of everyone involved and bind them closer together than they could have ever imagined.

Also by Joey Jones

LOSING LONDON

Losing London is an epic love story filled with nail-biting suspense, forbidden passion, and unexpected heartbreak.

When cancer took the life of Mitch Quinn's soulmate, London Adams, he never imagined that one year later her sister, Harper, whom he had never met before, would show up in Emerald Isle, NC. Until this point, his only reason to live, a five-year-old cancer survivor named Hannah, was his closest tie to London.

Harper, recently divorced, never imagined that work—a research project on recent shark attacks—and an unexpected package from London would take her back to the island town where her family had vacationed in her youth. Upon her arrival, she meets and is instantly swept off her feet by a local with a hidden connection that eventually causes her to question the boundaries of love.

As Mitch's and Harper's lives intertwine, they discover secrets that should have never happened. If either had known that losing London would have connected their lives in the way it did, they might have chosen different paths.

Also by Joey Jones

A FIELD OF FIREFLIES

 Growing up, Nolan Lynch's family was unconventional by society's standards, but it was filled with love, and his parents taught him everything he needed to know about life, equality, and family. A baseball player with a bright future, Nolan is on his way to the major leagues when tragedy occurs. Six years later, he's starting over as the newest instructor at the community college in Washington, North Carolina, where he meets Emma Pate, who seems to be everything he's ever dreamed of—beautiful, assertive, and a baseball fan to boot.

Emma Pate's dreams are put on hold after her father dies, leaving her struggling to keep her family's farm. When a chance encounter with a cute new guy in town turns into an impromptu date, Emma finds herself falling for him. But, she soon realizes Nolan Lynch isn't who she thinks he is.

Drawn together by a visceral connection that defies their common sense, Emma's and Nolan's blossoming love is as romantic as it is forbidden, until secrets—both past and present—threaten to tear them apart. Now, Nolan must confront his past and make peace with his demons or risk losing everything he loves . . . again.

Emotionally complex and charged with suspense, *A Field of Fireflies* is the unforgettable story of family, love, loss, and an old baseball field where magic occurs, including the grace of forgiveness and second chances.

Also by Joey Jones

THE DATE NIGHT JAR

An unlikely friendship. An unforgettable love story.

When workaholic physician Ansley Stone writes a letter to the estranged son of a patient asking him to send the family's heirloom date night jar, she only intended to bring a little happiness to a lonely old man during his final days. Before long, she finds herself increasingly drawn to Cleve Fields' bedside, eager to hear the stories of his courtship with his beloved late wife, Violet, that were inspired by the yellowed slivers of paper in the old jar. When Cleve asks her to return the jar to his son, Ansley spontaneously decides to deliver it in person, if only to find out why no one, including his own son, visits the patient she's grown inexplicably fond of.

Mason Fields is happily single, content to spend his days running the family strawberry farm and his evenings in the company of his best friend, a seventeen-year-old collie named Callie. Then Ansley shows up at his door with the date night jar and nowhere to stay. Suddenly, she's turning his carefully ordered world upside down, upsetting his routine, and forcing him to remember things best left in the past. When she suggests *they* pull a slip of paper from the jar, their own love story begins to develop. But before long, their newfound love will be tested in ways they never imagined, as the startling truth about Mason's past is revealed...and Ansley's future is threatened.

Also by Joey Jones

WHEN THE RIVERS RISE

Three hearts, pushed to the limit. Can they weather another storm?

High school sweethearts Niles and Eden shared a once-in-a-lifetime kind of love until an accident—and Eden's subsequent addiction to pain medication—tore them apart. Now divorced, their son Riley is Niles's whole world, and he'll do anything to keep him safe.

In constant pain, chronically tired, and resentful of Riley's relationship with his dad, Eden is a shadow of the woman she once was. When she meets Kirk, a charismatic drummer who makes her feel alive again, she's torn between evacuating with Riley before a hurricane hits and the exciting new life that beckons.

Reese has never quite gotten over the death of her father, a cop who was shot in the line of duty. Now a detective herself and the only special operations officer on the East Ridge, Tennessee, police force without children, she volunteers to go help as a potential category five hurricane spins straight toward the North Carolina coast.

As Hurricane Florence closes in, their lives begin to intersect in ways they never imagined as each is forced to confront issues from the past that will decide the future…their own, each other's, and Riley's.

Emotions swell like the rivers in the approaching storm in this poignant story of guilt, second chances, and the lengths we'll go to protect the ones we love.

Also by Joey Jones

WHERE THE RAINBOW FALLS

In the face of a storm, a father's love is the most powerful force.

With Hurricane Florence rapidly approaching the North Carolina coastline, all Niles North can think about is his five-year-old son Riley and how he wished he bent the law when he had the chance to evacuate him. Now, instead of being safe in Hickory with his dad, Riley is with Niles's ex-wife Eden, who's decided to ride out the storm at home with her drummer friend. Desperate to get back to his son as the storm waters rise, Niles begs Reese, an attractive police detective and rescue worker, to drive him back to New Bern.

Refusing to help Niles seems nearly impossible for Reese who quickly realizes she's in deeper than she should be—both professionally and emotionally—especially since she's drawn to almost everything about him. As the two undertake a perilous journey into the eye of the storm, Niles's worst fears come true, setting in motion a series of events that will change both of their lives forever.

Also by Joey Jones

ALONG THE DUSTY ROAD

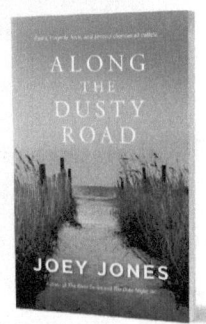

An unexpected love. A surprising second chance.

Everything Luke Bridges always wanted is in the small coastal North Carolina town where he has spent most of his twenty-six years—a fulfilling mental health therapy career, a loving family, baseball games with his dad, an adventurous beach life, and a close-knit group of friends. The only piece missing is someone to share it with, a genuine and lasting love that satisfies the soul.

He once thought Emily Beckett, the girl he dated ten years ago who has happened back into his life as his sidekick on the coed beach volleyball team, could be that someone. Emily has a seven-year-old son and an ex-husband with dangerous addictions. Although Luke enjoys spending time with Ayden, he has no interest in the challenges of being a stepfather.

Luke only dates women he can see himself marrying. With the "just friends" title firmly placed on his relationship with Emily, he agrees to a blind date with Mindy, his mentor's cousin. As he explores a connection with Mindy, the "just friends" veil with Emily is suddenly ripped away. Now he is torn between two very different women—one who might be perfectly right for him and one who doesn't seem to fit the mold but just might make his dreams of forever come true.

Fears, tragedy, love, and second chances all collide *Along the Dusty Road.*

THE ROOTS BENEATH US

Fate brought them together. Their pasts tried to tear them apart.

Leaving behind a career filled with danger and secrets, Piper Luck arrives in Duck, North Carolina, on her fortieth birthday, determined to build a new life. Starting with The Roots Beneath Us, a local course her friend and father figure swore would transform her, she embarks on a new journey. However, on the first day of class, only one other person shows up—a shy, guarded man.

Like Piper, Boone Winters just moved to the Outer Banks at the suggestion of his now deceased mentor and boss, who promised Boone a job when he arrived if he worked up the courage to leave an abusive relationship. The job: Build a luxurious oceanfront home. However, there are contingencies. He must attend The Roots Beneath Us program, have an accountability partner, and live alone.

With no other course participants, Piper becomes Boone's accountability partner. Together, they work through the course by facing their fears, setting goals, overcoming obstacles . . . and forging an unlikely friendship that evolves into something deeper. Nonetheless, when their previous lives resurface and threaten the tentative roots they've planted, they must each courageously confront their past demons once and for all in order to claim their future.